"Nicholas Mosley is a throwback, a modernist mastodon whose project for fiction surpasses in grandiosity that of any American writer I know."
—Tom LeClair, *Washington Post*

"The series of five fictions called 'Catastrophe Practice' may be one of the most important extended literary projects of this century, on a level with the multivolume universes created by Proust, Anthony Powell, Lawrence Durrell and John Updike."
—Joseph Coates, *Chicago Tribune*

"Nicholas Mosley is a brilliant novelist who has received nothing like the recognition he deserves—either at home in England or in this country."
—Robert Scholes, *Saturday Review*

"Switching perspective from one book to another, from one character to another, from a watchtower to a three-eyed sheep, from the Bible to a television flicker-switch, from the immediate to the eternal and back again, Nicholas Mosley is in the midst of constructing an answer as tricky and uneven, as holy, as powerful and as old-fashioned as prayer."—Craig Brown, *Times Literary Supplement*

ALSO BY NICHOLAS MOSLEY

FICTION

NONFICTION

CATASTROPHE
P·R·A·C·T·I·C·E

NICHOLAS MOSLEY

Introduction by John Banks
Postscript by the author

Dalkey Archive Press

Originally published by Martin Secker & Warburg Ltd., England, 1979
Copyright © 1979 Nicholas Mosley
Introduction copyright © 1989 John Banks
Revised edition copyright © 1991 Nicholas Mosley
First U.S. hardback edition, 1991
First paperback edition, 2001

Library of Congress Cataloging-in-Publication Data:

Mosley, Nicholas, 1923-
    Catastrophe practice / Nicholas Mosley; introduction by John Banks; postscript
    1988 by Nicholas Mosley. — 1st American ed.
        I. Title.
    PR6063.082C36   1989   823'.914—dc19   88-30391
    ISBN: 1-56478-252-2

Partially funded by grants from the National Endowment for the Arts, a federal agency and the
Illinois Arts Council, a state agency.

NATIONAL
ENDOWMENT
FOR THE ARTS

Illinois
ARTS
Council

Dalkey Archive Press
www.dalkeyarchive.com

To

VERITY

Supposing truth to be a woman — what?
Is the suspicion not well founded
that all philosophers, when they have
been dogmatists, have had little
understanding of women?

What meaning would our whole being
possess if it were not this — that
in us the will to truth becomes
conscious of itself as a problem.

NIETZSCHE

Introduction

Catastrophe Practice was the first book to be written in the series that carries its name. It was a seed for the other books — *Imago Bird, Serpent, Judith, Hopeful Monsters*. It was to be seen as a seed; but a seed is perhaps best looked at after its fruits.

The idea behind *Catastrophe Practice* was: in our lives we are all to some extent actors on a stage; we perform roles in accordance with 'scripts' that have been given us — by heredity, by upbringing, by society. But there is a part of us that knows that this is not quite the point; that what matters is what, as it were, goes on off-stage.

The characters in *Plays For Not Acting* struggle to convey this to an audience — 'You know don't you, that we are all for the most part stuck in this or that script; but the fact that we can know this, is not this the point?' This is how there might be being born, nurtured — although we seem unable to talk about this much — some understanding, pattern, of what might be being created off-stage.

In the short novel *Cypher* the actors are seen in what might be called their ordinary lives. Of course they are still actors! But because they are aware of this they carry with them the style — standing back from themselves, watching and listening — of whatever it is that might be being born.

Interwoven with the plays and the novel are four essays, the results of reading to discover what wider backing there might be for these ideas. It seemed that the need for a new form of understanding was not something arbitrarily imposed.

The title 'Catastrophe Practice' was suggested by a mathematical theory of the 1970s — Catastrophe Theory — which explained how evolution, change, might take place in sudden jumps. So — could not humans practise to be ready for such a jump? The title also arose from the idea that the human race has in fact reached a point at which old role-playing, old 'scripts', have become too dangerous: the liking for antagonism, for drama, for tragedy and farce, will have to be balanced by a further style of understanding if humans are not simply to blow themselves up.

Biologists tell us that there is always the chance of hitherto unnurtured seeds turning up. What humans can do is to prepare the ground — material or mental — on which one seed rather than another might grow.

I have made some slight alterations to the original 1979 edition. Now that the further works of fiction in the series, more straightforward in form, have been written, it is natural that there should be some modification to the seed.

Nicholas Mosley
London, 1991

Plays for Not Acting

SKYLIGHT
LANDFALL
CELL

To act is to do and to pretend.

What are we doing that is not
pretending when we know that
we are acting?

SKYLIGHT

Anthropologists explain how the rituals and myths of primitive people are expressions of ambiguities that a person feels but cannot readily comprehend — himself as an individual and yet a member of a group, as part of both a natural environment and a culture, as possessing instincts for self-preservation and yet for self-sacrifice for a whole. These impressions are inescapable yet disturbing: the mind tends to be logical yet processes that inform it apparently are not. For the mind to be placated as it were — for experience to seem not too much at odds with that which comprehends it — there have to be glimpses of a unity in which such ambiguities can be held. This, traditionally, has been a function of art. The myths and totems of primitive people are reconciling expressions of individuality-with-group, of consciousness-with-nature, of sacrifice-with-survival. If there cannot be a direct language with which to try to deal with these things, there can be a code.

In classical ages tragedy dealt with this kind of predicament — the way in which a person felt himself to be both a free and responsible agent and yet at the mercy of the gods — or of his past, or of society. What happened to him was ordained: yet he experienced it as his fault. By the stylised enactment of such predicaments on a stage an audience was comforted: an individual was reassured that his pitifulness was universal. His condition, however, still did not make much sense.

In an age when it was imagined that a man was no longer helpless but the potential master of his fate there was a decline in the force of tragedy but the experience of helplessness remained: then melodrama flourished, in which helplessness was acted by actors, and watched by audiences, as something that could not happen to them. There was a division between, rather than a co-existence within, the actor and that which he was acting; between what a person in the audience saw and

7

what he felt of himself; between people like 'us' and people like 'them'. In ages of so-called enlightenment, what audiences were apt to appreciate were characters like automata.

Comedy remained a reassurance, in which helplessness was portrayed, and pretensions of control were mocked, even by characters that seemed sympathetic. But with anxiety allayed by laughter there was still a gulf between the pleasure felt by an audience and the discomfiture shown by characters on a stage; still the division, that is, between 'us' and 'them'. Characters in a comedy, to be satisfying, had to be simple, all-of-a-piece; then ridiculousness could be condescended to, discomfiture could give pleasure: realities of feeling had been cut out. But the complexities of feeling of a member of an audience were real: ambiguities were lulled, but remained unassuaged.

Modern playwrights have written in some recognition of this — the gulf between the ways in which people are pleased to see others and the experiences they feel within themselves. There has been a Theatre of Cruelty — by which audiences are supposed to be bludgeoned into an increased sensitivity: a Theatre of the Absurd — in which what is communicated often beautifully (and thus comfortingly) is that people cannot communicate. In all this there is the impression that these playwrights know much more than they say: by their craft they presuppose the existence of order and meaning, yet their plays state nothing of that of which this order and meaning consist. The art of their productions, that is, belies their pretensions of meaninglessness. And this in fact seems to be a latter-day predicament: people can indeed be articulate about despair: what is difficult to be articulate about is the fact of their articulateness.

Brecht was a playwright who saw something of all this: who hoped that the point of a play might be not to try to reassure audiences but to make them think: to provide not comfort but change. A play, Brecht said, should be a demonstration: it should not be a presentation of characters simple and all-of-a-piece because this falsified reality: a play should be for a practical purpose and have a meaning. Imagine, Brecht said, there has been a street accident and an eye-witness is trying to explain to bystanders what has taken place. For this to be done properly — for bystanders to be able to make a correct assessment of what occurred — what is patently not required is for the demonstrator to struggle to make his characters simple and self-consistent: if he does — if the bystanders are sufficiently carried away to exclaim for instance 'What a fine portrayal of a chauffeur!' — then the point of the demonstration is lost, which is not to show off, but to explain an occurrence. A demonstrator should not 'cast a spell' over his audience: should not 'transport them from normality to higher realms'. Above all, he should not foster the delusion that the audience is watching anything other than an illusion. A demonstrator 'never forgets, nor does he allow it to be forgotten, that he is not the subject but the demonstrator . . . the feelings and opinions of the demonstrator and demonstrated are not merged into one'. For a latter-day predicament, Brecht realised — following on from those of primitive and classical ages — was to do not so much with ignorance as with knowledge: not a terror at almost unimaginable contradictions, but an inability to make acceptable sense of what in some ways was known very well — the fact that a person is not simple and self-consistent; he is aware of this himself; the part of him that is aware is different from the part it is aware of; his feelings both of control and of helplessness are valid. But there might be some chance now, in what Brecht called a 'scientific' age, for these complexities to be comprehended in some unifying form in which men might be able to observe, reconcile, even demonstrate themselves: instead of treating themselves — and thus the world — as either disastrous or absurd.

The practical purpose of Brecht's 'epic' theatre was, he used to say, the promulgation of Marxism — the furthering of the interests of the working class and the confounding of those of the bourgeoisie. But to anyone seeing or reading Brecht's plays this function is not clear: his working-class characters seem

9

neither less nor more inept than any others. Brecht explained that the hearts he wanted to change were those not of his characters but of his audience. But there was still the question — How could an audience be changed if what was being demonstrated was that, socially, people did not change? And Brecht saw himself above all as an agent of change: 'What matters most is that a new human type should be evolving, and the entire interest of the world should be concentrated on his development.' Towards the end of his life Brecht himself seemed to see this predicament; and to suggest that his commitment to Marxism, which could easily be put into words, might be a cover for something quite different, which could not. After his death there was a note found among his papers — 'An effort is now being made to move on from the epic theatre to the dialectical theatre; we envisage a sizeable transformation.' He did not live to elucidate what this transformation might be. But he left hints. In his last message to his Berliner Ensemble he wrote — 'Our playing needs to be quick, light, strong. This is not a question of hurry, but of speed; not simply of quick playing, but quick thinking . . . In the dialogue exchanges must not be offered reluctantly as when offering someone one's last pair of boots, but must be tossed like so many balls. The audience has to see that there are a number of artists working together as a collective ensemble in order to convey stories, ideas, virtuoso feats to the spectator by common effort.' This was more than a statement about technique: it was a statement about what technique should be about — an effort to express the 'more' that playwrights know but do not readily give substance to — the business of thinking, of imagination, of creativity itself. For it is here, in the recognition of a man's natural and inherent imaginative processes — a glimpse into the way in which he constructs his view of the world — that a man can stand back and see himself; can meet with others who are doing likewise; and thus have some freedom, being both separate from his hitherto controlling impulses and yet in contact with them, with a chance of changing them. And it is by men seeing themselves as all-of-a-piece that there is their solitariness and helplessness. What should be demonstrated in a play, Brecht seemed to suggest, was not a social blueprint for change, because this in fact does not bring change: but rather the condition through which, with humans, the idea of change exists — its style and substance — because this might bring change, through its recognition. Brecht quoted with approval the example of the Chinese actor who 'never acts as though there were a fourth wall beside the three that surround him; he expresses his awareness of being observed . . . observes himself . . . will occasionally look at the audience and say "Isn't it just like that?" at the same time observing his own legs and arms, adducing them, testing them, finally approving them'. This was the sort of, acting the sort of theatre, suitable for an audience of the 'scientific' age. It expressed the way in which people did in fact think — might in fact change — within some interaction (difficult to express) between the watcher and the watched; the 'I' that thinks and the 'I' that it thinks about; these both being observed, comprehended, from some further point of thinking. And it was by becoming as it were at home there — at this further point — that a person might become at home with others doing the same; rather than everyone being trapped in lonely self-projections. And it was by this becoming-accustomed that there might be the evolution of 'a new human type'. For the predicament of modem 'scientific' man was not only (nor even primarily) his alienation from society but this alienation within himself — the split between what he knew, especially about himself, and his ability to come to terms with this knowing. It was this that brought him to lack of communicativeness and despair; and to his cruel but futile rites to allay these. But if a man could no longer be comforted by traditional symbols, perhaps he could still be given hope by symbols from this further point of thinking — symbols which could move back from, look at, the old symbols, as well as that which they had once so helplessly (but now perhaps no longer) been about.

It seemed some sort of playwriting might be possible here — the 'more' that all artists know about being that which is expressed; the form involved with the content. Experiment in the theatre has for so long been about technique — shall the stage be here or there; shall actors enter through auditorium or roof; shall audiences be caressed or pelted. There have been theatrical companies like churches — and like brothels. But what if all this were taken for granted — life is like that, yes: there are explosions, bodies: queens do, at altars, raise their skirts to awestruck children. And marvels are performed in honour of marvels being meaningless. But still, what is our predicament? We know all this. And by knowing, we have the chance of knowing more. And on a stage, life not only happens but is observed. And this is a scientific age, in which we practise much observation. So what if, in a theatre, we did what in fact human beings do — what distinguishes them from animals. And if in thus watching themselves, human beings recognised themselves — as neither animals nor angels. An actor comes on: he is watched: he watches himself being watched: those who watch, watch him watching. This is a person's predicament — what is an act, what is not: what is 'true', what is 'false': not what will happen next, but what is happening now. This is a person's experience of himself; through it, his experience of everything. And being shown this, a member of an audience might indeed recognise himself — might even be encouraged to change — being presented with an experience of — not acting! There might indeed be something alarming here — man as his own myth or totem! But a man has always learned from myths — and from what alarms him. Once myths arose instinctively: they were expressions of complexities that could be held in no better way. Men are now conscious of the way their minds make myths: this itself has become a sort of terror. But there is still the chance — this is the predicament — for men as it were to make myths about myths; and in this, the chance of the 'new human type' evolving. If a man has the power to observe the controlling patterns of his mind it is here, and not in the patterns, that there is his freedom. The theatre has been accustomed to observe how people behave; what might now be observed is people's observing. A riddle, a sifting, has usually entertained: and a present one, at work on a past, might even seem truthful.

Riddle . . . . . to separate chaff from corn,
ashes from cinders etc . . .
test (evidence, truth)

SKYLIGHT

ACKERMAN
HELENA
JUDITH
JASON
ARIEL
JENNY

ACT I

SCENE: The terrace of a house on a mountain. On the right (audience's right) is a loggia with a balcony above it. Along the back of the terrace is a balustrade. On the left is a swing sofa. Centre, are two tables with the remains of drink and food. The ground is the rock of the mountain, grey and gnarled like the surface of a brain.

The backdrop is unlit. Then it becomes pink, like a dawn sky.

There enters, front left, a boy, Ariel, aged eighteen. He wears a coloured shirt and white trousers. He acts as if he had not expected to find himself on a stage.

Then he takes up the position of a dancer.

From behind the loggia comes the sound of 1920s' dance music.

Ariel breaks his pose and moves to the tables and takes food and eats. He picks up glasses and sniffs at them until he finds one from which he drinks. Then he turns to the loggia, right, and takes up a pose as if alarmed.

The music stops.

Ariel relaxes.

There come on through the loggia Ackerman, a man in his sixties, and Jenny, a girl of seventeen. They wear evening dress. Ackerman walks with a stick, but gives the impression of power. He has his arm round Jenny, who is pretty, but dazed as if on drugs.

Ackerman sees Ariel: hesitates: then comes with Jenny down the loggia steps to the front of the stage, right. He looks out over the audience.

Ariel takes food from a table and eats.

Ackerman speaks as if he were acting from a conventional script, but were finding the business of acting rather ridiculous.

17

ACKERMAN Each stone had to be brought up. There's a
quarry from the time of Charlemagne. They
still use primitive methods; pulleys and
ropes, with platforms of sticks. Like eagles'
nests. Men working in the sky. An amazing
sight. No one can see us.

He seems to listen for Ariel.

Ariel puts his hand on his stomach and doubles
up, as if in pain.

Ackerman continues —

Scorned a safety net. Said it would interfere
with their work. Great craftsmen. Magnificent physique. There was one called
Angelo. I'm not supposed to tell this story.
The whole building is said to be a folly — a
monument to paranoia —

Ariel has begun to tip-toe towards the swing
sofa, left. When Ackerman stops talking, he
stops — in the position of a dancer.

Though why it should be a folly to want to
get away from this world, I don't know, in
which we have to spend so much of our
time —

Ariel has moved on. When Ackerman stops, he
stops.

The work took six years. We were tactful
enough not to rest on the seventh —

This time Ariel has not moved.

Ackerman stands behind Jenny and puts his
arms around her.

I like to think of the building as of the same
stone as the mountain. The pale pink rose
of the dawn. With no road. Just a lift-shaft
like a flower —

He kisses Jenny's neck.

Ariel raises a foot and holds it as if he had
trodden on something and were in pain — or
like a dancer.

Ackerman gazes over Jenny's shoulder at the audience.

> That's where Angelo fell. Two hundred foot to the bottom. The body was never found. An underground river swallows its victims. Stay out late. Be naughty. Little girls are punished —

Ariel has been examining the sole of his foot.

Ackerman seems to listen: then continues —

> I like to think one could say — I'll give you all the countries of the world. But who would want them. Who would want them! I make motor cars. A cockleshell for Venus. There's room above the loggia —

He waits.

Then he turns to Ariel.

Ariel, holding his foot, has raised his head as if he were a statue.

Ackerman moves towards Ariel with his stick. It is as if he were acting anger that Ariel had been mocking him.

Jenny crouches at the front of the stage and holds her nose as if about to jump over.

Ackerman turns and looks at Jenny. He acts, somewhat clumsily, as if he is pulled each way between Ariel and Jenny.

Then Ariel falls, heavily, on to his face on the swing sofa.

The sofa bounces, and becomes still.

Jenny stands. She turns and looks at Ariel.

Ackerman goes to the balustrade at the back and looks over.

ACKERMAN   Did you hear it? Some signal. Some sign. They're all around, like wolves.

Jenny comes and kneels by Ariel.

Ackerman looks at the audience. When he speaks it is as if he is trying to get into some contact with the audience.

19

What can one get him? Brandy?

Ackerman waits. Then he goes and stands looking down at Ariel and Jenny. He raises the
back of Jenny's skirt with his stick.

They make the stuff in their own backyards.

Dirt gets in —

He looks out at the wings, right.

It was leaning over the pool one day when
it saw its own reflection in the water —

He lowers Jenny's skirt. He has been showing
increasing unease. He looks at the audience.
Then he seems to try to act again —

The sun comes up about an hour after first
light. Colours the old glaziers knew about.

Softness in hardness —

He turns to the wings, left; then to the loggia,
right.

After a time he shouts as if in desperation —

Stranger!

It is as if 'Stranger' were the name of someone
off-stage to whom he is calling for help.

From behind the loggia there starts up again the
sound of 1920s' dance music. There is the
scratchily recorded noise of a party in progress.
Ackerman looks at the audience: smiles; frowns.
Then he strides off through the loggia.

The music and the noise of the party cease
abruptly — with the sound of a needle being
scraped across a record.

Then there is a faint cry, as from a woman.
Ariel half looks up: then lies face downwards on
the sofa again.

The backdrop goes blank. Then it flickers.
Then a mountain, ringed with clouds, appears.
Jenny turns, sitting, with her back against the
swing sofa. The seat moves back, so that Jenny is
half collapsed.

She enunciates carefully — as if she is trying to

make a more successful job of acting than Ackerman had done, though not always keeping to a script.

JENNY   Take off your gas-mask, daddy. I don't want to be forcibly fed.

She sits up cross-legged.

On a dark night — at the edge of a wood — have you got water and oil?

She opens her mouth and gazes upwards.

Then she stares at the audience.

I'm a fish. At the bottom of the ocean. Where no light comes. And I see your pearly gates. With heads on spikes. And tongues like streamers. And when it rains they talk. With bloody music —

She stares at the audience.

Then she says in a matter-of-fact voice —

They've got dogs down there. One boy got caught on the wire.

She seems to search amongst the audience.

Was it you? Was it you?

She waits. Then acts —

My mother thinks this party's heaven. Twinkle twinkle cow bells.

She stretches her hands out in front of her, as if drugged.

Then she presses her hands against the ground as if steadying herself in a boat.

I wasn't going to jump. Or was I —

She slaps at the ground quickly as if something were climbing up to her.

Get off! There are too many of you!

Then she steadies herself and leans forward, smiling.

Hullo sun, can you hear me? Can I give you a hand up? I mean you give me a hand up? My slip. My Freudian slip.

She stares at the audience.

You can use your ears — your eyes —

She closes her eyes.

Can't you?

After a time there comes on through the loggia Helena, a woman in her fifties. She wears an evening dress. She pauses on the loggia steps, and looks at Ariel and Jenny. Then she takes up an attitude with an arm in front of her breasts like a statue of Venus.

When she speaks it is as if she were trying to get back to a script; but were soon becoming involved, like the others, in trying to convey some message or attitude that is more urgent.

HELENA   Oh what a relief! I thought someone had gone over. They did once. A workman.

She comes to the front of the stage, right, and looks out over the audience.

I'd hardly spoken to him. He used to bring me gifts. You know — each morning after breakfast —

She stares at the audience.

Then she moves off along the footlights.

Of course my husband didn't know. He thinks they're all perfect. They can fly. Just like himself.

She stands by the wings, left, looking out.

What can one get him, water? That sounds like a plant.

She waits.

Then she turns to Ariel and Jenny.

Angy's got a daughter who's on drugs. She once just touched her, and she jumped straight out of the window. She said she was a fish. I said — Why the window? She said — A goldfish.

She turns to the audience.

I do see, don't you —

She seems to search about amongst the audience.

>One should have a net. Like a tennis ball.

She waits.

>Is it you? Is it you?

Then she moves off round the stage again.

>I have said — No dogs. But he does so adore animals. He's had notices put up. But they just don't read —

She stops by the front of the stage again, watching the audience.

>They like — music.

After a time she puts a hand to her head and sways.

>The sun doesn't get filtered — at this high altitude.

She waits. Then she takes her hand away.

>He's building something half way up. Did you see?

She waits.

>I think it's a tomb —

She looks to the wings, right.

>— Or is it a laboratory?

Then she looks at the audience.

>Are you Angy's daughter?

JENNY   No.

Then she speaks as if she were questioning the script.

>Isn't that right?

HELENA   I was afraid you might be.

Helena remains staring at the audience. Jenny watches her. They both seem to have stopped acting. After a time Ackerman comes on to the steps of the loggia. He looks at Helena.

ACKERMAN   I've been calling —
HELENA   Oh what did you say?
ACKERMAN   Didn't you hear?
HELENA   Oh I see.

Ackerman comes down the steps.

ACKERMAN	Get rid of him —
HELENA	Throw him over —
ACKERMAN	Is that funny?
HELENA	Is it meant to be?

Ackerman watches Ariel; then the audience.
It is as if, although he finds acting and their scripts increasingly absurd, he hopes the audience may recognise this, and how it is difficult to communicate with them more directly.
After a time he takes from his pocket an apple. He turns to Helena and holds the apple out to her.

ACKERMAN Come on up! Good pony!

Helena, at the front of the stage, puts her hands across her breasts in the attitude of a statue of Venus.

HELENA Oh you are a baby!

ACKERMAN Give it a rub down. Make it feel safe.

Helena puts a hand to her head: she sways.

HELENA It was in its pram one day —

Ackerman puts the apple down carefully on a table.

ACKERMAN Be careful children! God is watching —

Helena takes her hand from her head. It is as if she has once more given up acting. She turns to Ackerman.

HELENA They like this?

ACKERMAN They seem to —

HELENA But they don't!

ACKERMAN So what's the difference?

After a time Helena turns and walks out through the loggia.
Ackerman looks at the audience. He murmurs—

ACKERMAN Ten minutes to go. Just time for a cup of tea —

He waits. Then he goes out after Helena, as if he has become too embarrassed.
After a time Jenny stands, goes to the apple

24

which Ackerman has put on the table, bends down to it, puts her ear to it, then picks it up and walks around with it.

JENNY Once, when my mother was having dinner with Mr Ackerman, she opened her napkin and a thousand dollars fell into her soup.

She takes a bite out of the apple: then spits.

Pips!

She examines the inside of the apple.

Oh Mr Ackerman, what big factories you've got!

She takes another bite: looks at Ariel: speaks with her mouth full —

What happened, did it get lost in the wash?

She swallows.

Who are you?

Ariel speaks from lying face down on the sofa.

ARIEL Ariel —
JENNY Who's Ariel?
ARIEL A member of the liberation army.

He sits up. He looks around the stage. He speaks as if he is more successfully trying to act not acting.

This place is going to be blown up. They're coming up through the sewers. Rats and frogmen. Breaking down the fences. Leaping up the waterfalls. On to the dry land —

He stands. He goes to the pillars of the loggia, and kicks them. He looks up at the flies.

Wood! Plastic!

He goes to the balustrade at the back and looks over.

This is where Angelo fell! Two foot from the bottom! Into the bog! The glory hole! On to a foam rubber sea!

When he looks at the audience, it is as if he hopes that something may be being recognised there.

Then he goes to the centre of the stage and squats down by what appears to be a crack in the rocks. He puts his fingers in, seeming to be trying to force the rocks apart.

Jenny watches him.

JENNY   I think you're one of the boring guests —
ARIEL   Well you've had your slice —
JENNY   What of —
ARIEL   The cucumber —
JENNY   But I haven't —
ARIEL   But you will.

Ariel seems unable to get the rocks apart. He looks up at Jenny.

Jenny puts her half-eaten apple back on the table.

Then she gets down on all fours.

JENNY   — I'm a Trojan horse —
ARIEL   — How many men have you got inside —
JENNY   — Please, mister, I was only doing forty —

Ariel stands. He looks round the stage.

ARIEL   Got the wire?
JENNY   What for —
ARIEL   To chop it off —
JENNY   To make it grow?

Ariel looks down at her.

ARIEL   We've got to try —
JENNY   Why?
ARIEL   Haven't we?

Jenny stands; then goes and sits on the swing sofa, left. She looks at the audience.

JENNY   What do they see?
ARIEL   Coloured lights, shapes, music —

Jenny begins to take off her dress.

She seems to quote —

JENNY   — The plains where they were born —

ARIEL	— The rings round Salamanca —

Jenny, with her dress off, puts her feet up.
Ariel goes and pulls the curtains that are round
the back and sides of the swing sofa so that Jenny
is half hidden.

JENNY	Do they get through?
ARIEL	One or two —
JENNY	They see it?
ARIEL	Or see they don't —

Ariel climbs into the swing sofa with Jenny.

JENNY	I thought it was a tomb.
ARIEL	Or perhaps it's a laboratory?

From inside, Ariel tries to draw the curtains
round the front of the sofa.

JENNY	— Pick it up by the feet —
ARIEL	— Hit it —

He manages to draw the curtains so that he and
Jenny are hidden.
The sofa rocks for a time; then is still.
The backdrop goes blank.
There are three flashes, as if of lightning, on the
backdrop: then after a time, three bangs.
The backdrop changes to a deep blue.
There comes on at the front of the stage, right,
Judith, a woman in her thirties. She wears a black
dress and has bare feet. When she reaches the
centre, she stops and looks at the audience. She
seems to be someone who has taken refuge on
the stage.
There come in through the auditorium a man
and a woman. They might be people who are
pursuing Judith. When they see she is on a stage,
they seem uncertain. Then they climb on to the
stage and adopt the roles of a Footman and a Maid.
Judith moves along the balustrade towards the
left. The Maid goes to the table, left, on which
there is drink and food. She picks up the table so
that she seems to bar Judith's way.

Judith stops. She turns and looks at the loggia. The Footman has gone to the other table, right, so that he seems to be barring Judith's way from the other side.

Judith comes to the front of the stage and looks at the audience. She takes off the belt of her dress, provocatively.

The Footman and the Maid put down their tables. They watch.

Judith goes to the loggia and leans with her back against a pillar. She dangles the belt from her hand. The Footman goes and stands in front of her and holds out his hand.

The Maid goes to the centre of the stage quickly and squats down by the crack in the rocks and puts her fingers in. Then she looks at the audience. Then she straightens, picks up her table, and carries it out through the loggia, right. The Footman goes and picks up his table and follows her out.

The backdrop goes blank.

Judith is left with her belt hanging from her hand.

After a time Helena appears from behind the loggia. She is pushing a garden chair on wheels. She acts as if she does not see Judith. She wears sunbathing clothes and dark glasses. On the chair there is a basket. She comes to the centre of the stage and puts the chair down carefully over the crack in the rocks. Then she sits on the chair and puts her feet up.

The backdrop changes to a bright gold.

Judith winds up her belt into her hand.

Helena takes from her basket a half-made tapestry, and needles and thread. She begins to stitch. After a time she puts her stitching down and gazes at the audience.

She enunciates carefully —

HELENA	— The same direction at both ends or in between —

Then she goes back to her stitching.

There are three loud bangs from behind the backdrop. Helena takes no notice. After a time she looks up.

She enunciates carefully —

A fate. A weaver of tapestries.

She closes her eyes.

After a time she sings, in a faded but passionate contralto, a few bars from the 1st Norn's song in Wagner's *Götterdämmerung* ('So gut und schlimm es geh' —').

Judith puts her hands over her eyes. Then she looks at the audience and smiles. Then she goes out through the loggia.

Helena stops singing. She looks in the direction in which Judith has gone. Then she goes back to her stitching.

From now until the end of the act it is as if the actors are finding and coming to terms with a style — moving between acting a script and not acting, and acting not-acting — which they hope will be, and demonstrate, what they wish to convey.

After a time the swing sofa begins to rock and bounce.

Ariel's head pops out through the curtains. He holds the curtains wrapped round his neck as if he were a clown.

Helena continues with her stitching.

ARIEL	Ariel —
HELENA	No!
ARIEL	Yes.
HELENA	Oh you did frighten me — .

She jumps, puts a hand to her heart, and acts as if she had been alarmed.

Ariel climbs out of the swing sofa. He arranges the

curtains carefully so that Jenny cannot be seen. He watches Helena. He murmurs as if quoting —

ARIEL   — Two arms, two legs —

Helena murmurs —

HELENA   — And one in between.

She is looking down at her finger as if she had pricked it with her needle.

Ariel waits. Then he seems to prompt her —

ARIEL   — Yes, I've been at school —

HELENA   Oh, what school did you go to?

ARIEL   I don't think it matters, do you, where you go to school?

Helena goes back to her stitching.

HELENA   You mean home environment's more important?

Ariel stares at her. Then he moves round the stage. He acts as if quoting —

ARIEL   — Huts. Watchtowers —

HELENA   — Ladies and gentlemen on the grass —

Ariel stands looking down at her.

Helena puts down her stitching. She closes her eyes. She acts as if she is having difficulty with her lines —

HELENA   I remember you in your pram. You looked up to the leaves, the shadows. Children see by what they learn —

Ariel waits. He seems to prompt her —

ARIEL   She went for the eyes?

Helena seems to say a wrong line —

HELENA   — It's been such ages —

ARIEL   Who, my mother?

After a time Ariel moves round the stage again. Helena goes back to her stitching.

ARIEL   And my father?

HELENA   Isn't he in a tomb —

ARIEL   Oh, I thought it was a monastery.

Helena puts down her stitching. She seems to be in despair.

30

HELENA	How did you get in?
ARIEL	I climbed.
HELENA	No one's ever climbed.

Ariel comes and looks down at Helena. He seems to quote —

ARIEL	— Except once at the time of Napoleon —

Helena closes her eyes.

Ariel watches her.

I thought I'd come to your party.

HELENA	Oh Pree will be pleased.
ARIEL	Why do you call him Pree?
HELENA	Paris, you know; gay Paree.

Helena seems to be overcome with embarrassment.

After a time Ariel moves round the stage again.

ARIEL	What does he do — you know — in that little room —

Helena opens her eyes. She seems to make a great effort.

HELENA	Oh Ariel I wish I knew! He used to go out mornings and evenings. And I always knew where he was! In the fields, the factories —

She puts a hand to her head; sways.

— Now he's most of the time in his room —

Ariel goes to the balustrade at the back and looks over.

ARIEL	I thought he might give me a job.
HELENA	Oh Ariel I don't think he does give jobs!
ARIEL	Not in his factories? I saw one on the road —
HELENA	With little flames coming out of the chimneys?
ARIEL	And ashes —
HELENA	There were ashes?
ARIEL	On the fields —
HELENA	The poor fields —
ARIEL	And men like snow.

Ariel comes back to Helena and stands over her.

And people on the roads with prams,

31

	pushing.

Helena goes on with her stitching.

HELENA	Oh Ariel, I sometimes think —
ARIEL	It might be better if —
HELENA	Rather than —
ARIEL	— What would have been the colour of her eyes, her hair —
HELENA	Sometimes at night —
ARIEL	You can hear him?
HELENA	It's terrible!

Ariel walks round the stage again.

| ARIEL | You mean, how much can we say? |
| HELENA | How much can we know. |

Helena looks out at the wings, left.

After a time Ackerman comes on through the loggia. He wears a white dressing-gown. He stands on the steps watching Ariel and Helena, who ignore him.

He begins to pace up and down the balustrade at the back. He declaims as if rehearsing a speech —

| ACKERMAN | Do you hear the rumble, the thunder, when the spirits come out and invade the upper air. And the young apes stir in the trees. And flop on the roads like parachutes. You tread on them they kick. With wings like snow. And in the ditches breed. With eyes blown out. And in no-man's-land at night you hear them calling — Good! — Good! — to put them out of misery. With your tongue a pistol. And their mouths, roses. |

He stops, by the wings, left, with his head up, as if hearing music.

HELENA	Look who's here!
ACKERMAN	Who's here?
HELENA	Ariel. Your grandson, Ariel.

After a time Ackerman comes to Ariel and holds

32

	his hand out.
ACKERMAN	You were in your pram. You looked up to the leaves, the shadows. Children see by what they learn. There was an accident! Between the rocks and the whirlpool, you had to be changed.
	Ariel frowns. Then he takes his hand.
ARIEL	I thought I'd come to your party —
ACKERMAN	— Oh Pree will be pleased! —
ARIEL	— Why do you call him Pree? —
	They both seem to have said the wrong lines. Then Ackerman says mockingly —
ACKERMAN	The sun doesn't get filtered at this high altitude.
ARIEL	I wondered if you could give me a job —
ACKERMAN	Oh I don't think I do give jobs.
ARIEL	Not in your factories —
ACKERMAN	Jokes —
ARIEL	Shit —
	They wait.
	Ackerman goes to the balustrade at the back and looks over.
ACKERMAN	How did you get in?
ARIEL	I climbed.
ACKERMAN	No one's ever climbed.
	They wait.
	Then Ariel turns to Ackerman; smiles.
ARIEL	I had irons —
ACKERMAN	On your hands —
ARIEL	And feet —
ACKERMAN	Your poor feet! —
	They wait.
ARIEL	And the people in the valley?
ACKERMAN	Want to get in —
ARIEL	For what —
ACKERMAN	— We haven't got —
ARIEL	So you provide —
ACKERMAN	— Waste from the factories. Jokes. Shit.

33

He watches the audience.

Helena has lain back as if she is asleep.

Ariel comes to the front of the stage and looks at the audience with Ackerman.

ACKERMAN   We call them the fossils. To prove that the world was not made the other day.

Ariel looks down over the footlights. Ackerman puts an arm round him. They stand together looking out.

After a time Ackerman acts —

ACKERMAN   — The king sat here, with his courtiers. Two eyes and a nose, with a room behind —

He turns, with Ariel, to the loggia, right.

    — Where Harlequin kept Columbine —

He turns to the swing sofa, left.

He takes his arm away from Ariel's shoulder. He remains looking at the swing sofa.

ARIEL   They rub together —
ACKERMAN   Keeps them white.

Ariel looks at the audience as if to see if there are any results from some experiment.

Ackerman goes to the swing sofa and pulls back one of the curtains. He stares down.

Ariel murmurs —

ARIEL   — I can destroy you —
ACKERMAN   — I can climb down —

After a time Ariel calls —

ARIEL   Oh you are an old fraud! I'm sure you're frightfully good at it really!

Ackerman closes the curtain. He shouts —

ACKERMAN   On guard!

He turns and faces Ariel.

Ariel hesitates: then he crouches and holds on to his leg as if he had been hit there.

ARIEL   You go for the legs —
ACKERMAN   Tap the ground.
ARIEL   You've got to give warning.

Ackerman comes to Ariel and bends down as if

	to examine his leg.
	After a time Ariel murmurs —
ARIEL	Did you see it?
ACKERMAN	Underneath the chair?
	Ackerman looks towards the wings, right.
	Ariel says loudly, as if to divert the attention of anyone who might be listening —
ARIEL	— I don't see why there shouldn't be parasites in an industrial society —
ACKERMAN	— Of course you young men want to give them cups of tea —
	Ackerman turns back to Ariel.
	Ariel puts an arm round his shoulder.
ARIEL	Wouldn't it be better if —
ACKERMAN	Instead of her arms, her hair —
ARIEL	A bit of rope —
ACKERMAN	Wire —
ARIEL	Wine — ?
ACKERMAN	Wire!

They seem to be trying not to laugh. They begin to hobble off the stage through the loggia. Ackerman has his arm round Ariel. At the top of the loggia steps Ariel turns and looks back at the audience.

ACKERMAN	They protect themselves —
ARIEL	By rubbish?
ACKERMAN	Don't they like it?
ARIEL	But if they see it —
ACKERMAN	One or two get through.

Ackerman takes his arm from Ariel's shoulders. He looks at Helena. Helena has her eyes closed, lying back in the garden chair.
Ackerman nods at Ariel: then he goes off through the loggia.
Ariel goes and stands behind a pillar. It is as if he were imagining he were off-stage.
The backdrop goes blank.
Then there appears the huge outline of a tree.

After a time Jenny pushes back the curtains of
the swing sofa. She looks out tentatively. She
buttons up her dress.

JENNY Oh Mrs Ackerman, I did so love your party —
She climbs out of the sofa.
The garden! The tree! Especially the
Chinese lanterns.
She looks round the stage.
Oh I know I ought to have gone!
She looks down at Helena.
But I'm so in love with Ariel.
Helena does not move.
Jenny goes to the loggia and looks out at the
wings, right.
She sees Ariel. Ariel makes a move as if to stay
hidden behind the pillar.

JENNY You know, last night, he hardly knew what
he was doing. He walked up and down on
the parapet. He said he was a bird —
She comes and looks at the audience. She seems
to quote —
— Stand back, you go over —
She waits.
Then she walks round the stage. She seems to
make a great effort to explain —
We had this child in its pram. We took it to
the airport. It was a bright spring day.
There were aeroplanes flying —
She stops and looks amongst the audience.
Was it you. Was it you —
She moves round the stage again.
I went ahead. Ariel was following me.
Wires had to be attached from the suit-
cases to the pram —
She stops; looks out at the wings, left.
What's that burning?
She waits: then moves round the stage.
They'd been watching for people like us.

36

She seems to be finding it increasingly difficult
to know which way to face or how to convey
her meaning.

    Mrs Ackerman —

She looks at the audience.

    What have they given her, do you know?

She tries to lift Helena's chair by its handles.

    There were men in the control tower —

The chair seems too heavy: she puts it down.
She looks towards the loggia, right —

    It was a small room, with fir trees —

She turns to the audience.

    You can't taste it, touch it, smell it —

She raises her hands, as if surrendering.

    Don't shoot! I'm pregnant!

After a time the Footman comes on through the
loggia. He stands on the top of the loggia steps.
He watches Jenny.
Jenny looks amongst the audience.
The Footman goes to Helena's chair.
Jenny lowers her hands.
The Footman wheels Helena's chair towards the
back of the loggia.
Just before Helena and the Footman go off Jenny
yells —

    They can make you say anything!

Helena sits up gripping the sides of the chair as if
terrified.
Jenny smiles.
Then the Footman wheels Helena off.
Jenny goes and leans with her back against the
proscenium arch, left. She looks up, as if basking
in the sun.
From now on, it is as if the actors were confident
they had found a style proper for what they are
demonstrating.
After a time Ariel runs on from behind the pillar
of the loggia.

He goes to the balustrade at the back and climbs on to it and walks along holding his arms out like a bird. Then he jumps off and goes to the crack in the rocks and squats down by it and puts his fingers in.

Jenny remains with her eyes closed. Then she holds her hand out as if she were trying to make shadows with her fingers on a wall.

After a time Judith comes on from behind the loggia. She wears her black dress. She moves along the balustrade. Then she turns to Ariel.

JUDITH	Ariel —
ARIEL	Yes —
JUDITH	When you see your father, will you tell him I've done his socks and they're in the oven —

Ariel is facing the audience with his eyes closed. Judith puts a leg up on the balustrade as if about to climb over.

— And would he never, never do this to anyone again.

Ariel does not move.

Judith seems to become interested in what he is doing with the crack in the rocks. She climbs down from the balustrade. She walks about the stage, acting as if she were not interested in what she is saying.

You know, when I was on that ledge, there was a humming bird in front of a flower. And its wings moved so fast that you couldn't see —

She comes and looks over Ariel's shoulder.

And my body, which I hate, had wires attached to its shoulders —

She looks up at the audience.

So that when you pulled, you could see —

She waits.

The back of your own head? Angels?

After a time she moves off round the stage again.

  I do wonder if you'll get that job! It's so difficult, nowadays, with so many opportunities open —

Ariel suddenly yells —

ARIEL He's in the pub!

Judith stops. She stares at the audience.

After a time —

JUDITH Don't shout —

ARIEL Don't *shoot* —

JUDITH — I'm pregnant.

She seems to find it difficult not to laugh — or cry. Then she goes to the balustrade and puts a leg up and climbs over.

At the far side, she is on a slightly lower level to that of the stage. She walks off, left, with just her head and shoulders visible above the balustrade. She is like a target on a fun-fair shooting range. Ariel watches where she has gone.

After a time Jenny, with her back against the proscenium arch, left, holds out her hand and lets fall from it a pendant which dangles on the end of a chain.

JENNY Look —

ARIEL What —

JENNY He gave me last night —

Ariel gets up and stands by Jenny, and takes hold of the pendant dangling from her hand.

ARIEL It's an egg.

JENNY He said —

ARIEL What —

JENNY Put it in —

ARIEL Where?

JENNY It's a bomb —

ARIEL A laboratory?

He lets go of the pendant. He looks at the audience.

Jenny moves off round the stage like a water

39

	diviner with the pendant dangling from her hand. She speaks as if she were trying out some formula —
JENNY	— Couldn't we have committees, you know, representation at every level —
ARIEL	— The more houses they build, the more places there are in the evenings —
JENNY	— Till we're all in one room —
ARIEL	Like a telephone box?

Ariel goes to the balustrade at the back and looks over. Then he looks up to the flies.

Jenny, walking round the stage with the pendant swinging from her hand, stops above the crack in the rocks, where the pendant becomes still.

JENNY	— Mrs Ackerman uses them for her headaches —
ARIEL	— Mrs Ackerman gets them from her landlady —
JENNY	'Landlady' can't be 'headaches' —
ARIEL	Why not?

Jenny lowers the pendant towards the crack in the rocks. The backdrop flickers. Then the image of the tree goes out. There appear swirling red lights as if of a town burning. Ariel looks at the audience.

JENNY	— Put a banana beyond the bars of a cage —
ARIEL	— With a packing-case, a stick —
JENNY	— Sit in the packing-case using the stick —
ARIEL	— On the banana —

He seems to be finding it difficult not to laugh. Jenny raises the pendant from the crack in the rocks. The lights on the backdrop become set, like lava.

Ariel comes to the front of the stage and looks over the footlights.

Jenny declaims —

JENNY	— A sort of tightness round the throat —
ARIEL	— Mouth —

JENNY	— Eyes —

Jenny lowers the pendant into the crack in the rocks again.

Ariel looks at the backdrop.

Jenny raises and lowers the pendant several times; the backdrop remains the same.

ARIEL	Can't you —
JENNY	What —
ARIEL	Tell them a story?

Ackerman appears on the balcony above the loggia. He is holding what appears to be an old-fashioned gas-mask. He prepares to put it on.

Jenny winds the pendant up into her hand.

JENNY	Once upon a time, children, when apples hung from trees —

Ackerman puts on the gas-mask. He adjusts the straps.

Jenny watches Ackerman.

— And its mouth was the same as its anus —

Ackerman stares out over the stage in his gas-mask.

ARIEL	It comes in here: goes out there —
JENNY	And in between —
ARIEL	They came on once or twice; one or two —
JENNY	Didn't they?

Ariel looks at the audience.

After a time Jenny goes behind a pillar of the loggia. She appears to be taking her dress off. Helena comes on through the loggia with her hands over her ears. She acts —

HELENA	Oh I do hate fireworks! They should send them up in paper bags, like the Chinese —

She takes her hands away from her ears.

She looks at Ariel, then at Ackerman.

Then she says in a matter-of-fact voice —

Have you taken the pin out? —

ARIEL	Pin in —
HELENA	I thought we were doing —

41

ARIEL	What —
HELENA	Put us out of —
ARIEL	— It in —
HELENA	— Yes —
ARIEL	— Misery?

There are three loud bangs from behind the backdrop. Jenny comes out from behind the pillar. She carries her dress in her hand. She watches the backdrop.

The backdrop begins to change back to the swirling lights of a town burning.

Ackerman, in his gas-mask, begins to droop over the balustrade as if he were being asphyxiated.

Jenny turns to the audience. She stamps her foot by the crack in the rocks; but nothing happens.

ARIEL	It's inside —
HELENA	— Outside —
ARIEL	You can't taste it —
HELENA	Touch it —
JENNY	Smell it?

Ackerman has slumped in his gas-mask as if he has been overcome by fumes.

The others seem to have given up acting.

ARIEL	There are too many of them?

Ariel goes to the balustrade at the back and looks over. Then he looks at the audience.

Helena looks up at the flies.

Jenny holds her stomach as if she might be ill. Then she seems to give up acting again.

The lights in the backdrop become set, like red-hot lava.

After a time there comes on from behind the loggia, right, Jason, a man in his forties. He wears dark trousers and a white shirt. He carries a coil of wire over his shoulder. It is as if he might be a stage technician.

He walks to the crack in the rocks and looks down. Then he looks up at the flies.

42

The others act as if they do not know whether or not he is supposed to be part of whatever they are or are not acting.

Jason puts his coil of wire down on the ground. He takes from his pocket a penknife and begins to trim an end of the wire as if preparing to make an electrical connection.

Ariel seems to be amused.

Jenny looks at Jason.

Ackerman is slumped in his gas-mask.

Helena is staring at the audience.

Jason, having trimmed the wire, squats down as if to make an electrical connection within the crack in the rocks.

HELENA Won't you stay to lunch?

Jason looks up; looks round; then he goes back to making his connection in the crack in the rocks.

After a time Ariel calls —

ARIEL I say, is this place going to be blown up?

Jason pauses: looks up at Ariel: then goes back to his electrical connection. Then he stands. He moves to the balustrade at the back, paying out the wire behind him.

On the way he glances up at Ackerman. When he is by the balustrade he turns and looks at Ariel. He holds out the wire coiled in his hands. After a time Ariel points at himself questioningly. It is as if he were asking — Me? Then he goes and stands by Jason. He raises his hands and acts —

ARIEL — They usually give you more time, you know —

Jenny says as if she were not acting —

JENNY There's someone down the cliff?

Ariel looks over the balustrade. Jason has made a loop with the wire as if to put it round Ariel to lower him — or to rescue someone from down the cliff.

43

HELENA	Perhaps it's a goat —
JENNY	— Joke?
HELENA	— Goat! —
JENNY	That'll attract them —?

Helena speaks to Jason.

HELENA	Or you mean, what's it tethered to?

Ariel lowers his head. He looks up at the flies.

ARIEL	Isn't that music?

Jason throws the looped end of the wire down over the cliff. Then he jerks on the end of the wire that is attached to the crack in the rocks. Jenny ducks with her hands over her ears.
The others are still.
Then there comes on at the back of the balustrade, left, Judith. She still wears her black dress. She moves along on the level slightly below that of the stage.
When she comes to where she is close to Jason and Ariel, she speaks to Helena.

JUDITH	I'm so sorry. I never thanked you for your party —

She waits. The others do not move.

I did so enjoy it. Especially the Chinese lanterns.

She puts a foot up on the balustrade as if to climb over. She seems to wait for someone to help her.

I do hope you don't mind. I spent the night in your little room.

She looks up at Ackerman.
After a time, Jason puts out a hand to help her over. As she takes his hand, and steps over the balustrade, she puts out a hand and strokes Ariel's cheek. Ariel jerks his head away.
Judith looks at Jenny.
Helena watches the audience.
After a time Jason says awkwardly —

JASON	Oh, Mrs Ackerman, my —

He waits.

— Wife? Mistress? Mother?

Then he turns to Ackerman, and holds out a hand as if about to introduce Judith to him. Then he seems to get an electric shock from the wire that he is holding. He drops it. He looks where the wire goes down over the back of the balustrade. Then he looks up at the flies.

Judith goes and stands underneath Ackerman, looking at him.

Ariel goes and looks down at the crack in the rocks.

Jenny has straightened. She watches Jason.

JENNY   — Now you see it —

ARIEL   — Now you don't —

HELENA   Don't you get any farther —

JENNY   — Father?

ARIEL   Farther!

Jenny murmurs —

JENNY   Son and —

After a time, Ackerman takes off his gas-mask. He is red in the face and sweating.

HELENA   Shouldn't you be saying — Won't you come and see me have my bath?

Jason is looking up at the flies.

JASON   Oh. Yes —

Jenny moves quickly and puts a hand on Jason's arm.

Helena turns to Judith.

Judith is looking up at Ackerman.

JUDITH   Won't you come and see me have my bath?

She turns with her back to Ackerman, and looks at Jenny and Jason.

Ackerman makes a lunge over the balcony and takes hold of Judith violently by the hair.

Judith opens her mouth as if to scream.

Jason looks down at the crack in the rocks.

The CURTAIN comes down

ACT II

The CURTAIN rises as if unexpectedly before the lights in the auditorium have gone out. Judith is on the garden chair, left of centre, with Jason bending over as if he has been embracing her. Jason straightens: he looks at the wings, right. The lights in the auditorium go out.

The SCENE is the same, but as if at night. The backdrop is a dark blue: the surface of the rock is silver. The loggia is hung with coloured lights. The swing sofa has gone. The wire still trails from the crack in the rocks to the balustrade at the back.

Judith lies back in the chair with her eyes closed.

Jason walks up and down. It is as if he is lecturing.

JASON   They were in their natural surroundings —
          imagining — this or that is going on. Is it
          murder. Is it someone else's wife. We
          found — if there was no misery — no one
          turned up. My wife, she likes a good
          murder. Will he strike? In capital cities, all
          over the world, people turned up.

He stops by the wings, left, looking out.

          The rewards were — pain, deprivation.
          They knew where they were. I am alive:
          you are dead. Mummy. Mummy.

He moves on.

          We found happiness, if it was to be held,
          was against a blue background — a mother
          and child, a tree, a woman on the bed. But
          with enough room — this was the point —
          for a man to stand back: and then move on
          — was this the point? — within his hands,

his head. I have gone now, Mummy, Mummy. You are on the bed.

He comes and stands by Judith, looking down. The problem was, to get people at the right place at the right time. So that when there was the crack in the rocks, the avalanche — ah, was that what it was! some would say, standing back; and then move on, their hands within their heads. And some, when the rocks came down, the avalanche —

He looks at the audience
— the fighting in the streets: the people in the valley —

Judith speaks without opening her eyes.

JUDITH   — You drip, drip, making patterns in the snow like pee —

JASON   — would say: exactly.

He moves on.

JUDITH   — Would stay. Exactly.

Jason appears to be thinking.
After a time —

JASON   But what no one ever knew, was whether these theatres ever existed, or if they were just in the mind —

He stops; staring at the loggia.

JUDITH   — Which stayed alive —
JASON   — In the mind — ?
JUDITH   — Of the people.
JASON   But that you can't say. Exactly.

After a time, he moves on.
In the silence, Jason and Judith glance at the audience as if they might observe what people in the audience might be making of what they are saying: as if they are still carrying out an experiment.
Judith sits up and arranges her skirt.

JUDITH   Well, Mr and Mrs Ackerman are sort of gangsters, millionaires. They don't have

	much feeling —
JASON	— Just a lift-shaft —
JUDITH	— Like a flower.

Jason goes to the balustrade at the back and looks over.

JASON	And Ariel —
JUDITH	What —
JASON	Will he get that job?
JUDITH	I don't see why not. His father came to save him –

Jason turns to her.

JASON	And arrived too late —
JUDITH	You were ill. In a monastery —
JASON	— Furry friends came to visit me —
JUDITH	I came to visit you!
JASON	— In your skirt —
JUDITH	— My little skirt! —
JASON	— Your tongues like bells —

They wait. They seem to be listening.

JUDITH	Ah, when you're middle-aged, it's not your fault!

Jason moves round the stage again. He acts —

JASON	— I didn't sleep with her, if that's what you mean —
JUDITH	— I do think Jenny's attractive. It's a mistake, perhaps, to be so young —

Jason stands by the wings, left, looking out.

JASON	They didn't have any children —
JUDITH	Who?
JASON	The women.
JUDITH	But they did. They wanted something different.

Jason seems to think. He looks at the audience. Then he walks up and down again as if lecturing.

JASON	The brain is in two halves, so the left doesn't do what the right is knowing. The left side talks, gives names —

He stops, faces the audience, and holds out his

left hand

    — left of the brain, that is —

He rotates clockwise so that his back is to the audience. He lowers his left hand and holds out his right.

    — but this works the right, so there's no contradiction.

He lowers his right hand. He looks at Judith.

    The right side doesn't speak much: knows what things are for —

He turns clockwise so that he is facing the audience again.

    — but this works the left, so that if you're watching, which you are —

He holds out his right hand; then his left.

Then he stares down as if fascinated or bewildered by the two of them side by side.

After a time —

JUDITH	You drip, drip —
JASON	What does he make?
JUDITH	Who?
JASON	Mr Ackerman.
JUDITH	Chemicals.

Jason looks at the audience. Then he puts out his hand against the vertical plane above the footlights as if he were feeling there a glass partition or a screen.

JASON	Shake it —
JUDITH	Like a cage —
JASON	A sieve —
JUDITH	A riddle —
JASON	A heartbeat.

Ackerman comes on from behind the loggia. He wears an old overcoat over trousers and slippers. He seems to wear no make-up. He appears old. He looks at Jason. Then he walks along the balustrade at the back.

ACKERMAN	They've turned the heating off. I don't

know why. Wouldn't be a bad thing if they
did. Stupid buggers.

He turns and watches Jason.

Jason is still looking at the area above the footlights as if it might be a screen containing
switches and dials.

ACKERMAN   I'm your version of me —
JASON   They're their version of them —
ACKERMAN   Wouldn't be a bad thing if they were; if they
                saw —
JASON   What: rubbish?

Ackerman comes to the front of the stage and
looks at the audience. He seems to act; Jason
seems to be not acting.

ACKERMAN   — There's a boy down there on the wire —
JASON   Do you remember when we went climbing?
ACKERMAN   You dangled on a rope —
JASON   I fell. Was resurrected.

Ackerman and Jason stare at the footlights. It is
as if they were watching the vertical screen
above the footlights containing dials.

ACKERMAN   — Death, disease —
JASON   — Get down off your knees —
ACKERMAN   Which —
JASON   Both.

Ackerman and Jason wait. They watch the
audience.

ACKERMAN   One or two —
JASON   Get through.
ACKERMAN   We didn't know them —
JASON   Didn't we?

After a time Judith speaks with her eyes closed.

JUDITH   You can sing, can't you? Dance?

Jason speaks as if his sentence were the first line
of a song —

JASON   — There was a busload going over the Alps —
ACKERMAN   — And an old lady wanted to pee — ?
JASON   — So I said — Milk? Sugar? —

ACKERMAN	— The water's boiling —
	They stare at the audience.
	After a time Jason looks down over the footlights.
JASON	Something open —
ACKERMAN	Like a hook —
JASON	Like a woman —
	They wait.
ACKERMAN	Try it in second.
JASON	Now?
	Ackerman moves away. He stands by the loggia looking up. He declaims —
ACKERMAN	— Ariel will have great opportunities!
JASON	— The first age since that of Charlemagne! —
	They wait: they seem discouraged.
ACKERMAN	We're not characters.
JASON	Are we?
	After a time —
JUDITH	I'm cold —
ACKERMAN	I'm hungry —
JUDITH	I'll warm you —
JASON	I'll wash it up.
	Ackerman leaves the loggia and goes to Judith and rumples her hair.
	Judith jerks her head away.
	Ackerman goes to the wings, left, and looks out.
	Judith sits up and arranges her skirt.
JUDITH	Is all this being taken down?
JASON	Yes there's a man underneath in a monastery.
JUDITH	I thought it was a tomb.
ACKERMAN	No, it's a laboratory.
	Jason turns from the footlights and watches Judith.
	Judith speaks formally —
JUDITH	You know how, in occupied countries, and the enemy are in the front row — well, if anyone knows the code, why don't they know the message?

ACKERMAN	Such as —
JASON	Because —
JUDITH	— What are you doing tonight? The names of your dearest friends —
JASON	— What would be passed on, would be —
ACKERMAN	Don't tell her! —
JUDITH	I see.

Judith lies back and closes her eyes.
Ackerman comes to the front of the stage and looks as if at the screen above the footlights.

JASON	— I'm cold —
JUDITH	— I'm hungry —
ACKERMAN	They have to do it themselves —
JASON	— I'll warm you.

Ackerman puts a hand out over the footlights.
Behind him, Judith jerks her head away.

ACKERMAN	You see?
JASON	What —
ACKERMAN	More than we can say?

Ackerman looks towards the wings, right.
After a time Jason goes and sits on the steps of the loggia. He faces left across the stage. He acts like a story-teller: or as if he were embarking on another experiment.

JASON	We'd gone through the gamut of determinism, free will: come to the point — you know — you alter what is known. Well one of us, call him me, said — Granted the future goes its own way —

He waits.
He and Ackerman stare at the audience as if waiting for a reaction.
Jason continues —

We took a child, in its pram, to the airport —
Ackerman seems to be watching dials above the footlights.

They'd been watching for people like us —
Ackerman turns to Judith, who is lying back with

her eyes closed.

> There were aeroplanes flying —

Ackerman puts a hand out, tentatively, towards
Judith: then he turns and looks at the audience.

> In each, there was a connection between
> the pilot and the ground —

Ackerman takes his hand away.

Helena appears on the balcony above Jason's
head.

Jason continues to watch Ackerman.

> We put the child, in its pram, by the
> control tower —

Helena is wearing her clothes from the last act.
She gazes out across the stage theatrically. She
appears to be somewhat drunk.

JASON   Wires had to be attached from the suit-
            cases to the pram —

HELENA   Jason —

JASON   Yes —

HELENA   How did you find your father?

Judith speaks with her eyes closed.

JUDITH   — With a stick, a packing-case, and a
            couple of oranges —

Ackerman turns and looks at Helena. He speaks
as if he is amused.

ACKERMAN   — Sit in the packing-case using the stick —

JUDITH   — On the banana —

HELENA   But Jason, what else could he do?

After a time Jason seems to carry on with his
experiment.

JASON   Still, in the air, there were aeroplanes
            flying —

HELENA   You know how much he wanted this part!

Jason seems to give up. He leaves the loggia
steps. He goes to the balustrade at the back and
looks over.

Judith speaks with her eyes closed.

JUDITH   Leave it to the dogs' home —

53

JASON	Build a library.

Helena puts a leg over the balcony as if she is about to climb over.

HELENA	But if we're not characters —

Ackerman speaks to Jason —

ACKERMAN	Where's Ariel —
JASON	Ask Jenny —
HELENA	What are we?

Judith speaks as if answering Ackerman.

JUDITH	In the park.

Helena, as if drunk, seems about to fall over the balcony.

Ackerman goes and stands underneath her and puts his hands up as if to help her on to his shoulders.

Judith sits up and arranges her skirt. She speaks again formally.

JUDITH	You know the experiment with the dog —

Helena gets a foot down on to Ackerman's shoulder.

Show it a circle, give it food: show it an oval, give it —

Jason looks down at the wire which trails over the balustrade. He seems to be considering whether or not to touch it.

JUDITH	Bring the two closer and closer together —
JASON	— You'll betray me —
JUDITH	— You'll make me —
JASON	— You'll stand on those steps and say —

He puts his hand on the wire.

Helena gets both legs down over Ackerman's shoulders.

JUDITH	It's dead —
JASON	It's not.
JUDITH	What —
JASON	The baby?

Ackerman and Helena move off round the stage with her on his shoulders like elderly acrobats.

	Judith lies back with her eyes closed. She acts —
JUDITH	— The people on the roads! With their little tails going! —
JASON	— There were not many left to tell the tale.
	Jason pulls the wire up and coils it. Then he comes to the front of the stage carrying the wire. One end remains fastened to the crack in the rocks. He looks down over the footlights.
JUDITH	A connection —
JASON	Conception?
JUDITH	Connection!
JASON	I know they're somewhere —
JUDITH	Like a bird?
	Helena, on Ackerman's shoulders, looks up to the back of the auditorium. She speaks in a young girl's voice.
HELENA	— Mummy —
ACKERMAN	— Yes?
HELENA	— What's that person in the trees?
ACKERMAN	It's the light of our lives, darling.
	Ackerman moves with Helena to the balustrade by the wings, back left. He seems to be trying to set her down there.
JASON	Ooops —
JUDITH	Oopla —
JASON	Upsadaisy —
	Jason seems to get an electric shock from the wire that he is holding. He drops it down over the footlights. Then he looks out over the audience.
JUDITH	— It goes on all the time —
JASON	Like music?
	Ariel comes on from the wings, back left. He wears a duffle coat. He seems to have stopped acting. He goes to Ackerman and seems to have a conversation with him.
	Helena is still on Ackerman's shoulders. She is trying to get down. After a time, Ariel helps her

	down on to the balustrade.
	Judith calls —
JUDITH	Louder!
	Ackerman stops talking to Ariel. He turns to Judith.
	Jason squats by the footlights.
JASON	Can you hear?
	Helena enunciates carefully, as if relaying what Ariel has been saying —
HELENA	— My — men — are — outside —
	Jason takes hold of the wire over the footlights and pulls at it gently, as if it were a fishing line.
ACKERMAN	You telephoned —
JASON	What —
ACKERMAN	Exact time and place.
	Helena enunciates carefully —
HELENA	Do — not — leave — this — building —
	She climbs down from the balustrade.
	Jason lets go of the wire. He stands. He looks amongst the audience.
ACKERMAN	Got it?
JUDITH	— The tanks are in the streets —
JASON	— There are people dying.
	They wait.
	Ariel goes out at the wings, back left.
	Ackerman remains at the back as if he is off-stage, watching.
HELENA	Harry —
JASON	Yes?
HELENA	Will you hold her for a moment please?
	Jason turns to her.
JASON	She's my child?
	Jenny comes on from in front of the loggia, right. She wears a T-shirt and jeans.
	She comes to the front of the stage and begins undressing.
JENNY	God, do you know how often I have to do

56

this? Every day. Morning and evening. —
Where's the fire. In your great big beautiful
eyes —

When she is in her underclothes she looks at the
audience. The others have paid no attention to
her. She goes and stands by Jason.
Where do they come from?

JASON	How did we do it —
JENNY	If it helps them.

They wait.

JUDITH	Perhaps if we don't watch —
JENNY	I'm burning!

Jenny doubles up, holding her middle.

Jason squats down by the footlights with his
back to the audience, facing the stage. It is as if
he were about to lower himself down by the
wire over the footlights.

HELENA	But Harry, they'll kill you —
JUDITH	What is this, a hairdresser's?

Jason is watching Judith.

JENNY	Who're you talking to —
HELENA	The barman?

Judith gets up off the chair and goes and stands
by Ackerman. She faces Jason.

JENNY	Now you see it —
HELENA	Now you don't.

They wait.

JENNY	Leaping up the waterfalls
JASON	On to the dry land.

They wait.

JENNY	I think it's when it touches —
HELENA	What —
JASON	Not another world?
JENNY	The walls fall down?

They wait.

HELENA	It's when you're dying.
JENNY	Trying —
HELENA	Dying —

They wait.

JASON   Don't touch!
JENNY   They're in the building —
HELENA   They're from outside.

They wait.

JENNY   You step back —
HELENA   You go over.

Judith puts her head on Ackerman's shoulder.
Then the lights on the stage go out.
There run on from the wings, left, Ariel pursued
by the Footman and the Maid. They catch him;
they scuffle; they seem to be trying to prevent
him reaching the crack in the rocks.
Ackerman moves along the balustrade and
begins to dismantle a section, right of centre.
Judith goes to help him.
Jenny moves across the front of the stage to the
proscenium arch, left, and leans with her back
against it.
Jason turns to the front of the stage where the
wire goes over. He looks down.
Helena remains by the wings, back left.
Ackerman and Judith arrange the bits of the
dismantled balustrade to make it seem as if
someone had fallen over.
Then the lights come on.
Everyone becomes still.
Ariel, centre, is held by the arms by the Footman
and the Maid. He watches Jason.
After a time, the Footman and the Maid let Ariel
go. They turn and watch the audience.
Jason takes hold of the wire that goes over the
footlights.
Jenny, by the proscenium arch, left, watches
Jason.
Ackerman and Judith continue to arrange the
bits of the balustrade as if someone had fallen
over.

Ariel goes and crouches by the crack in the rocks.

Ackerman and Judith go to the loggia, right, and look up.

Helena has not moved.

The lights go out.

Jenny goes and sits on the garden chair.

Ackerman and Judith reach up and begin to dismantle the huge toy-like blocks of which the loggia is made.

The Footman and Maid come to the footlights, right and left, and look out over the audience. The Maid puts a hand in her pocket as if she holds a gun there.

Ackerman and Judith carry blocks from the loggia and place them round the garden chair like prehistoric stones.

Jason crouches by the footlights, holding the wire, and turns with his back to the audience.

Ariel and Helena have not moved.

The lights come on.

Everyone is still.

After a time Helena joins Ackerman and Judith by the loggia. They continue to dismantle the huge toy-like blocks of the loggia. They place them round Jenny in the chair.

Ariel is squatting by the crack in the rocks facing Jason. He has his hand on the wire.

ARIEL	— Johnny —
JASON	— Yes —
ARIEL	— Don't jump. Your old grandmother, in Australia, has a message for you —

Jason is holding the wire with his back to the audience as if he is about to lower himself over a cliff. He turns and looks down over the footlights.

ARIEL	— You might hit a little doggy in the road —
JASON	Oh really!

59

The lights go out.

Ackerman and Judith and Helena continue arranging the blocks of the loggia around Jenny. The Footman and Maid, at the footlights, stare out over the audience. They both have their hands in their pockets as if they might be security men, or terrorists.

Jason lowers himself over the footlights. He looks down.

JASON   It's a sort of —

ARIEL   What?

JASON   Museum. Huts, watchtowers. Ladies and gentlemen on the grass.

When he is in the auditorium, Jason coils the wire at the front of the stage.

The lights come on.

Ariel is crouching by the crack in the rocks. He looks up at the flies.

ARIEL   That's brilliant!

The Footman and the Maid, right and left, watch the audience.

Judith and Ackerman and Helena, having arranged the blocks of the loggia like primitive stones around Jenny in the garden chair, stand back as if to admire their work.

Helena goes to Jenny and stands with her hand on the back of her chair.

Judith and Ackerman go and stand by the broken balustrade.

Jason begins to walk off at the front of the auditorium, left.

Ariel is facing the audience.

ARIEL   See if they can fly —

He waits.

Now!

The Curtain begins to come down.

There are three loud bangs, from the flies, as in the first act.

The Footman and the Maid duck.

The Curtain stops.

Jason, at the front left of the auditorium, stops.

He looks at the stage.

Ariel looks at the audience.

The Footman and the Maid look up at the flies.

Ackerman looks over the broken bit of the balustrade at the back.

Judith watches Helena and Jenny.

Jason murmurs —

JASON   Ten minutes to go.

He looks at the audience.

Just time for a cup of tea?

The Footman and the Maid have straightened.
They take their hands out of their pockets and raise them: they have no guns.

Helena and Jenny are posed within the circle of stones.

Ariel, by the crack in the rocks, takes his hand from the wire.

The Curtain continues to come down.

The Footman and the Maid seem uncertain; then they move off into the wings, right and left.

Jason walks out through an exit at the back of the auditorium, left.

The Curtain stops a few inches above the ground.

Ariel can be seen, on his hands and knees, to have one hand on the wire: he is peering underneath the Curtain into the auditorium.

Then the lights in the auditorium come on.

The lights on the stage go out.

The CURTAIN remains a few inches above the stage.

ACT III

The lights on the stage come on while the Curtain is still a few inches above the stage.

The CURTAIN rises.

SCENE: the same. A cold grey light. The backdrop is unlit, so the material it is made of is showing. The broken pieces of the balustrade are arranged as at the end of the last act. The wire still trails from the crack in the rocks over the footlights and into the auditorium. The dismantled blocks of the loggia are in their semi-circle like prehistoric stones.

Jenny is lying in the garden chair within the circle of stones. She is in her underclothes. Her eyes are closed. She seems to have taken over the role of Judith in the last act.

Helena is standing by the broken balustrade, looking over. She wears an old overcoat and trousers and carries a travelling bag on a strap over her shoulder.

Judith is seated on one of the blocks, left. She is in her underclothes, and has on her lap a pair of jeans which she seems to be altering or mending. She speaks as she sews.

JUDITH   And when I'd come into the kitchen he'd got them even there, with little stalks sticking out like apples. And when I'd say — For God's sake, if you want to speed up nature —

She bites her thread off: holds the jeans up to the light.

— he put them in the fridge.

She puts the jeans down: tries to re-thread her needle.

He called it proterogyny — of the female sexual organs.

She manages to thread the needle.

    If you don't eat it up for dinner —
She sews.

    — bombs: seeds: apples —
She holds the jeans up again. She puts the needle in her mouth.

    — you'll get them back for tea.
She puts down the jeans. She puts the needle away. She rummages in a travelling bag that is beside her on the ground.

    How many did he have with him, do you know? I think it was a number. Or was he on his own? I think it was a number. There are enough in the streets, God knows. In the valleys. Leaping up the fences. Breaking down the waterfalls. On to the dry land.
She has taken from her travelling bag an automatic pistol, which she holds on her lap and dismantles.

    What were they doing in a place like this? I think they were imprisoned. Or were they protected? I think they were imprisoned. You were in that chair. Then I was in that chair —
She uses Jenny's old T-shirt, taken from the bag, to clean the pistol.

    Put enough of us together —
She holds the pistol up towards the wings, right, and looks through the barrel.

    — in a telephone box —
She squeezes the trigger.

    — Help! He pushed me! —
She lowers the pistol.

    It's an overcrowded profession.
She reassembles the pistol and puts it back in her bag. Then she stands and struggles to put on the jeans, which are Jenny's, and thus too small for her.

wouldn't it be for the best if —
She faces the audience.
    — With your hands, your hair —
She manages to get on the jeans.
    — you think you're so morally superior —
She raises the T-shirt; she struggles to pull it over her head: for a moment it is as if she were being tortured.
    — Oh no I didn't —
    — Oh yes you did —
Helena leaves the balustrade and comes towards her. She speaks in a masculine voice.

HELENA   — Either of you two girls coming with me across the park? —

Judith manages to pull the T-shirt down over her face. She says with relief —

JUDITH   — Freddie knocks his bowl over, and then he can't drink.

Helena looks to the wings, left. Then she moves round the stage.

HELENA   They didn't have any children. Or they didn't have any children —

She stops by Jenny and looks down at her.
    — The people on the roads. With their little tails going —
She looks at the audience.
    — The queens of Egypt, on their beds.
She goes to the balustrade at the back and looks over.
    What did they give her, do you know?

JUDITH   Coloured lights, shapes, music —

Helena turns to the ruins of the loggia, right. She acts —

HELENA   — When she came in —

Judith acts as if following Helena's lead —

JUDITH   — With his arm around her —
HELENA   — And they were looking up —
JUDITH   — Our skirts —

64

HELENA	— Our little skirts! —
JUDITH	— Their tongues like bells! —

Helena comes to the footlights and looks at the audience. She speaks in her ordinary voice.

HELENA	Have you looked in her bag?
JUDITH	God, aren't there enough people in this town looking in people's bags!

She comes and looks on the floor by Jenny.

HELENA	It has to be in the dark —
JUDITH	Why?
HELENA	Or how can you look for it?

Judith seems to quote —

JUDITH	— There's an underground river —
HELENA	— Disgorges its victims.

Helena moves off round the stage. Then she faces the ruins of the loggia again and acts —

	— I was in the back of the van —
JUDITH	— He asked for water —
HELENA	— His head was in my lap —
JUDITH	— They'd kept the engine running.

Then Helena goes and looks over the balustrade. She says in her ordinary voice —

HELENA	Don't blame yourself, lovers quarrel.

Judith acts —

JUDITH	— I was in my pram —
HELENA	— Then I was in my pram —
JUDITH	— Till we're all in one room —

Helena faces the audience.

HELENA	You don't get to where you want to go, if you think you know where you're going.

Jenny speaks with her eyes closed.

JENNY	I'm not asleep, if that's what you mean.

Judith has been looking on the ground around the chair.

JUDITH	It's all in your head —
HELENA	Your pretty head —
JUDITH	Your tongues like music.

After a time Jenny sits up and mimes arranging

	her skirt as Judith has done in the last act.
	Judith has turned to the audience.
JENNY	You know how, he said, you're in a wood, and you come out on to a cornfield —
JUDITH	Weren't you a singer?
HELENA	I used to dance.
JENNY	— And in front of you there's the sun, so that you can't see —

Helena comes to the footlights.
She leans forward and screws up her eyes as if she were trying to read something on a wall in front of her —

HELENA	— I am the — conscience of — my unhappy — family —
JENNY	— A pit —
JUDITH	— A tomb —
HELENA	— A garden —
JENNY	Whether or not you've dug it yourself —
JUDITH	— Don't push me dear, I'm peeing.

They wait.
Then Jenny makes a noise as if she might be imitating music, or a machine-gun —

JENNY	Da da di dum dum. Da da di da —
HELENA	You can't say that!
JUDITH	It's people!

Jenny lies back with her eyes closed.
Helena looks down over the footlights.
Judith watches the audience.
It is as if Helena and Judith were seeing through the screen that Ackerman and Jason were looking at in the last act.

| JUDITH | In the end — |
| HELENA | Is it people? |

After a time Ariel comes on from behind the ruins of the loggia. He wears his white trousers and his coloured shirt. He holds his left forearm with his right hand. The sleeve of his shirt is torn and bloodstained.

66

He moves along the balustrade till he comes to the place where it is broken. He stops.

A spotlight comes on him from above the stage.

After a time Judith goes to him, and takes his arm and examines it.

Jenny speaks with her eyes closed.

JENNY You saw them, what were they like?

ARIEL Two eyes and a nose, and a room behind.

JENNY You were with them, what did they do?

ARIEL One or two on street corners.

JENNY You brought them —

JUDITH I brought them!

JENNY They followed you —

JUDITH But what do we do?

After a time Helena turns and looks at Judith. Judith has taken off Ariel's shirt, and is trying to make a sling with it.

Helena moves off along the footlights towards the left. She acts —

HELENA — There was one took out his eyes —

Jenny speaks with her eyes closed.

JENNY — Said Mummy, open your mouth —

JUDITH — And in she popped them.

Ariel leaves Judith and comes down towards the footlights.

He stares at the audience. He acts tragically —

ARIEL — They were coming across the ice —

JUDITH — The barrel got so hot —

ARIEL You couldn't see —

JENNY — Pee — ?

JUDITH See!

Helena puts her head in her hands.

Ariel watches the audience.

ARIEL They cared?

JUDITH They listened —

JENNY They were seeing —

After a time Judith goes into the wings, back left, and seems to be trying to drag a heavy object on

to the stage. It comes half into view. it is the
swing sofa. She struggles with it: then she sits on
it and rests.

Helena murmurs —

HELENA   It's when you're working —
JENNY   Dying —
ARIEL   Knowing?
JUDITH   Handing on —

Ariel is watching the audience.

ARIEL   — Where did he put it, do you know?
JENNY   — In some hole, I think, by the lavatory.
ARIEL   — Who's going to get it, do you know?
JUDITH   — Some grandson, I think, in Australia.

They wait.

ARIEL   You throw your sticks on the ground —
JUDITH   Upsadaisy!
HELENA   You create it?

They wait.

JENNY   You stand back —
ARIEL   You go over.

After a time there come on from the wings, back
right, Ackerman, followed by the Footman and
the Maid who carry a stretcher. On the stretcher
there is a blanket covering what seems to be a
body. They are like a funeral cortege.

They come and stand awkwardly by the broken
part of the balustrade.

Judith watches them. The others ignore them.
Helena takes her head from her hands.

HELENA   Are we gods and goddesses?

After a time Jenny sits up. She and Ariel and
Helena speak to the audience as if they found
what they were saying once more embarrassing.

ARIEL   — We'd introduced a strain —
HELENA   — Into a culture —
JENNY   — You do it yourself —
ARIEL   — In laboratory conditions —
HELENA   — What hurts you; makes you grow —

68

JENNY	— To see, whether or not —
ARIEL	— Oi! They're getting into government! —
HELENA	— There could be tested —
JENNY	— They like it?
HELENA	— What might make for tolerance, under-standing —
ARIEL	— Radio-active waste: cancer-carrying bacteria —
JENNY	— In the outside world —
HELENA	— It kills them?

They wait. Ariel and Helena watch the audience. Jenny lies back.

After a time Ackerman and the Footman and Maid with the stretcher move on and stand outside the circle of stones, as if waiting to be let in. Judith stands; drags the swing sofa slightly further on to the stage; gives up and sits on it.

Jenny sits up.

Ariel and Helena speak to the audience again with slightly different words and emphases —

ARIEL	— We'd introduced a strain —
HELENA	— Into a culture —
JENNY	— You do it yourself —
ARIEL	— In laboratory conditions —
JENNY	— It hurts you?
HELENA	— To see whether or not —
JENNY	— Oi! They're getting into government!
ARIEL	— There could be tested —
HELENA	— Do they like it?
ARIEL	— What might make for tolerance, under-standing —
HELENA	— Radio-active waste; cancer-carrying bacteria —
ARIEL	— In the outside world —
JENNY	— It kills them.

Ariel and Helena watch the audience, as if waiting to see the results of an experiment. Jenny lies back with her eyes closed.

Judith sits on the swing sofa. She smiles.

After a time —

JUDITH   Ariel —

ARIEL   Yes?

JUDITH   Don't you think you've got the right man?

Ackerman leaves the Footman and the Maid. He comes and joins Ariel by the footlights and looks with him at the audience.

ACKERMAN   You can make him smile —

ARIEL   — Can't you —

HELENA   — Dance —

ACKERMAN   — A bit of wire through the mouth, the eyes —

Ariel puts a hand to his face as if he were grieving.

ARIEL   One knee slightly bent. The arms in the position of a man in —

ACKERMAN   Power —

ARIEL   Pain —

ACKERMAN   Power!

After a time Ackerman seems to prompt Ariel.

ACKERMAN   Footprints in the —

ARIEL   Snow —

ACKERMAN   Blood —

ARIEL   Snow —

They wait.

Ariel takes his hand from his face. It seems as if he might have been laughing.

Ackerman goes back to the Footman and Maid. Ariel calls after him —

ARIEL   — I'll be at the second milestone —

ACKERMAN   — I'll be at the fourth —

ARIEL   — Then run —

ACKERMAN   — I can't

ARIEL   — Why not —

ACKERMAN   — Arthritis —

Ariel seems to be controlling laughter with difficulty.

The Footman and Maid, with their stretcher, step inside the circle of stones. They are squashed up against Jenny on the chair.
Ackerman watches them.
Ariel puts a hand out over the footlights. He gets hold of what seem to be the bars of a cage. He speaks as if he is not acting —

ARIEL   At the back of the vocal chords?
ACKERMAN   A sort of tongue, you move around.

Ariel seems to shake, gently, the bars of the cage.

ARIEL   Not a language?
JUDITH   A kiss —
JENNY   A bit of old boot —
HELENA   A landfall.
ACKERMAN   A cell.

Jenny gets up from the garden chair. She goes and sits on the steps of the ruined loggia, right.

ARIEL   Now you see them —
ACKERMAN   Now you don't —

The Footman and the Maid place the stretcher on the chair. Then they turn to Ackerman.
Ariel calls, to his front —

ARIEL   How are you two doing?
ACKERMAN   All right.
ARIEL   Wife and kids?
ACKERMAN   All right.

Ariel takes his hand away from the footlight.
Helena turns from the footlights. She goes to the back of the stage and faces front.
Judith speaks from the swing sofa, back left.

JUDITH   That one worked then.

Ackerman goes and joins Helena at the back of the stage.

ACKERMAN   How was that for you?
HELENA   Oh wonderful!

Judith watches Ariel.

JUDITH   And will there be a child?
JENNY   Oh what shall we call it!

71

	Ariel moves round the stage.
ARIEL	Remember, in politics, nothing is ever said.
	In politics, remember, nothing is ever said.
	They wait; occasionally glancing at the audience.
JENNY	What happened?
ARIEL	Slipped and went over.
JUDITH	Will it get better?
ARIEL	How do we know —
JENNY	How can we bear it!

After a time, Jason comes on from behind the ruins of the loggia. He wears an old overcoat. It is as if he were about to go home.

He stands watching the others, who have turned away from the footlights.

Then he calls —

JASON   Oi! You can't just leave it — ! How is it? Or he or she. Oh —

He looks at the audience.

The others are still.

Jason comes forward. He stares at the audience; then down over the footlights. Then he squats down where the wire goes over the footlights. He takes hold of it.

      — They were mucking about one day —

He pulls the wire in.

      — In the fields, the factories —

He stands: coils the wire.

      Said — Don't look now, Daddy; something's burning —

He lays the coiled wire at the front of the stage. He speaks as if not acting.

      It was too expensive a system anyway.

He turns to the Maid and the Footman who are in the circle of stones.

      Where were you two sitting?

The Maid and the Footman stare at him.

Jason looks amongst the audience.

After a time he goes to the crack in the rocks and

	takes a screwdriver from his pocket and squats down as if to disconnect the wire there.
	Jenny calls —
JENNY	It is still breathing!
	Jason looks up at the audience.
	Then he goes to the circle of stones and takes the blanket off the stretcher. Underneath are two pillows.
	He gives these to the Footman and the Maid.
JASON	You've got clothes, haven't you? Wine — ?
JUDITH	Wire?
JASON	Wine!
	Jason goes back to the crack in the rocks. He squats down.
JUDITH	Oops!
JENNY	Oopla!
JUDITH	Upsadaisy!
	Jason disconnects the wire.
ARIEL	See you —
ACKERMAN	In the pub?
HELENA	At the airport!
	Jason stands, and comes back to the Maid and the Footman in the circle of stones.
JASON	Does the light hurt you? The air?
	He waits.
	Would you like a bath?
	The Maid and Footman watch him.
	Helena murmurs —
HELENA	Pick it up in your arms —
JUDITH	— With soft lights, sweet music —
JENNY	— Don't hit it!
	After a time Ackerman says awkwardly —
ACKERMAN	And the rest —
JASON	Are buried beneath the tree.
	They wait, as if taking care not to look at the audience.
ARIEL	There were aeroplanes flying —
HELENA	One went over —

JUDITH	One went into a tree —
ACKERMAN	We can try again —
JENNY	Can't we?

Jason goes to Jenny on the steps of the ruined loggia and rumples her hair. Jenny moves her head away.

JASON In love, remember, not much is ever said.

He turns to Judith.

In birth, love, not much of pain is remembered.

Helena is by the balustrade, facing the circle of stones.

Judith is sitting on the swing sofa, left, facing the circle of stones.

Jenny is on the steps of the loggia, right, facing the circle of stones.

HELENA	One or two —
ACKERMAN	Got through.
JENNY	Are we eggs and fishes?

Ackerman is by the footlights facing the circle of stones.

Ariel is by the footlights facing the circle of stones.

Jason looks down at Jenny.

ARIEL	What's the advantage —
JUDITH	You can bear it —
JASON	It'll survive?

Jason looks at Judith. He smiles.

Judith, on the sofa, smiles back at him.

Jason holds out a hand to the Maid and the Footman as if to usher them off the stage.

The Maid and the Footman remain within the circle of stones.

Jason lowers his arm.

Everyone except the Maid and the Footman go off the stage.

The CURTAIN comes down.

LANDFALL

The word 'alienation' has had other vogues than that of being used to describe Brecht's acting technique ('the demonstrator and demonstrated are not merged into one'): Hegel and Marx used it to describe the predicament of a man in modern society being cut off from, yet dominated by, his environment: Sartre used it both in this way and, as Brecht seemed to try to do, in the way of describing a man's difficulties in being at one within himself. Being-at-one, Sartre said, was a characteristic of the unconsciousness of a thing: the fact that a human being had consciousness meant that there was a division between the self that was conscious and the self it was conscious of: consciousness consisted as it were of this gap: it was a lack, an anxiety, a 'nothingness' because it was not a 'thing'. It was by virtue of his no-thing-ness that a man had freedom: he could move, decide, choose: but because he could not become an object in himself (and thus be-at-one with himself) his choosing, and what was chosen, were still within a condition of nothingness — and thus were absurd. Haunted by the pain of this a person tried to find some object in an 'other': but this 'other' was trying to find some object in him: so there was collision between persons as if two bodies were trying to occupy the same space at the same time. This was hell. Sartre saw human violence as inevitable not just because of economic scarcity (there would always be too many people fighting for too few goods) but because of this primary predicament in which a man could not be at peace with others because he could not be at peace with himself. Men did in fact form groups: they transferred their anxieties on to groups: but the cohesion of a group was ensured by the threat of violence to an enemy without and to a potential traitor within. This indeed is a description of much in modern politics. Sartre's logic however depended upon verbal tricks. The jump from the recognition that a man is not a 'thing' to the despair that he is therefore 'nothing' — the assumption that duality, distancing, are the same as vacuity, lack — these are personal presupposi-

77

tions, using logic as a weapon, and it is on them that Sartre's pessimism rests. Sartre talked of his deep disgust with himself — the 'dull and inescapable feeling of sickness' which 'perpetually reveals my body to my consciousness'.[1] Given this controlling feeling, it is likely that a man's experience of himself should seem absurd. But this is an affliction, it is not a necessity — this supposed inability of consciousness to heal or surmount its own split.

One escape from despair at the predicament of consciousness was to make a scapegoat of science — to blame scientific ways of thinking for a man's alienation from society and within himself. At the time when Sartre and Brecht were beginning to write their novels and plays Husserl, a philosopher, was launching a full-scale attack on science. From the days of Galileo, Husserl said, thinking had taken a wrong turn: there had been an insistence that nothing should be taken as 'real' except that which could be described in terms of measurements and equations: but these latter were abstractions and not the stuff of actual experience. Experience was to do with sense-impressions and feelings — upon which measurements and equations were imposed. It was within the ambit of this peculiar transposition by which abstractions were called objective and actual experience was doubted as illusory that life, not surprisingly, appeared absurd. Husserl suggested that a form of science should be attempted in which abstractions should not dominate ways of thinking about experience: that since 'objectivity' was in fact structured by the 'subjectivity' of minds, what might be studied, once this was admitted, were relationships between the two — the forms of 'subjectivity' that, by their prevalence, made the experience of 'objectivity' possible. Advantage could be taken of the very 'lack of coincidence' within the self that had caused Sartre such despair; since it was by this that a man might be able to study, with his mind, his mind's phenomena. And Sartre's further despair that each man's consciousness was inextricably at loggerheads with others', as if in a game of violent musical chairs, could be countered by the actual experience that each individual 'knows himself to be living within the horizon of his fellow human beings with whom he can enter into actual, sometimes potential, contact: as they can do (likewise he knows) in actual and potential living together'.[2] It is true that each man remorselessly confers his own meanings on experience: but amongst these meanings there are criss-crossings, sometimes collisions, sometimes connections: these form the web of a communal ('objective') subjective world. It is here that people can meet — can get pleasure, even, from some such banging into each other as in musical chairs — by the ability to stand back and observe, even laugh at, themselves. It is within this sort of dexterity — the ability to transpose, to create from, a situation of potential violence — that there can be valid freedom and healing and choice.

Another way of asserting that consciousness need not involve despair was not to berate science but to ask that its attitudes should be taken more seriously. Jacques Monod, a biologist, has said that it seems likely that the need for a man to try to explain his existence is 'inborn, inscribed somewhere in the genetic code'.[3] It was this that had given impetus to the projections of myths and religions — for huge philosophical systems like that of Marx. These have been necessary for the formation of societies, which in turn have been necessary for survival. But in the course of evolution there has been selected an aptitude for scientific method — 'the systematic confrontation of logic and experience' — and it is this that now seems necessary for survival. The old myths have become too dangerous: in an age of H-bombs, societies requiring enemies and scapegoats are unfitted for evolution. But at some level the animist traditions of thousands of years remain: scientific method, although practised in special disciplines and honoured by lip-service almost universally, is divorced from ways in which people ordinarily feel and behave. Western societies, Monod said, still 'present as a basis for morality a disgusting farrago of Judaeo-Christian religiosity, scientific progressism, belief in the "natural" rights of man and utilitarian pragmatism': and Marxist societies still 'profess the materialist and dialectical religion of history. All these systems are 'outside objective knowledge, outside truth, and strangers and fundamentally hostile to science . . . The divorce is so great, the lie so flagrant, that it can only obsess and lacerate anyone who has some culture and intelligence or is moved by that moral questioning which is the sole source of all creativity.' 'Modern societies have accepted the treasure and power offered them by science: but they have not accepted, have scarcely even heard, its profounder message — the defining of a new and unique source of truth, and the demand for a thorough revision of ethical premises; for the complete break with the animist tradition, the definite abandonment of the "old covenant" and the necessity of forging a new one.'[4] This was a fine cry — similar to those which called for a new covenant in art, in literature — and it came from a scientist at grips with actual processes of creation. But the old questions remain — of just what is this new covenant between scientific method and daily life to consist? what is the style of the 'profounder message' after the 'revision of ethical premises'? Monod, like Brecht — like the old animist theologians before them — found it easier to talk about what faith does not refer to, rather than about what it does. But again, he gave hints. Evolution through natural selection — one of the basic tenets of modern science — is, in the case of man, hardly 'natural' any more: it is not the 'fittest' in any traditional sense who are now most likely to survive: 'even genetic cripples live long enough to reproduce', and the qualities of 'intelligence, ambition, courage and imagination' upon the favouring of which the future of the race would seem to depend, whilst still having personal advantage, have now no obvious genetic advantage — 'the only kind that matters for evolution'.[5] This deposition of nature has come about through the agency of modern science: but science has as yet no alternative to the 'naturalness' of selection. Men have not thought it proper ('who would wish or dare?') to take the place of nature in this way: and in this, given their confusions, they are probably right. But it is in the facing of this sort of situation that there is the chance of some new covenant. At the moment there are only taboos: there is no structure of thinking or of language with which to deal with these things — to deal both with the judgements arrived at through scientific knowledge and, at the same time, with the value judgements of ethics — although these latter have a status as it were equal to that of more precise scientific knowledge since they too have evolved through processes of natural selection — as has the ability to learn. This is the area, the gap, in which there might be the rainbow-bridge of a new covenant — the ability to become accustomed to talking, with authority, a language which will refer to all these forms of knowledge at the same time.

An attempt to describe the style of some new covenant — and incidentally to face the question of the possible forms of man-made selection — has been that of Karl Popper, a philosopher of science. (These names — Husserl, Monod, Popper — are brought in here like harbingers of some spiritual-scientific football team because this is the sort of thing, it seems to me, that they are — having perhaps little direct contact with each other, but forming, in my mind at least, the vastly exciting web of a communal 'objective' subjective world: it being by such connections, influences, ramifications of attitudes and ideas that life becomes ordered and creative and as it were scores goals.) Scientists are not, Popper says, taking observations and constructing from them a world of objective truth though it is often supposed that they are: what they are in fact doing is making imaginative conjectures and then making observations to test these against experience with the purpose of eliminating those conjectures which are shown to be false. Men learn from a process of making mistakes: 'the quest for certainty for a secure basis of knowledge has to be abandoned': 'what may be called positive is *only* so with respect to negative methods'. Even our knowledge of ourselves is all such 'decoding or interpretation'. But although both 'the amoeba and Einstein . . . make use of the method of trial-and-error elimination, the a moeba dislikes to err while Einstein is intrigued by it: he c onsciously searches for his errors in the hope of learning'.[6] The style of a new covenant between scientific method and daily life, that is, might be something to do with this attitude towards mistakes — to learn how to use them, rather than be haunted by them: to see them as a means for improvement, rather than a being enmeshed. But this is not a common attitude: there seems to be a greater attraction, at the moment, in the security of being enmeshed. Popper suggests that there should be a recognition of three distinct worlds — 1. the world of physical objects: 2. the world of states of consciousness: and 3. the world of objective contents of thought — 'especially of scientific and poetic thoughts and works of art'. This 'world 3', as Popper calls it, is man's special accomplishment: it is the tangible representation of the world of communal subjectivity in which he can move and have a choice: it is man's creation, yet it has its own autonomy: it is a world of man's ideas, yet held objectively in books and records and symbols. This world 3, perhaps, contains the means by which a man can stand back and see himself: by which he can be in relationship with others without the absurdity of collision. And it is here, perhaps, that natural selection can still properly take place. There can be evaluation and elimination of the products of the imagination: there need be a violation of neither knowledge nor ethics. 'It is only science which replaces the elimination of error in the violent struggle for life by non-violent rational criticism and which allows us to replace killing (world 1) and intimidation (world 2) by the impersonal arguments of world 3.'⁷ But still, it is in worlds 1 and 2 that people have to live: and it is here that the question again is posed — might there not be some acceptable attitude to selection here, if only there were a language by which humans could embrace the apparent complexities of their nature?

A scientist who moved from a study of societies to a study of personalities (the better, perhaps, to understand societies) is Gregory Bateson — anthropologist, ecologist, psychologist — who in his collection of essays *Steps towards an Ecology of Mind* has suggested how a man's lack of coincidence with himself might be a means of not just accepting but being able to grow in consciousness and learning. There is Learning I (these code-words, like those of Popper's 'worlds', are the sort of cries that footballers use when more elegant speech is not useful) — there is Learning I, which is the sort of learning available to animals as well as to humans and which depends on the responses to stimuli becoming habitual. There is Learning II, which is an accomplishment of man, and depends on a man's ability to stand back from the processes of Learning I and to see its patterns — and in this at least in some sense to be free of them. And there is Learning III, which is rarely glimpsed by men, but perhaps is that which may be necessary for survival. Learning III is a standing back from the patterns of Learning II — in the same way that Learning II is a standing back from Learning I — it is the chance for a man to see not just the patterns of his behaviour but also the patterns of his ability to see — and by this, not just to be free of patterns, but possibly to influence them. For what he will then be in contact with, Bateson suggests, is a network of 'propositions, images, processes, natural pathology and what-have-you' that is like 'some vast ecology or aesthetics of cosmic interaction': not only within the mind, but in connection with the world outside of which the mind is conscious: some circuitry going between, and around, these inside and outside worlds. And insofar as a man knows himself to be part of, representative of, these interactions, then he is not helpless: it is only when he supposes himself to be single and all-of-a-piece that he is. A simple or 'unaided' consciousness is likely to be 'only a sampling of different parts and localities of this network' and thus a 'monstrous denial of the integration of the whole': 'from the cutting (or limitation) of consciousness, what appear above the surface are *arcs* of circuits instead of either the complete circuit or the larger complete circuit of circuits'. Also — 'unaided consciousness must always tend towards hate, not only because it is good common sense to exterminate the other fellow, but for the more profound reason that, seeing only arcs of circuits, the individual is continually surprised and necessarily angered when his hard-headed policies come back to plague the inventor'.[8] To get beyond 'good common sense' — beyond the patterns of Learnings I and even II that cause such anguish — to be able to consider some 'circuit of circuits' — it is in this effort that there is freedom, fellowship, lack of hate; and thus the chance to survive. But still — how are people who wish to make such an effort not to be wiped out by those who do not?

Scientists who deal with physical workings of the brain find some such kinds of circuitry in fact: the brain with its immensely complex system of fibres and connections and branches and switches through which impulses pass and are activated or eliminated or stored is like Popper's World 3 or Bateson's 'vast ecology': as a result of scientific observation there appear to be correlations between patterns formed in the brain and patterns perceived in the world outside. J. Z. Young, an anatomist of the brain, has written, 'The combined evidence from histology, physiology and training experiments shows that there is some connection between the shape of the cells in the nervous system and the thing that can be learned by it.'[9] Patterns are formed in the brain: the brain itself works by processes of elimination and selection: innumerable small-scale experiments are carried out to determine what shall live and what shall not. 'Each cell leads to two possible outputs, and learning consists in closing one of these.' This is the physical counterpart of Popper's suggestion that we learn through our mistakes. There are, in the brain, processes of larger interrelation like Bateson's 'circuit of circuits' or Learning III — perhaps thwarted at the moment by our present language which finds it difficult to embrace seeming opposites from a higher point of view. There are circuits of interrelation for instance between 'pleasure' and 'pain'; between 'good' and 'bad' — 'good' being that which helps an organism to survive but 'bad' (in the sense of that which gives pain and thus instruction of what to avoid) being necessary too: for without such warning, how could an organism survive? And so 'bad' can be 'good': but without an understanding of how to see, and describe, the larger interconnectedness appertaining to these processes — to gain a further vision perhaps of a higher 'good' and 'bad' — how can sense be made? And how can an organism not let itself be destroyed in the confusion? But it is in just such areas that there are taboos. J. Z. Young has noted that there is in conventional thought 'a resistance to recognising that good and bad, pleasure and pain, need to be considered in one category'.[10] There are also the taboos (as Monod noted) in facing the problems, natural or unnatural, of selection. It is 'a fundamental instruction of every species that from time to time it shall discard nearly the whole organism and start again'.[11] It is by means of death (and birth) that there is kept alive the continuing strain which, in terms of evolution, is what matters rather than the individual. The taboos arise because it is difficult for a man to think of himself (once he has broken away from religious and political animism) as anything other than an individual. But the means are there. If he were able to see himself, scientifically, as representative of a potentially greater strain — it is this, as well as providing comfort in the face of individual death, that might enable him, since he would know that part of this potential were inside as well as outside him, to come to terms with himself; and thus, of course, with the world.

The 'objective' world of ideas has become so vast, and the imagery used to describe even specific corners of it so complex, that it is not surprising that men have not caught up with scientific attitudes in their hearts and daily lives; that they still serve what Monod calls their 'disgusting farrago'. Popper noted in his World 3 the existence of 'works of art': Bateson suggested that art was a mode by which glimpses of Learning III could be given expression; J. Z. Young, following practical experiments with the brain, noted 'art, literature and aesthetics . . . are major contributors to human homeostasis' (an organism's continual adaptation of itself in order to stay alive). A philosopher who has tried to describe such a relationship between science and art is Susanne Langer. Symbolism is an element, she says, in all cognition — scientists use symbols to formulate their experience — but some further imagery is required for the mind to be able to cope as it were with these symbols. 'They and they only originally made us aware of the wholeness and overall form of entities, acts and facts in the world: and little though we may know it, only an image can hold us to the concept of a total phenomenon against which we can measure the adequacy of the scientific terms with which we describe it.' 'We are actually suffering from a lack of suitable images of the phenomena that

85

are currently receiving our most ardent scientific attention — the objects of biology and psychology. This lack is blocking the progress of scientifically oriented thought towards systematic insight into the nature of life and especially of mind.'[12] What is required for the evolution of liveliness, that is — for the jump across the gap between scientific attitudes and daily living — is not just the images used by scientists, because these are specialised; but images as it were of these images (where has this cry been heard before?): and it seems possible that men have the ability to provide these, because they can stand back and observe something of the processes of their own minds. The creation of such images, traditionally, has been a function of art. But art in this age of complex self-awareness and self-reflection, is not, currently, finding its own life-springs, however much these are needed to describe the 'total phenomenon' of science. But they are there. The 'image of feeling created by art . . . seems to me capable of encompassing the whole mind of man, including its highest rational activities. It presents the world in the light of a heightened perception, and knowledge of the world as rational experience. Rationality, in this projection, is not epitomised in the discursive form that serves our thinking, but is a vision of thinking itself — of a vital movement outstripping the sure, deep rhythms of physical life — so its tensions against those rhythms are felt as keen and precarious moments within the very limits of supportable strain.'[13] *A vision of thinking itself* — this too is a cry, an image, that has been used before — by Brecht, by philosophers and scientists quoted above, by almost anyone who is anxious about the condition of modern living and modern thinking in which art has little content and science little shape. To bring the two together — to provide for both art and science an encompassing covenant — this might be an activity indeed almost as difficult to speak about as the qualities of old (or new) divinities.

Writers have been quoted by random selection here — Popper, Monod, Bateson, Young, Langer — random in that they were come across by this writer at least without plan but selected in that, it seemed, they all were connected by the same authority and liveliness and thus seemed to form, and not just in the writer's mind, their psycho-celestial football team. And this was the sort of occurrence that the writers themselves seemed to describe — the way that out of the activities of randomness there are formed structures as of a mind and by a mind: that such is life: all these writers in their different disciplines so unpremeditatedly but so luminously making connections — a state of affairs like Hermann Hesse's Glass Bead Game, the cosmic interaction of some World 3 Cup or indeed the conception and parturition of these plays. Or like a molecule of DNA — the structuring and ordering of cells for survival — while most of the rest of the world — the world of running down, of entropy — goes its way. Means of communication have become so deafening: what is called 'negative entropy' (life!) so bemused: that perhaps language has had to become more and more a protection (see *After Babel* by George Steiner, that notable winger): and those who still wish to communicate truly — who wish to move in a world other than the conditioning-and-response of Bateson's Learnings I and even II — have to live as it were in an occupied country; cautious of speech in case it will be too easily understood and misinterpreted; tapping on cell walls for their communication; the walls of language being thus useful, even if they are for protection. And this coded language being called a meta-language (such phrases are bleak enough, goodness knows, to put off stray enquiry agents) in that it will be talking not only about facts but also the language usually used to talk about (or hide?) the facts: 'If we want to speak about the correspondence of a statement to a fact we need a meta-language in which we can state the fact (or the alleged fact) about which the statement in question speaks, and in addition can speak about the statement in question' (Popper).[14] And only thus are we dealing with the question of 'truth'. Well, what jailer will understand that? But the point of all this is that it is only by such practice, by such sleight-of-mind, that statements can be given a form beyond individual predilection: that beyond cacophony there can be living connections. Higher abilities of learning, of consciousness, can in truth be like components of a genetic code: the authority that they carry, and transmit, may survive — even within, and going on from, a body that has sickness. A body may have to have sickness — may have to die — so that, through the code, what lives is re-shuffled and re-formed — for evolution. That which a body itself has learned of course may not survive — for this there has to be some concurrence with chance, a concurrence between what occurs genetically and what, in the world, has happened that will make such a result of chance be best fitted for survival. Acquired characteristics cannot be handed on: what can occur is that what has been learned can become the ground upon which one chance seed (of which there are myriads) rather than another might grow. And so, still, it can be upon what has been learned, upon what has been made of the environment, that the distinction between what will survive and what will not will largely depend. And so it is as if there were some ability to hand down what has been learned, since that which is not fitted to experience may simply die. And experience can be chosen. And there can be an environment either friendly, or hostile, to seeds, not just in the world, but in minds. Nowadays there are few illusions about the attractiveness of death in the outside world; also in the mind. We live in societies in which death is the chief allurement and entertainment: guns hang down like breasts on street corners; legs on posters explode like wounds. It is as if some tired old species knew it had to die: was thus just arranging in the usual way (extinction) for its improvement. What is not known, of course, is whether the whole species has to die — or just attitudes which have made death so attractive. In either case, genetically, processes remain the same — something has to be broken up, re-shuffled, re-formed, for survival. To describe that which survives — for which the reshuffling, breaking up, takes place — there can be symbols of symbols: DNA, germ-cells, negative entropy, even divinities! But the characteristics of persons who choose to become involved in such liveliness rather than deathliness — in a chance of survival — will be, roughly, the same: the ability to move between different levels of consciousness; the attempt at language capable of embracing seeming opposites from a higher point of view; the acceptance of errors as the purveyors of learning rather than traps; the becoming at home in such systems and codes of transformation. It may be, of course, that the invasions of entropy will be too strong: the lively, along with the deathly, will be destroyed. But at least there is the hope (in the mind?) that subtlety (like that of a wrestler?) will result in the violence of deathliness being turned back only to destroy itself. For it is in subtlety, in art, that there can be said — All right, if you want to die, do it! — with the intention, perhaps, of achieving the opposite. On the grid, the riddle, of chance, of evolution, there is anyway nothing better to be done: men have to hang on, like sperms (do not thousands have to die? in the womb? in the mind?) for the sake of the survival of — everything.

NOTES

1 Quoted in Philip Thody, *Sartre* (London: Studio Vista, 1971), 41.
2 Edmund Husserl, *The Crisis in European Sciences and Transcendental Phenomenology*, trans. David Carr (Evanston: Northwestern Univ. Press, 1970), 164.
3 Jacques Monod, *Chance and Necessity*, trans. Austryn Wainhouse (London: Collins, 1972), 156.
4 Ibid., 159, 160.
5 Ibid., 152, 153.
6 Karl R. Popper, *Objective Knowledge* (Oxford: Clarendon Press, 1972), 37, 20, 36, 70.
7 Ibid., 84.
8 Gregory Bateson, *Steps towards an Ecology of Mind* (London: Intertext, 1972), 118, 119, 277.
9 J. Z. Young, *A Model of the Brain* (Oxford: Clarendon Press, 1964), 164.
10 Ibid., 196.
11 Ibid., 287.
12 Susanne Langer, *Mind: An Essay on Human Feeling*, 2 vols. (Baltimore: Johns Hopkins Univ. Press, 1967), I:xviii.
13 Ibid., 150.
14 Popper, 46.

LANDFALL

BARMAN   who played   ACKERMAN

HARRY   who played   JASON

CHAR   who played   HELENA

OLDER HOSTESS who played JUDITH

YOUNGER HOSTESS (SOPHIE) who played JENNY

BERT   who played   ARIEL

WALDORF
GEORDIE   two of whom were the
SMUDGER   FOOTMAN and the MAID
NORBERT

ACT I

Before the lights in the auditorium are out, the CURTAIN collapses. It lies at the front of the stage.

The stage is in darkness. Then neon lights flicker and settle into a glow.

The SCENE is a refreshment room — as if at an old country house, or at a small local airport.

On the right are a plate-glass window and a glass door. On the left is a stone gothic doorway.

There is a bar along the back. To the right of the bar is a machine which could be a coffee machine or a juke box. To the left of the bar is a hatch to a food lift.

There are two stools in front of the bar. Centre, are two tables with four chairs round each.

Harry is standing by the window, right, looking out. The glass is opaque, or as if there were a mist beyond the window. Harry is a man in his forties. He wears an old overcoat.

The Barman, a man in his sixties, is crouching behind a table, left, with his hands over his ears. He straightens, dusts himself, looks at Harry. Then he looks up at the flies.

The characters alternate between acting realistically and theatrically; sometimes they seem to be not acting at all. Always it is as if they are trying to convey some message which can be conveyed in no better way.

BARMAN   Headache?
                He puts a hand to his head: then answers himself —
                No.
                He faces the audience. He acts —
                — Is this a dagger? —
                He answers himself —

No.

He gets into the position of someone preparing to play a golf shot, to the right. He speaks as if giving a military order —

— Over the hill, two hundred yards —

He acts as if beginning to play the golf shot.

Then he stops and looks at Harry: he calls —

— Open —

He stands with his hands on his hips. He mouths, almost inaudibly —

— Fire?

Harry turns and looks at him.

The Barman looks up to the flies. Then he begins to back away as if something were falling towards him from the sky. He ducks behind the table, left, with his hands over his ears again.

Harry watches him.

After a time the Barman stands up and dusts himself. He takes up an attitude of boxing.

> There's a weathership out in the Atlantic. It's surrounded by vastly superior enemy forces —

He mimes boxing.

Then he stops. He looks at Harry.

After a time he puts a hand to his mouth and shouts —

> Mind that donkey!

HARRY
> You mean, I'm talking the hind leg off a donkey?

The Barman stares at him.

Then he moves round the stage.

BARMAN
> I've got to get this place cleaned up. They're coming in here — up through the sewers. Rats and frogmen. Breaking down the fences. Leaping up the waterfalls. On to the dry land.

He straightens the curtain at the front of the stage so that it is in a line along the footlights.

I had a small business once. I used to go out mornings and evenings. And I always knew where I was. Now they're getting into government. And I'm most of the time in my room —

He stops and looks over the footlights.

What do you think this is, a Sunday School?

He puts his hands on his heart.

Come along then. Coop! Coop!

After a time he holds his hands out in front of him as if they contained a bird. Then he opens his hands and shakes them. He looks to the back of the auditorium as if the bird has flown away there.

HARRY	Are there aeroplanes flying?
BARMAN	Yes, there was one in nineteen hundred and two I think.
HARRY	What happened?
BARMAN	It went into a tree.

He turns from the audience and goes behind the bar and puts glasses and bottles from the shelves on to the counter.

Harry comes to the bar and sits on a stool.

After a time he says as if it were the name of a game —

| HARRY | — Can I have a drink? — |

The Barman seems to follow his lead —

| BARMAN | — No I haven't got any change — |

The Barman places the bottles around on the counter as if he were arranging pieces for a game.

Harry watches him. Then he murmurs —

| HARRY | On this strange landscape — |
| BARMAN | Do I know you? |

Harry and the Barman look at the pieces on the counter. It is as if they are uncertain of the nature of the game.

Harry seems to quote —

HARRY	— Open your mouth —
BARMAN	— And in she pops them —

After a time Harry bangs on the counter and yells —

HARRY	Can we have some discipline in this establishment!
BARMAN	Coming, sir! Sorry!

The Barman takes a glass and fills it.

Harry looks round the room. He says tentatively —

HARRY ·	What is it, a hairdresser's?

The Barman pushes the full glass towards him.

Harry says more confidently —

Broken needles everywhere! Shit —

BARMAN	We had a party last night, sir. A lot of young gentlemen —

Harry seems to quote —

HARRY	— On a dark night —
BARMAN	— Just down from the trees —

Harry pores over the counter.

After a time the Barman goes to the machine at the end of the bar, right, and pulls a lever.

The machine emits a puff of steam.

The Barman carries two mugs from the machine and sets them down in front of Harry. Harry watches them. Then he murmurs —

HARRY	Where did it go —
BARMAN	You remember?

He looks to the back of the auditorium.

Harry does not look up.

The Barman moves off round the stage again.

You know what this place once was? A bloody great house with lawns and gardens. A polo ground. A moat —

He wipes his hands on his body as if disgusted.

HARRY	No, I think those stories were greatly exaggerated —

Harry turns away, as if he were bored with the rules of the game.

96

BARMAN	Coming and going all night.
HARRY	With a little black bag —
BARMAN	An aerial —
HARRY	Like the Defence Ministry?

They wait. It is as if the Barman is not quite sure if the game is over.

BARMAN	Would you like a drink? —
HARRY	Oh this one's on me.

The Barman seems to quote —

BARMAN	— Have you got water and oil —
HARRY	— Don't look now, Daddy —

Harry picks up a mug and drinks.

After a time the Barman comes to the front of the stage. He acts —

BARMAN   We're off to Rome! The hula girls beneath the palm trees! A few minutes to go! Just time for a cup of tea! Hold on to me, daddy, or we'll never cross the road. What did you say this place was? We're outside our own hotel, daddy —

He stares out above the audience.

Harry speaks with his back to the Barman and the audience.

HARRY	You live here?
BARMAN	In a room downstairs —
HARRY	It wasn't a big house. A lawn and garden —

The Barman interrupts —

BARMAN	She won't speak to me —
HARRY	Who?
BARMAN	My wife.

Harry seems to try to go on with his story —

HARRY   — Aeroplanes flew over. There were connections between the control-tower and the ground —

The Barman interrupts —

BARMAN   I've got this daughter, see, aged fifteen. They have her out in front of class. She wears a belt, black stockings, and something

97

	loose round the top —
HARRY	She lay in her pram —
BARMAN	Children see by what they learn —
HARRY	What did she learn —
BARMAN	The sun doesn't get filtered —
HARRY	— At this high altitude?

They wait.

After a time the Barman goes to Harry and swats him on the shoulder as if there were an insect there. Then he mimes picking off the insect and dropping it on to the ground.

The glass door opens, right, and a girl comes in. She is dressed in the uniform of an air hostess. She carries a folder with papers. She comes to the centre of the stage and stands there looking through her papers.

The Barman watches Harry.

Harry has turned to the Hostess.

After a time he says as if he is trying not to act —

| HARRY | I'm looking for my wife — |
| HOSTESS | Oh, do you know what plane she's on? |

Harry puts his hands to his head. He gets up and walks round the stage as if in despair. After a time he calls —

| HARRY | No! |

The Hostess acts as if she is near to tears.

| HOSTESS | — Then I'm afraid I can't help you — |

Harry comes and takes her papers out of her hand and leafs through them.

The Barman turns to the audience. He acts as if he were ad-libbing —

| BARMAN | The Lord of the Manor could have any girl he wanted on his wedding night. On his wedding night he wanted this girl. The problem was to get her into the manor past his wife — |

Harry jabs a finger at the papers he is holding.

| HARRY | After — |

98

HOSTESS	What —
HARRY	— Because I don't love you —

The Hostess takes her papers back. She looks through them.

BARMAN	— There were two staircases, or spirals, the one going up, the other down. They were joined, but they never met. Occasionally there were windows —

He looks up to the back of the auditorium. He waves —

Coo-ee!

Harry is watching the Hostess.

HOSTESS	When they come in?

Harry says as if quoting —

HARRY	— Don't I know you —

The Barman speaks as if to the audience —

BARMAN	But if they separated, they died —

Harry turns away from the Hostess. He seems to finish the Barman's line.

HARRY	— Or immediately formed another attachment.

The Hostess goes out through the gothic door, left.

Harry goes and sits on a stool at the bar.

After a time the Barman, facing the audience, calls —

BARMAN	How're you doing?
HARRY	All right.
BARMAN	Wife and kids?
HARRY	All right.

The Barman goes back to the bar. He puts away the bottles and glasses.

BARMAN	— You've got to live —
HARRY	Where is the necessity.

The Barman goes to the food lift on the left of the bar and opens the hatch and shouts down in a mock upper-class voice —

BARMAN	Will you come up here a moment please?

He listens; then shouts —
>And bring your tennis things —

He closes the hatch. He turns to Harry.
>The smell down there! Honestly!

He tidies the glasses and bottles at the bar.
>I read a book the other day. There was this headmaster, see, aged fifteen. He had them out in front of class. He'd been given carte-blanche by the parents —

The gothic door opens, left, and the Char comes in. She is a good-looking woman in her sixties. She wears a fur. She speaks with an upper-class accent.

CHAR   Did you hear that bang?

BARMAN   Yes I thought it was one of me legs coming apart.

CHAR   How is the poor little thing?

BARMAN   It's breathing.

The Char glances at the audience. Then she comes to the bar and sits on a stool by Harry. The Barman faces her across the counter.

BARMAN   Sign here, please. In blood. You know the symbols? Dip the pen in the inkwell —

He acts ghostly laughter.

Then he looks down at the counter.
>There's one stipulation. You must bring her home before morning.

HARRY   Why?

CHAR   I've lost my keys.

HARRY   You want to sleep at my place?

They wait.

After a time the Barman comes round to the front of the bar. He acts —

BARMAN   The riders are over their handlebars! Their arses are up around their ears. Hooray! Hooray! Down falls the cherry blossom! —

He waves his arms. He waits.

100

	Then he yells —
	You've got a spare, haven't you? A jack? —
	The Char and Harry remain with their backs to the audience.
CHAR	A man came to see me the other day —
HARRY	And had he?
CHAR	He said he'd come to mend the lights —
	She waits.
	No.
	She looks at the Barman.
	He had some wire; and one of those hats, you know, like witches.
HARRY	And two barrels like imitation leather suitcases?
	They wait.
	The Barman seems to be in despair. He acts, facing the audience —
BARMAN	— What would you do if a black man wanted to marry your daughter? But a black man doesn't want to marry my daughter! What is this, the pharmaceutical industry?
HARRY	There was a game of rugger the other day and one of the front row forwards became pregnant.
CHAR	Why do you talk like that?
HARRY	What —
	The Char seems to copy the Hostess —
CHAR	Do — you — know — what — plane — she's — on —
	Harry stares at her. Then he turns from her and gestures round the room.
HARRY	We lived here one summer, she and I. It was a small house, with a lawn and garden —
CHAR	You had a child?
HARRY	It was in its pram. It looked up to the leaves, the shadows. Children see by what they learn —
CHAR	What would it have learned?

HARRY	A sort of terror, breaking.
	He turns to the Char and tries to put an arm round her.
	The Char pushes him away.
CHAR	No —
HARRY	Why not —
	The Char seems to quote —
CHAR	— Because I don't love you —
	They wait.
	It is as if a cue has been missed.
	Harry turns to the Barman —
HARRY	This is impossible.
	The glass door, right, opens and the Hostess comes in. She turns and holds the door as if there were a wind blowing from outside.
	There come in through the door, as if there were no wind, Waldorf and Geordie, an older and a younger man. They are dressed in fashionable clothes. They carry briefcases. It is possible that one of them might be a woman.
WALDORF	No questions —
GEORDIE	No questions —
WALDORF	Just say we're delighted to be here —
GEORDIE	We're delighted to be here —
WALDORF	I had a grandmother, or something, who was born in this part of the world —
GEORDIE	He had a grandmother, or something, who was born in this part of the world.
WALDORF	Lead on —
GEORDIE	Who —
WALDORF	I've forgotten.
	They go to the table, right, and put down their briefcases. Then they look round the room.
	The Hostess has managed to close the glass door. Then she turns to Harry.
	Harry, at the bar, is looking at the gothic door. The Barman has gone to the machine at the back and is facing it as if it were a pin-table. He pulls a

102

	knob. A few lights come on; then fade out.
GEORDIE	Where's the car —
BARMAN	No car.
GEORDIE	Can I telephone?
BARMAN	You can try.

Geordie has gone to the machine where the Barman is standing. He seems to be waiting for a telephone to be free.

The Char is watching Harry.

Then the Char and the Barman seem to talk as if prompting Waldorf and Geordie.

CHAR	— Where's the child —
BARMAN	— Where's the money —
CHAR	— At the airport — ?

The Hostess comes and stands by Harry. She stares at him. After a time Harry seems to quote —

HARRY	— I love only you, you see, I've never loved anyone else in my life —

Then he knocks the papers the Hostess is holding out of her hand: they fall to the floor. He and the Hostess stare at one another as if in hostility.

The Barman leaves the machine. He comes and stands by Waldorf at the table, right.

BARMAN	And where have you been? Bangkok? Honolulu?

Geordie picks up the handpiece of a telephone which is on the right side of the machine. He begins to dial. The Barman speaks looking at the audience.

> Put a nosebag on him and you couldn't tell him from the one-legged horse.

Waldorf is sitting facing the audience.

Geordie continues dialling — a dozen or so numbers.

The Barman listens, standing by Waldorf.

> Once one didn't wake up for three days.
> Papers piled up against his front door. They

couldn't get past his milk bottles!

The Hostess has got down on her hands and knees and is picking up her pages from the floor. Harry watches her.

Geordie has finished dialling.

The Barman speaks to Waldorf.

BARMAN	Like some soap?
WALDORF	And water.
BARMAN	How many lumps?
WALDORF	Four.

Harry puts out a foot and, balancing delicately, lifts up, from behind, the skirt of the Hostess, who is collecting her papers from the floor.

The Hostess becomes still.

The Barman moves back to the machine. He waits for Geordie, who is listening to the receiver. After a time Geordie puts the receiver down as if there had been no reply.

The Barman rolls his sleeves up. He takes hold of the machine.

BARMAN   Now comes the big moment of the day. I love this machine, but I can't satisfy it! I push it here — pull it there —

He struggles with the machine: bangs it. Then he puts his arm round it as if trying to lift it. Then he bows his head and puts an ear against it.

      — Bitch! I know you've got it!

Then he seems to cry.

The Hostess has stood up. She grabs a bottle from the bar and hits at Harry with it.

Harry holds her arm: smiles.

HARRY   Was there a lady on your aeroplane?

After a time Geordie seems to think that Harry is talking to him.

GEORDIE   Was there a lady on my aeroplane?

The Barman speaks excitedly with his ear against the machine.

BARMAN   I can hear it — kicking!

The Hostess puts the bottle back on the bar.
Geordie is staring at Harry.

GEORDIE   What time does it open?
HARRY   What —
GEORDIE   The museum.

Harry stares at him.

Then the machine makes a whirring noise, as if of a ticker-tape machine, or computer. The Barman raises his head. He waits while a bit of paper comes out. Then he takes the bit of paper and seems to be reading it.

The Char says to Harry —

CHAR   My husband doesn't get home till ten.
HARRY   What else does he do?
CHAR   He's a university lecturer.

Harry is watching the Barman.

The Barman screws the bit of paper up and throws it to the floor.

Harry clutches his arm where the Hostess has hit at him. Then he falls on to his hands and knees on the floor. He crawls to where there is the piece of paper.

Waldorf has looked round at Harry; then at the Char; then at the Barman; then at Geordie.

Geordie comes and stands behind him.

Waldorf faces front. He acts as if he has had a cue, and is lecturing —

WALDORF   I want to say something about the decent things of life. There has to be some morality beyond that of power and money. There was once the English gentleman. He had long hair and wore a beard. He had nothing to do with tradesmen. He marched through the streets on Sundays —

He breaks off as if he is uncertain that he has done the right thing.

Harry picks up the piece of paper and sits at one of the tables, left, reading it.

105

The Hostess, who has been watching him, goes out of the gothic door, left.

Then Harry screws the piece of paper up and throws it on to the floor again.

The Char comes and sits at the table, left, with Harry.

CHAR   He's — the only word I can think of — arid. I want to have a relationship with him, but I can't. He wants me to dress up as Napoleon. I want to say — Kissey kissey make-up — but I can't.

HARRY   You want him back?

CHAR   Yes.

HARRY   Then lay a trap —

CHAR   How?

HARRY   Dig a pit. Cover it with old milk bottles. Then when he comes to fetch his clothes —

CHAR   He won't —

Harry shouts —

HARRY   Then sell them!

Geordie, standing behind Waldorf as if he were a hairdresser, has been watching Harry and the Char.

After a time —

WALDORF   Is he one of ours?

GEORDIE   I think so.

WALDORF   And him?

GEORDIE   I don't know.

WALDORF   The woman?

GEORDIE   It was agreed —

WALDORF   What a place!

GEORDIE   That's why they chose it.

WALDORF   Why?

GEORDIE   I promised never to tell.

WALDORF   Then never, never do —

The machine makes a whirring sound, as if it were a fruit machine. Then it is silent.

The Barman has remained standing, in front of it.

Then he murmurs —

BARMAN	Ever try it?
HARRY	No.

The Barman yells like a fielder in a cricket match —

BARMAN 'Owzat!

Then he turns to the audience.

Some team, I think. On Sundays.

He squats down, with his hands out towards the audience, like a wicket-keeper. Behind him the machine makes a loud tinkling noise, as if coins were pouring out.

Geordie, behind Waldorf at the table, right, brushes at Waldorf's collar and straightens his hair.

He looks at the audience as if it were a mirror. The Char speaks to Harry.

CHAR I remember you in your pram.

HARRY No!

The Barman, crouching, makes a noise, as if he were imitating music, or a machine gun —

BARMAN — Da da di dum dum. Da da di da —

The char seems to change her tune.

CHAR — Ah there was a spirit in those days!
The boys with their little tails going!
Their drums like bells! —

HARRY And you were left with an only son to bring up?

CHAR As a matter of fact he did very well in the war —

HARRY That's why he had to go for a quiet pull in the pub —

CHAR You're not just doing this to be nice to me, are you?

The Barman straightens and looks at the flies.

BARMAN It goes on all the time. Like seeds. Like parachutes.

He waits. He looks at the audience.

Leaping up the waterfalls. Breaking down
the walls.
Then he goes behind the bar. He acts —
— Good evening, sir, and what can I do for
you? I hear you've got some Pakistanis on
your billiard table. You won't be able to get
into your own pockets next —
He laughs.
Harry gets up from the table, left, and goes and
sits at the bar.

HARRY   If only she'd say something — !
BARMAN   Didn't she? What —
HARRY   What were you doing last night. The names
of your dearest friends —

Geordie speaks over Waldorf's head, facing the
audience.

GEORDIE   Put your tongue out —

He mimes wiping the corner of Waldorf's mouth
with a handkerchief. He puts his hands on
Waldorf's shoulders.

Got your umbrella?

Geordie takes a newspaper from one of the briefcases and rolls it up and puts it under Waldorf's
arm. Waldorf stands. Then Geordie leads Waldorf
to the back of the stage on the right. He seems to
be posing him there.

BARMAN   You'd still have to go —
HARRY   Grow?
BARMAN   Go!

Harry looks round.

HARRY   On this strange planet.

The Barman, behind the bar, takes a plug and
wire and plugs the wire into a socket on the wall
at the back.
Then he comes from behind the bar and sits on a
stool in front, by Harry, watching the machine as
if it were television.
The glass door opens, right, and a woman in the

dress of the Hostess comes in. She stands looking down at her papers.

Harry turns to her: seems about to speak: then stops.

There come in through the glass door, right, Smudger and Norbert, an older and a younger man. They are dressed in holiday clothes. They carry travelling bags and a radio. It is possible that one of them might be a woman. They walk one behind the other. They act —

SMUDGER   Mule train halt!

NORBERT   We're outside our own hotel, Daddy —

SMUDGER   What do you think the poet was trying to say?

NORBERT   The nature of time, and of human responsibility.

They put down their bags and radio on the table, right. They look round the room. Waldorf is posed with the newspaper under his arm. Geordie is standing looking at him as if he were a statue.

The woman like the Hostess looks up at Harry. She is older than the original Hostess.

HOSTESS   Hullo —

HARRY   Hullo —

HOSTESS   I was afraid you might not remember me —

HARRY   Oh yes, I loved only you, you see. I never loved anyone else in my life —

The Hostess puts her head in her hands.

HOSTESS   I feel so guilty!

Smudger goes and looks at Waldorf's feet, as if he were a statue and there were an inscription there. He seems to read —

SMUDGER   — The column, drawn by six white horses, rose to a height of several thousand feet —

He looks up at Waldorf.

              — Slowly our forefathers moved down the Mall —

Norbert watches Smudger.

109

NORBERT   — There were not many left to tell —
                 He breaks off. It is as if he and Smudger had been
                 trying out some code.
HARRY   That's not right, is it?
                 The Hostess looks up at Harry.
HOSTESS   No.
                 The Barman leans forward and gives the machine
                 a bang.
                 Geordie has been watching Smudger and Norbert.
GEORDIE   What's he carrying?
                 Smudger and Norbert look at Waldorf.
SMUDGER   A wireless?
                 Harry speaks to the Hostess.
HARRY   A child?
NORBERT   A rolled-up newspaper?
                 The Hostess turns towards the gothic doorway,
                 left. Then she looks back at Harry.
                 Smudger holds his hand out to Waldorf.
SMUDGER   Smudger —
                 Waldorf relaxes: takes his hand.
WALDORF   Waldorf —
                 Smudger turns to introduce Norbert.
SMUDGER   Nobby —
                 Norbert holds out his hand to Waldorf who
                 comes forward and takes it.
WALDORF   Wally —
                 He turns to Geordie —
                     Geordie —
                 Geordie comes up and holds out his hand.
SMUDGER   Smudger
NORBERT   Norbert —
                 Geordie takes Smudger's hand: then Norbert's —
GEORDIE   That's not right is it?
                 They wait.
                 The Barman leans forward and gives the machine
                 a bang.
                 The Hostess moves towards the gothic door;
                 then stops and looks back at Harry.

110

Waldorf, Geordie, Smudger and Norbert have settled down round the table, right. They repeat, as if jokingly —

SMUDGER	Smudger —
WALDORF	Waldorf —
SMUDGER	Nobby —
WALDORF	Wally —
GEORDIE	Geordie —
SMUDGER	Smudger —
NORBERT	Nobby —
GEORDIE	George —

They stop.

There is suddenly deafening music (a military march) from the machine as if it were a juke box. Harry puts his hands over his ears.

The Hostess goes out through the gothic door, left.

The Four sit round their table, right, and seem to confer, quickly, amongst themselves, under cover of the music.

The Barman has gone behind the bar. He pulls the electric plug out.

The music stops.

The Four at the table stop talking.

Harry remains with his hands over his ears.

After a time the Four at the table, right, speak as if in a comic routine they have learned.

WALDORF	— Where's the child —
SMUDGER	— Where's the car —
NORBERT	— Where's the money —
GEORDIE	— At the airport.

Norbert lifts the radio from the floor on to the table. He pulls up the aerial, carefully. The Four continue to talk as if in obviously assumed voices.

SMUDGER	— I'll be at the second milestone —
WALDORF	— I'll be at the fourth —
GEORDIE	— Then run —
WALDORF	— I can't —

NORBERT	— Why not —
WALDORF	— Arthritis.

Norbert has put an ear to the radio. He seems to be tuning it.

The Barman has been watching the Four at the table. He glances at the Char, who has turned to look at him.

Harry takes his hands away from his ears. He looks at the Barman.

After a time the Barman begins to shake up and down as if he were on a train. He comes from behind the bar as if moving down a corridor. He takes a pad and pencil from his pocket and stands by the table, right.

He watches Norbert who seems to be tuning the radio. He seems to be trying to see what Norbert is doing.

BARMAN   You know, in the old days, they took on water south of Carlisle. There was a trough.

A little nozzle —

He jerks his hips forwards and holds his behind.
Do you mind!

Norbert looks up at him.

Harry looks at the Char. The Char looks at Harry.

The Barman bends down to the radio: he shouts as if into it —
— How're you doin' Nob, all right?

He seems to listen to the radio.

Then he shouts again —
— Wife and kids?

Geordie answers as if for Norbert.

GEORDIE   All right.

The Barman straightens. He moves back, walking ordinarily, to the machine at the right of the bar.

He murmurs to Harry —

BARMAN   Know how the post office works? The telephone — ?

He touches the machine. A green light comes on.

112

He turns to the audience.

There are these particles, see, going through you all the time. Like seeds. Like parachutes —

He waits.

He seems to quote —

— And where were you on the night of the thirteenth —

HARRY   I don't know —

BARMAN   But you would if you were —

HARRY   What —

There are three flashes from the machine, as if it were taking photographs.

The Barman waits.

The Four, at the table, right, talk in turn into the radio — as if it were a microphone, and they were establishing through it, by code, a programme in a computer.

SMUDGER   — I'm interested in the marketing of these self-reversing spectacles —

GEORDIE   — Actually, on my way here, I saw a cloud in the shape of a bird —

WALDORF   — When we came to the barricade against its soft grey walls we battered —

NORBERT   — There were not many left to tell the tale.

After Norbert has spoken, it is as if the programme has been set.

The Four move back slightly from the radio.

The Barman, at the bar, speaks facing the audience —

BARMAN   There was a young couple lived here after the war —

Harry speaks watching the machine.

HARRY   What did they do —

BARMAN   Worked in the fields. Kept animals.

The Char, at the table, left, bends down, and picks up off the floor the piece of paper from the machine that the Barman and Harry have earlier discarded. She seems to read it. Then puts it in her pocket.

BARMAN	What did you call them —
HARRY	Spot. Beauty.
BARMAN	Aeroplanes flew over —
HARRY	We shot one down —
BARMAN	What with —
HARRY	Ack Ack —

The Char seems to be trying to look under the table, right, where the Four have put their bags. Then the green light on the machine goes out. The Barman goes to it and takes from a slot what seems to be a set of photographs. He looks at them.

HARRY	They'd lost their child.
BARMAN	It was in its pram —
HARRY	There was a bomb. Or was it crossing the road —
BARMAN	How can God let such a thing happen?
HARRY	You believe in God?
BARMAN	If I say no —
HARRY	Then what's the difference.

The Barman comes to the counter. He pushes across to Harry what seems to be the set of photographs.

Harry takes them: turns them this way and that. Then he stands, looks round on the floor. He speaks while he searches.

HARRY	On a temporary overflow airport, put up to be out of the likelihood of fog, there met, for the purposes of history, four travellers, or representatives, of the antique style —

He seems to be looking for the piece of paper he has earlier discarded.

  — Taffy Evans, Smudger Smith, Nobby Clark and Geordie —

He looks at the audience.

  — Also undercover agents, from the

114

liberation army —

He turns to the gothic doorway, left.

> — It was not known, at this stage, if the mysterious sixth person was with them —

The Char says to the Four at the table, right —

CHAR   Excuse me, I couldn't help overhearing your conversation —

The Barman says to Harry —

BARMAN   You were meeting her here?

HARRY   Yes.

BARMAN   When —

HARRY   Today.

Harry looks at the set of photographs he is holding.

> Not only did the negotiators go to their destination blindfold, but their wives were under the impression that they were making arrangements for divorce —

He throws the set of photographs on to the ground. Then he looks at the Char.

The Four at the table, right, have been acting as if with increasing tension.

The Char gets up and goes over to them, carrying her chair. She sets her chair down by them. She seems to be trying to see under the table. She acts —

CHAR   — My father was a vicar in the West Country. Each morning he'd run down towards the sea. If the seagulls got him, I'd climb into his bed —

The Four have not made room for her. She is squashed up against them awkwardly.

> — He'd tell me of the great world outside. Of goblins, and dragons —

She seems to be groping, with her foot, for one of the bags under the table.

The Barman has been watching her. After a time, he calls out to her —

BARMAN	— And you, madam, what did you do in the war —
CHAR	— I opened my Bible and my eye fell on one Samuel fifteen —
BARMAN	— Is that the same as quarter past Samuel one? —

He laughs manically.

Then he leaves the bar and comes to the front of the stage and looks at what the Char is doing.

The Char has got hold of one of the bags with her foot.

The Barman looks at the audience.

CHAR	It's about Agag, who was hacked to pieces.

She seems to be having difficulty in dragging the bag towards her.

After a time the Barman acts, as if in panic —

BARMAN	It wasn't like that! No!

He goes to the centre of the stage and begins to mime, violently, a waiter as if in a Charlie Chaplin film going in and out of swing doors in a restaurant carrying trays.

He shouts —

This one — was this one's —

He stops, looking at the audience. He speaks as if in despair —

— this one —

Then he seems to avoid, just in time, someone coming the other way —

— in this one's —

He seems just to avoid the door again. Then it is as if a door hits him in the face. He staggers: collapses in front of, almost on top of, the table, right, where the Four and the Char are sitting. The Char, with a foot, manages to push the bag at her feet towards him so that it is in front of him when he falls.

He speaks quietly, facing the audience —

— official residence!

116

Lying on his side, the Barman unzips the bag and feels inside quickly. Then he becomes still.

He stares at the audience.

Smudger begins to sing in a quiet voice —

SMUDGER   I was walking down the street and I was walking down the street and I wanted a cup of tea and I wanted a cup of tea —

He puts one of the briefcases by the radio on the table.

Geordie stands.

GEORDIE   — Pip! Pip! —

Waldorf moves towards the plate-glass door, singing quietly —

WALDORF   — And I poured two spoonfuls into the pot, and I poured some water into the pot —

He stops by the plate-glass door.

Smudger puts the other briefcase on the table.

NORBERT   — Boom boom —

Smudger goes and joins Waldorf by the glass door.

GEORDIE   Don't look now, but we're outside our own hotel, Daddy —

Geordie and Norbert have stood. They move towards the plate-glass door.

They have left the case by the radio on the table. It is as if the case might contain a bomb, which might be about to be set off by the radio.

The Barman erupts into activity. He hurls the bag that he is holding towards the door, right. Smudger catches it. Then the Barman hurls himself on the Char and knocks her off her chair and lies on top of her on the ground. Then he jumps up and takes the other bags and briefcases and throws them to the Four by the door. They catch them. Then the Barman picks up the radio. He looks around as if to see where to throw it. He turns to Harry. Harry has his back to him; he is watching the gothic door, left. The Barman acts

117

with decreasing assurance. After a time he puts
the radio down at the very front of the stage.

Then he lies on top of the Char again.

The Four by the plate-glass window stand
holding their suitcases.

After a time Harry walks round the stage as if
trying to re-establish the scene.

HARRY   The anaesthetist was here. Walls of dull
grey steel. Curtains of stone. Forty years in
the hospital service. Married. With children.
Taking a whiff every now and then. To keep
up appearances —

He stops by the Barman and the Char.

After a time the Barman stands up; dusts himself.
Rats ran in their cages. Connections between
the cortex and the ground —

Harry waits.

The Char stands up: dusts herself.
The sister was here. With her strong brown
arms. For the crowds at the railway station.
The seeds in the wind —

The Char goes and sits on a chair, left.

Harry turns to the gothic door.
The surgeon was here. Saw a gap in the
clouds. Took aim —

He remains watching the gothic door.

After a time —
And the students. The eternal trump cards.
With their strings of sausages —

He turns to the Four by the plate-glass.

After a time he continues —
Oh God, let it not have two arms, two heads —

He waits.
Let it have three.

The gothic door opens, left, and the Hostess
comes in. She leads by the hand Bert, a tall young
man in white overalls. She is the younger,
original Hostess. She leads Bert towards the

centre of the stage. Then she stretches up and kisses him. Then she looks at Harry.

Harry watches her.

The Barman has gone behind the bar. He tidies up bottles.

After a time the Four by the window, right, seem to try out, tentatively, ways of establishing communication with Bert.

WALDORF — My dear fellow, did you have trouble getting through? —

SMUDGER — I'm interested in the marketing of these self-reversing spectacles —

Waldorf has pushed against the glass door, right. It seems locked.

GEORDIE — Actually, on my way here, I saw a cloud in the shape of a bird —

NORBERT — When they came to the barricades against its soft grey walls —

The Four move towards the wings, front right, as if they might be looking for somewhere to get out.

Bert speaks facing the audience.

BERT Johnny —

HARRY Yes?

BERT See any of the old crowd now?

HARRY No.

BERT Taffy or Smudger?

HARRY No.

Harry is looking at the Hostess.

Bert is groping for the chair, centre, where the Char is sitting. He appears to be blind.

The Char gets up. She joins the Barman behind the bar.

BERT Johnny —

HARRY Yes?

BERT Remember the sundial?

HARRY — While there was still time —

BERT And the swing —

HARRY	There was a swing?
BERT	You went up to the leaves, the shadows —
HARRY	I fell, was resurrected —
BERT	You were fed and kept alive —

Bert sits in the chair that the Char has left.

Harry puts out a hand to the Hostess. She comes and takes it.

BERT	I know a place —
HARRY	What —
BERT	You know. Young people —

The Four by the plate-glass have come to the front of the stage, right. They look out at the wings, tentatively.

Harry and the Hostess seem to quote —

HARRY	— The more houses they build —
HOSTESS	— The more places there are in the evenings —
HARRY	— Till we're all in one room —
HOSTESS	— Like a telephone box?

The Hostess puts her head in her hands, as if embarrassed.

The Four are watching Harry and the Hostess.

BERT	Johnny —
HARRY	Yes?
BERT	There were two climbers on the north face of the Eiger. They'd scorned the safety net that would take them to the top —

Harry interrupts —

HARRY	Oh both —
BERT	What?
HARRY	Sorry —
BERT	One fell, and dangled on a rope. The other couldn't lift him. He either had to cut the rope, in which case only one would die —

He puts a hand to his head.

After a time —

HARRY	Oh, the mother —
BERT	Why —

HARRY	— had they got married in the first place?

The Hostess leaves Harry. She goes to the gothic door, left. She turns and looks at the Four, right.

Bert speaks as if with increasing difficulty —

BERT	A man, on his honeymoon found he wanted his wife to die. The child that was then conceived became a danger to its mother —

He stops.

There is a long silence.

Then Bert speaks with a hand over his eyes.

You're in some sort of trouble, can I help you?

After a time the Four realise he is talking to them.

WALDORF	We want to get out —
BERT	You can't —
SMUDGER	Why not —
BERT	My men are outside —

Harry has been watching the Hostess.

Bert speaks with increasing confidence.

You should have been at the control tower this morning. They thought it was a game, but it was not.

GEORDIE	What happened?
BERT	They were shot.

The Barman, behind the bar, takes a dust sheet and throws it over the machine, the lights of which have gone out.

GEORDIE	I'm going —
WALDORF	You can't —
NORBERT	Why not —
SMUDGER	You should have been at the control tower this morning —

The Hostess goes out through the gothic door, left.

Harry takes the table, left, and turns it on its side. Then he takes the three chairs and puts them this way and that on the table, as if he were constructing a shelter.

BERT	Up to now men have been able to die —
HARRY	Now they cannot.

Harry stands back and looks at his shelter.
Bert takes his hand from his eyes.

BERT	Johnny —
HARRY	Yes?
BERT	Don't jump —

Harry goes to the table, right, and takes it to build up his shelter.

Your old grandmother, in Australia, has a message for you —

Harry puts the table on top of his shelter.

— You might hit a little doggie in the road.

HARRY	Oh really!

He stands back and surveys his tower, or shelter.

BERT	I could have given you an address —
HARRY	— What would have been the colour of her eyes, her hair —
BERT	Let it have three?

Harry goes and collects the chairs from where the table was, right, and makes his shelter more solid.

BERT	Spit then —
HARRY	Spit?

Harry goes to the front of the stage and looks at the curtain which is stretched along by the footlights.

BERT	A bird, a camel —

Harry takes hold of the curtain and drags it to his shelter. He tries, with difficulty, to throw it over the structure to form a roof like that of a nomad's tent. It floats. At the third attempt he succeeds in getting it over the shelter. He walks round, tucking it in at the base.
Bert, by the footlights, puts his hand to his eyes. He rubs them. Then he takes his hands from his eyes: blinks. It is as if he can see.
Harry stops by him.

HARRY	A miracle?
BERT	A coincidence —
HARRY	One or two.
BERT	Get through.

Smudger speaks from the back loudly —

SMUDGER	What is he, schizo?
BERT	Yes, he thinks that everything in the world exists for him and he can save it.
WALDORF	Isn't that a contradiction?
BERT	No, I've often found selfishness goes with altruism.

Bert is watching the audience.

Harry has finished arranging his shelter. It is like a nomad's tent. He walks round it.

HARRY	I sometimes think nothing has ever happened. No one has been raped, or driven into a ravine. Two football teams have run on to the field of play and have run straight off again. An alderman has waited on the steps of a guildhall for lunch —

The Char calls from the bar —

CHAR	And the long jump. How do you do the long jump?
HARRY	You have a run. A take-off board. Then you wiggle your feet in the air —
CHAR	And the discus. How do you do the discus?

Geordie suddenly goes to the gothic door, left, and goes out.

They wait.

The Barman has been putting away bottles and glasses behind the bar.

Harry murmurs —

HARRY	— Furry friends will visit me. Dancing girls in red and brown —

Then Geordie comes in again at the gothic door, left. When he sees the scene it is as if he had not expected it. He looks back the way he has come. Then he comes into the room leaving the door

123

open behind him: he touches the food-hatch, the bar, as if they might not be real.

Through the gothic door which Geordie has left open there can be glimpsed the figures of the two Hostesses, off-stage. The younger Hostess seems to have her hand on a light switch. Then the older Hostess ducks out of sight.

NORBERT   What's the treatment?

BERT   See if you can spot it —

The neon lights go off.

There is a dim light from beyond the plate-glass window.

After a time, the older Hostess comes in through the gothic door. She stands in the centre of the stage, with one hand across her chest, as if posing. Then a spotlight comes on her from the flies.

HARRY   Hullo —

HOSTESS   Hullo —

HARRY   I was afraid you might not remember me —

HOSTESS   Oh yes. I believed everything you said, you see —

HARRY   What did I see?

HOSTESS   I loved you, would never leave you —

HARRY   I said that?

The light from behind the window becomes brighter.

The older Hostess begins to undress.

Harry says as if amused —

HARRY   — The front knee slightly bent. The arms in the position of a man in —

HOSTESS   — Power —

HARRY   — Pain —

HOSTESS   — Power! —

She stops undressing.

Harry is looking up at the flies.

After a time the Hostess turns to the bar at the back.

HOSTESS   This is impossible!

124

The spotlight goes off.

At the bar, the Barman and the Char, together with Norbert, seem surreptitiously to have been having a drink. They seem to try to hide their glasses. Then they gather round Geordie, who seems to be ill.

HOSTESS   He wants to keep all his balls up in the air at the same time —

WALDORF   — Bitte, wo ist die Toilette —

SMUDGER   — Chocolates, cigarettes — !

NORBERT   — Son équipe de football a gagné une grande victoire —

The Hostess turns to Bert —

HOSTESS   The curtain —

BERT   Customs —

HOSTESS   Curtain!

From the bar, there is a sound of giggling.

The plate-glass window has become brighter.

Harry looks towards the plate-glass. He calls —

HARRY   Sophie — !

The younger Hostess answers from the wings, right —

SOPHIE   Yes?

Harry looks at the audience.

HARRY   War has been declared!

The light from behind the plate-glass becomes brighter.

Harry goes and stands with his back to the plate-glass window. He turns and faces the older Hostess, to the left. He puts a hand to his eyes, as if to shield them from light, but the light is behind him.

The Hostess turns to Harry. She is in her underclothes. She strikes a seductive pose, her hands behind her, leaning back against the tables and chairs.

HOSTESS   Do you want me blindfold?

Harry takes his hand from his eyes and puts it in

125

his pocket. It is as if he might hold a pistol there. He is smiling. Then the Hostess leans forward with her arms behind her like a bird.

Shall I say my prayers?

Bert leaves his chair and goes to the wings, front left, and picks up a rifle there and seems to load it. Harry murmurs —

HARRY   We've only got ten minutes!

He seems about to take his hand out of his pocket. Then the light from the plate-glass window becomes blinding. Harry leans forward peering at the Hostess.

HARRY   You're my wife?

Bert sits on the ground with his rifle, with his back against the proscenium arch, left.

The Hostess, with her back to Bert, and facing Harry, stretches her hands out towards him.

HARRY   You're my child?

A second CURTAIN, the colour of gold, comes down.

ACT II

Bert is still sitting with his back against the proscenium arch, left. He holds the rifle on his knees. He appears to doze.

The CURTAIN rises.

SCENE: the same. The stage is still lit, but not so brightly, from light beyond the plate-glass window. Waldorf, Smudger and Norbert are by the window looking out. They cast long shadows to the opposite wall. Geordie is sitting against the wall by the machine, right.

The Barman and the Char are at the bar, as if poring over papers.

The table and chairs, covered by the original CURTAIN, are in the structure of a nomad's tent, left of centre.

WALDORF	It's the sun.
SMUDGER	It looks like the sun.
NORBERT	What does the sun look like?
WALDORF	Round. A sort of yellow.
	Norbert turns and makes patterns with his hands with the shadows that he casts from the window to the opposite wall.
SMUDGER	Perhaps it's the Aurora Borealis —
WALDORF	What is the Aurora Borealis?
SMUDGER	High speed particles, like, come down through the atmosphere, like —
	He looks up at the flies.
	Norbert has been making shadows move to and fro across Bert's face. Bert, with his back against the proscenium arch, left, appears to be asleep. Waldorf watches: then he makes a gesture for Smudger to get down. They get on to hands and

127

knees. They begin to crawl past the plate-glass window towards the front of the stage — as if keeping out of sight, or out of the light. When they reach the front, right, they turn and look back.

Norbert has knelt down by Geordie, who appears to be ill.

At the bar, the Barman and the Char are poring over their papers.

CHAR You change —
BARMAN If you like —
CHAR There are connections —
BARMAN In the fields. The factories —
CHAR What specifications?
BARMAN The lesser for the greater. Blood and bone.

Norbert, helping Geordie, has begun to crawl past the plate-glass window to join Waldorf and Smudger at the front of the stage.

CHAR Efficiency. Economy —
BARMAN Call them by different names —
CHAR What —
BARMAN Spot. Beauty.

The Barman mimes tidying papers.

Norbert and Geordie have managed to join Waldorf and Smudger by the footlights.

The Four sit with their backs to the audience. The Char has been watching where they have cast shadows to the left. She calls —

CHAR I saw you!

Norbert is forcing Geordie's head down on his knees. Waldorf and Smudger are holding his arms and legs. It is uncertain if they are helping or hurting him.

The Char has her back to them.

Where did you find them?
BARMAN Just down from the trees.
CHAR — On a dark night —
BARMAN — Can you tell the difference?

The Barman comes from behind the bar and stands by the Char and puts an arm round her shoulders. They face where the shadows have been, left.

CHAR	Come along then. Coop. Coop —
BARMAN	Wire floor. Netting. All amenities.

They seem to be waiting for more shadows on the wall.

CHAR	What do you feed them?
BARMAN	Waste from the factories. Jokes. Shit.

Waldorf, Smudger and Norbert let go of Geordie. They recline, by the footlights, right, their backs to the audience.

They watch the Barman and the Char.

The Barman and the Char face the audience.

CHAR	And where does it come in —
BARMAN	What —
CHAR	Gas. Electricity —
BARMAN	Little pipes. Like music.

The Char looks up at the flies.

CHAR	And it goes on all the time —
BARMAN	You don't taste it, touch it, smell it —
CHAR	And if the head breaks off?
BARMAN	It stays inside.

The Barman and the Char turn to the plate-glass window.

It is as if they have been uncertain, but have now decided, that this may be the front of the stage.

CHAR	What do they see?
BARMAN	Coloured lights, shapes, music —
CHAR	— The plains where they were born —
BARMAN	— The rings round Salamanca —

The Char looks at the Four by the footlights.

CHAR	I thought it would be more —
BARMAN	What —
CHAR	You know. Two by two. In a sack.
BARMAN	That didn't pay.

The Char turns and looks at the shelter, left.

CHAR	— Rubs them together —
BARMAN	— Keeps them white.

Then the Char faces the audience.

The Barman stands watching the plate-glass.

At the front of the stage, right, Norbert has turned and has stretched a hand out over the footlights. There seems to be no light on it. Norbert examines his hand. Then he looks up at the flies.

The Barman, watching the plate-glass, seems to be prompting someone —

BARMAN	— Got a job for you — Just down from university —

Bert, by the proscenium arch, left, seems to wake up with a jerk.

He raises his rifle and fires three shots up at the flies.

There is a distant cry, as if from a woman: then, briefly, the sound of 1920s' dance music.

Then the music stops.

Bert looks at the Four by the footlights, right.

Norbert is watching him.

Geordie still has his head down by his knees.

Waldorf and Smudger are miming smoking.

The light from beyond the window grows less bright.

Lights come on from above the stage.

Bert seems to go back to sleep.

After a time a flap is raised in the covering of the shelter, left, from the inside, and Harry puts his head out. He looks at the audience. Then he crawls out. He wears his old overcoat. He does not seem to have much on underneath. He crawls to the front of the stage and looks at the audience.

HARRY	You know how, you're halfway up the mountain — and the ivy's running out — and the balcony's a lifetime above — and

there's a bloody great dragon below — and
they begin to jump about like fishes —
He closes his eyes.
Well she wasn't like that, no.
He looks at the audience.
If she were the sun and moon, and I were
gravity —
He crawls round and mimes collecting fire-
wood. When he seems to have collected a
bundle he sits cross-legged at the front of the
stage facing the audience and mimes making a
fire. He mimes lighting it and blowing on it.
After a time there appears at the doorway of the
shelter the head of Sophie, the younger Hostess.
She watches Harry. She crawls to the front of the
stage. She is in her underclothes. She speaks
facing the audience.

SOPHIE   You know how, you've got a man and a ball
on the ends of a chain, and you whirl round
and round; and then you let go —
She closes her eyes.
Well he wasn't like that, no —
Harry has been miming taking a frying pan and
holding it over the fire. He mimes dropping
some bacon into it.
Sophie looks at the audience.
If he were the stream where I was born, and
I were fishes —
After a time, Harry holds the pan out to Sophie.
Sophie mimes taking a bit of bacon out of the
frying pan and putting it in her mouth. She
chews. Harry mimes taking a bit of bacon out of
the frying pan. He seems to burn his fingers. He
waves his hand about. They eat.
After a time the Char, who has been facing the
audience, exclaims —

CHAR   Did you see that — !
BARMAN   She hit him — ?

The Char turns to Sophie and Harry.
The Barman leaves the plate-glass window. He goes behind the bar.
    They separate —

CHAR   Or die?
BARMAN   Or immediately form another attachment.
Harry and Sophie eat.
Then they mime finishing their breakfast, tidying up, and sitting around as if wondering what to do.
Bert speaks as if still half asleep.

BERT   Johnny —
HARRY   Yes?
BERT   Got a job for you —
Bert stretches.
    For a nice boy. Just down from the university —
Sophie is reclining on one elbow, as if facing the fire.
    Did he or didn't he do his mother —
Bert stands.
    Did or didn't he have a beard —
Harry is watching Sophie as if he were an artist and she were his model.
Bert calls.
    Oi! They're on the green! They're getting into government!
He watches Harry.
    Their washing's hanging out!
He waits.
    Do you want your children to see it?
Harry mimes as if he might be making a drawing of Sophie.

BERT   You've had the girl —
HARRY   That was yesterday —
BERT   You said it was for ever —
Harry mimes putting his drawing-board down.
He looks at Bert.
Bert speaks mockingly.

132

	— Go through that door —
HARRY	— Along a corridor —
BERT	— In through another door —

Harry stands.

He says to Sophie.

HARRY   Don't move! There are people watching —

Then he speaks to the audience.

The smell down there, honestly!

Waldorf, Smudger and Norbert look up at Harry.

Geordie turns and looks at the audience.

Bert has put his rifle down at the front of the stage, left. He goes to the Barman, takes him by the shoulder, and places him in front of the machine which is covered, right. The Barman stands there as if he were a waxwork.

Bert goes to the Char and takes her behind the bar where he places her with her elbows leaning on it: it is as if she were representing the Barman. Then Bert goes and squats down facing Sophie in the place that Harry has just left.

Harry speaks as if to the Four on the right.

HARRY   What have you been eating, toadstools?

He puts his hands to his head.

Didn't you hear us tapping?

Waldorf, Smudger and Norbert watch him.

You had food, didn't you? Wine —

He looks down at the audience.

You were kept alive — Kept animals —

He turns to the back of the stage.

Put your feet exactly where I do.

He begins to move towards the Barman at the back. He seems to expect the Four to follow him, but they do not. He stops with his back to the audience, one foot in front of the other, as if he were on a tight-rope.

After a time Bert, the Char and the Barman seem to prompt him, mockingly —

133

BERT	— I wouldn't be in his shoes — !
CHAR	— You should hear him at night — !
BARMAN	— It's terrible — !

Harry moves on to the Barman at the back. He
stands in front of him.

After a time the Four get up and follow him.
Norbert supports Geordie. They move past the
plate-glass window as if they are nervous of the
light.

Harry speaks facing the Barman. He acts as if he is
a guide of a party on a tour.

HARRY   We now come to Napoleon's tomb.
Napoleon was born in 1821, after a dis-
tinguished career in the Indian Civil
Service —

He waits.

Smudger has put a hand in front of the plate-
glass. He looks to the left. There is no shadow.

HARRY   Every time he farted another couple of
noughts were knocked off —

Norbert and Geordie have come up behind
Harry.

Waldorf and Smudger join them.

HARRY   Note how the rocks are carved into the
fantastic shapes of great statesmen.

After a time Harry turns and looks at the shelter,
left.

NORBERT   What about suffering children.
HARRY   What about suffering children?

He moves on and stands in front of the Char.
Norbert raises the dust sheet over the machine,
quickly, and looks behind it.

Harry speaks facing the Char.

We now come to the hall of mirrors, where
everyone sees what they like. The man on
the meat hook, with his balls against his
eyes —

He stares at the Char.

134

	Geordie cries —
GEORDIE	I saw her!
HARRY	And wherever you go, they follow you. Note the particularly fine modelling round the breast and thighs —

Geordie is looking at the gothic doorway, left.

| HARRY | First century A.D. Defaced by early Christians. |

Harry moves on. He stands looking down at Sophie and Bert.

Bert is squatting watching Sophie, as Harry had done, as if he were an artist and she were his model.

Waldorf and Smudger have moved across the stage to the gothic door, left. Smudger puts a hand on the handle of the door. Waldorf puts out a hand as if to stop him.

Harry notices them.

Waldorf and Smudger pretend to fight, like fractious children, as if to cover what they have been doing. Then they join Norbert and Geordie, who have followed Harry.

Norbert has taken his hand from Geordie's shoulder. Geordie has stopped acting as if he were ill.

Harry looks down at Bert and Sophie.

| HARRY | The disrobing room, or bridal chamber, in which all opposites are revealed. The warp and the woof. The warp and the woof. And you look for a tennis ball at a depth of six inches. And it is behind your nose all the time. As is the space from the sun to the furthest stars. And if you touch it, it turns to gold. Never before seen in public — |

He turns out of the wings, left, and returns with a photographer's lamp which he sets up on its stand by the group watching Bert and Sophie. He points it down at Sophie.

— And never again.

He takes the wire of the lamp and goes behind the bar and seems to plug it in there. Then he sits on a stool at the bar with his back to the audience. The Four who are round Sophie and Bert watch them as if in uncertainty.

Harry speaks to the Char who is behind the bar.

HARRY Those old buggers are made of concrete.

The Barman leaves his position in front of the machine and goes and stands in front of the plate-glass window looking up at the flies.

Geordie puts out a hand and touches the photographer's lamp.

NORBERT Is he watching?
GEORDIE No.

Norbert squats down and looks at Sophie.

Geordie switches on the lamp.

The lights above the stage go out.

Sophie reclines in the circle of light.

HARRY — I had a bus-load, once, going over the Alps —

BARMAN — And an old lady wanted to pee — ?

Bert stands, stiffly, and joins Harry at the bar.

BERT — So I said — Milk? Sugar? —

CHAR — The water's boiling —

Bert sits with Harry at the bar.

The Char moves from behind the bar. She goes to the shelter of tables and chairs, left, and drags from it, with difficulty, its covering of the original curtain. She drags this over to the Barman, right. They look up at the flies above the plate-glass window.

Waldorf, Smudger and Norbert are squatting on the perimeter of the circle of light, watching Sophie.

Harry calls out savagely —

HARRY — Have you got her buttocks in? Her breasts? —

The Barman crosses to the old shelter, left. He takes from this a chair, which he carries over to the Char, right. The Char sits on it. The Barman arranges the old curtain around her as if it were a cloak. Then he stands back and looks at her. It is as if she might be a figure in a church.

Harry murmurs —

— Humiliation. Redemption —

BERT — The names of your dearest friends —

The Four remain squatting around Sophie.

After a time —

SMUDGER   Get hold of her arms —

WALDORF   Put her feet up —

NORBERT   Has she swallowed it?

GEORDIE   What would it have been called.

Sophie kneels, facing front. She puts her hands across her breasts.

SOPHIE   As a matter of fact, they do want some re-assurance, you know —

WALDORF   Such as —

SOPHIE   What were you doing last night, the names of your dearest friends —

SMUDGER   Get the head out —

WALDORF   Pin in —

GEORDIE   Do you tell them?

NORBERT   No.

Smudger bends down and puts his ear against Sophie's stomach —

Waldorf, on his knees, comes behind Sophie and puts his hands on the fastening of her brassiere at the back.

WALDORF   — Nasty slippery things —

SMUDGER   — With moustaches —

Smudger straightens. He takes hold, delicately, of the straps of Sophie's brassiere from the front. Gently, as if they are defusing a bomb, they try to take off Sophie's brassiere without disturbing her breasts or arms.

137

WALDORF	Now —
SMUDGER	Good girl —
WALDORF	A big 'un —
GEORDIE	Begin?
NORBERT	— Big 'un!

They manage to get Sophie's brassiere off. Smudger holds it up, with finger and thumb, at arm's length. He stands. He looks at it.

SMUDGER	A cloud —
WALDORF	A camel —
SMUDGER	Two arms —
NORBERT	Two heads?
GEORDIE	And in between?

Smudger moves to the front of the stage as if to drop the brassiere down over the footlights. Waldorf stands: follows him.

Sophie remains with her arms across her breasts. She is gazing up at the back of the auditorium as if she has seen a vision there.

Geordie is by the lamp.

Norbert remains kneeling.

As Smudger reaches the footlights the brassiere seems to jerk out of his hand: he grabs at it; half catches it; succeeds in tossing it to Waldorf, who catches it.

Then it seems to jerk out of Waldorf's hand.

Waldorf ducks; Smudger ducks; as if a huge bird were flying above them. (Waldorf has screwed up the brassiere in his hand.)

Then Waldorf and Smudger straighten, and look out over the audience as if the bird had flown away there.

They are half smiling; as if it had been a game. Geordie and Norbert have remained still.

Sophie remains staring out over the auditorium. In the confusion, Harry has changed places with the Barman, right, so that it is he who is standing in front of the Char, looking down on her.

138

The Barman has gone behind the bar: then he has gone off stage — if possible without being seen. After a time Geordie turns off the photographer's lamp. The stage is now lit just by a faint light coming from beyond the plate-glass window.

After a time the Char looks up at Harry.

CHAR   And the girl?
HARRY   Which —
CHAR   Both —
HARRY   Oh she was all right!

He puts his hand in the breast pocket of his overcoat as if to find money or a chequebook.

CHAR   Make it out in the name —
HARRY   Don't say!

Harry says mockingly —

            — A crate of champagne? A donation to
            your favourite charity?

The Char smiles.

CHAR   Your friends?

Harry moves round stage. He goes in and out of the figures of the others who have remained in the positions they were in when the photographer's lamp went out.

He acts —

HARRY   — On such a night as this — the fields dirty
            with snow — the factory chimneys like
            men's legs — I and my love have been
            separated for many a long year —

He looks at the audience —

            — I have seen — children with dogs' heads
            and fins of fishes —

He looks at Waldorf and Smudger —

            — The skull of the observatory — the spire
            open to the wind —

He looks at Norbert and Geordie —

            — The lights in the sky like pin-tables —

He looks at Sophie —

— Five paces to the wire, and five paces
back again —

After a time Bert speaks from the bar —

BERT   Harry —
HARRY   Yes?
BERT   Got a cigarette?

Harry feels in his pockets. Then he goes to Bert
and mimes holding out a packet.

BERT   You'll get me into trouble you know!

Bert mimes taking a cigarette.

HARRY   Ah, it's Christmas —

Bert mimes lighting the cigarette.

Harry mimes putting the packet away. He
watches Bert.

              Do you ever see her now?
BERT   Yes, I sometimes see her.

Bert moves from the bar. He bangs his arms
about as if he is cold. Then he seems to remember
he is supposed to be holding a cigarette. He
mimes brushing burning ash off his clothes.

HARRY   Look, when she comes tonight —
BERT   They're coming tonight?
HARRY   Give us ten minutes —
BERT   Put in a good word for me, will you?

Bert mimes smoking, keeping his hands cupped
round the cigarette as if it were after dark and he
did not want to be seen.

              I don't agree with what they're doing here,
              you know —
HARRY   Why, what are they doing — ?
BERT   Seeds, fertilizers. The lesser for the greater.
              Blood and bone —

Harry watches him as if amused.

HARRY   But the news is a little better, don't you
              think?

Bert half sings what seems to be a line of a song —

BERT   — I was only under orders —

Harry seems to finish the couplet —

140

HARRY	— And she was over the age of consent —
	Bert mimes dropping his cigarette on the ground and stamping on it. He looks at the plate-glass, right. He murmurs —
BERT	— Content? *Content?*

Then he goes over to Sophie who is still kneeling looking over the audience as if she were entranced. He clasps his hands to his head and acts dramatically —

Oh my God! What have they done to you? —
The light from behind the plate-glass becomes brighter. He looks at it.
He acts —

— You must walk — ! Don't let me down — !
He waits.
The light seems to have become steady.
He murmurs —

And so on.
Then he goes to the old shelter, left, and begins to dismantle it.
After a time the Char stands, taking the old curtain from her shoulders, and kicks it so that it is along the bottom of the plate-glass window. Then she goes to Harry, at the bar, and seems to whisper in his ear.
Harry looks behind the bar. Then he climbs up on the bar and looks underneath it. Then he looks round the stage.
Smudger breaks his pose by the footlights. He goes to the shelter which Bert has been dismantling and takes a chair from it. He carries the chair to the back, by the gothic door, where he sits.
Waldorf breaks his pose. He takes a chair from the shelter and follows Smudger and sits.
Geordie and Norbert remain where they are: but they glance at each other, uneasily.
Harry goes and opens the hatch of the food lift

and looks down.

Then he looks at Sophie.

It should become apparent, now, that the Barman is no longer on stage; and it is as if Harry has been looking for him.

Sophie stirs. She stands, rubbing her legs as if they had gone to sleep. She tries to keep her hands over her breasts.

Then she hobbles over to the chair by the window, right, that the Char has left.

She stands by it. She turns to Harry.

SOPHIE	Hullo —
HARRY	Hullo —
SOPHIE	I was afraid you might not remember me —
HARRY	Oh yes, I loved only you, you see —
SOPHIE	I've brought you some socks —
HARRY	How terribly kind!

Harry comes over and sits on the chair, right, facing Sophie.

HARRY	And how are the children?
SOPHIE	All right.
HARRY	Wife and kids?
SOPHIE	All right.
HARRY	But we can't talk —
SOPHIE	No.

Waldorf and Smudger, by the gothic door, left, seem to be acting as if they had stopped acting. They are miming reading newspapers; drinking cups of coffee; tying up shoe-laces, etc. They are half-hidden by the partly dismantled shelter.

After a time Sophie and Harry continue —

SOPHIE	So what do we do?
HARRY	Stand back to back —
SOPHIE	Turn —
HARRY	Take a step forward —

They suddenly seem overcome by giggles.

They collect themselves.

Bert has been watching Waldorf and Smudger.

142

BERT	Got it?
WALDORF	What —

Sophie speaks to Harry.

SOPHIE	The pram?
HARRY	The baby?

Bert has picked up Sophie's clothes from the ruins of the shelter. He carries them over and holds them out to her.

Sophie takes them.

Then Bert goes over to Waldorf by the gothic door, left, and holds out his hand.

Waldorf mimes putting down his paper. He speaks as if he is guessing the answer to Bert's question — 'Got it?'

WALDORF	— You're in some sort of trouble, can I help you — ?

Bert remains with his hand out.

Smudger mimes putting his paper down.

SMUDGER	He came in here. He was looking for his child —

After a time Waldorf holds out his hand and lets fall from it, into Bert's hand, Sophie's brassiere, which he has been holding.

Bert goes to Sophie and gives the brassiere to her. Sophie takes it.

Then Waldorf and Smudger go back to their acting of having stopped acting.

Sophie, with her clothes, goes behind the bar. Norbert and Geordie, who have remained in their poses since the photographer's light went off, now stand, take two of the chairs, and a table, and set them up by the dismantled shelter, left. They sit.

Geordie says tentatively —

GEORDIE	I went out through that door —
NORBERT	In through another door —

Smudger interrupts —

SMUDGER	Plenty more in the medicine cupboard! —

143

Geordie and Norbert look round as if to try to find out what they should be doing.

GEORDIE   There was a girl —
NORBERT   What did she say —

Waldorf interrupts —

WALDORF   Miaow, pussy pussy, down boy, cheep —
GEORDIE   Asked me my name —
NORBERT   What did you tell her —
SMUDGER   You touched the light — ?

Waldorf and Smudger mime putting their papers down as if they are irritated, or bored.

The light from beyond the plate-glass window has become brighter.

Geordie turns and talks to Harry, right.

GEORDIE   I was in a playground, alone. There was a chute with grey-green sides and a bed like water. I said — wrap your legs round me and we'll go over the rim of the world —

The Char goes to the remains of the shelter, left, and takes from it the table which she carries to the right and places as it was at the beginning of Act I.

HARRY   Say after me —
GEORDIE   Say after me —
BERT   You can't!
HARRY   Why not?

Harry and Bert are by the plate-glass window, right. Sophie, behind the bar, has been putting her uniform on.

The Char collects the remaining four chairs from the shelter, left, and puts them round the table, right. The tables and chairs are now roughly as they were at the beginning of Act I.

The Char goes behind the bar. She puts on a white coat like that of the Barman.

Norbert speaks from the table, left, facing the audience.

NORBERT   I was in a cell, alone. There were other cells

144

	around me. I thought — I will communicate through the walls. The sounds will stand for words and the words for meanings. I thought — An orchestra. Then I realised — rats!
WALDORF	Where's the barman?
SMUDGER	He was here a moment ago —
WALDORF	Now he's not.

Waldorf giggles.

Bert speaks to Harry —

BERT	They have to do it on their own.
HARRY	All scientifically controlled experiments can be repeated —
BERT	Repeat it then.

Harry turns to the bar. The Char watches.

A Hostess, in her uniform, moves from behind the bar and goes and stands by the plate-glass window staring out.

This is the older Hostess who has changed places with Sophie behind the bar — if possible, unseen.

Harry stares at her.

After a time Bert comes to the front of the stage and seems about to speak to the audience. Then he stops. He turns to the plate-glass window.

| BERT | Ladies and gentlemen, we now come to the practical part of our demonstration — |

He turns to the audience.

We have seen how comforting can be the suffering of pain —

He walks round the stage as if looking for something on the floor at the back in the corners.

Now we can see how pain can eliminate —

He comes back to the audience —

— You like it?

He watches the audience. Then he walks along the footlights, looking at the floor.

— Nothing can be done against moral or

145

religious principles. The exceptions are children and lunatics —

He comes to where the Barman had left the radio in the first act. He picks it up and faces the audience.

    — Is that your child?

Harry is still staring at the back of the Hostess facing the window, right.

After a time Smudger, from the back, calls as if he is fed up —

SMUDGER	Yes!
BERT	Can it talk?
SMUDGER	Yes!
BERT	What does it say —

He waits, holding the radio, by the front of the stage.

Smudger comes forward to the footlights.

He takes the radio from Bert. He fiddles with the knobs.

SMUDGER	It won't —
BERT	Won't talk?
SMUDGER	No.
BERT	It's dead.

Smudger turns to the plate-glass, right.

    Your baby's dead.

Bert faces the audience.

    Give it your breast —

Smudger hesitates.

Then he smiles, holds the radio like a child.

Bert paces around the stage again, stamping on the ground, as if to test whether it is secure.

    There are some who say — We shall not make love upon the stage! But are we then automata —

He stops; facing the plate-glass.

    The subject thinks nothing, feels nothing —

Harry has moved closer to the Hostess at the

146

plate-glass window, watching her.

After a time Waldorf, as if fed up, calls loudly from the back —

WALDORF   You know what this place is, don't you?

Smudger answers in the same manner —

SMUDGER   I should do. I run it!

WALDORF   You run it!

He stands. He comes forward to the footlights. He and Smudger face the audience. They act mockingly, as if they think they know what to say.

SMUDGER   — Don't touch! —

WALDORF   — He's been outside! —

SMUDGER   — His men are outside! —

WALDORF   — It's burning!

They smile.

Geordie has his head in his hands. Norbert watches him as if he is also in pain.

The older Hostess turns from the plate-glass window and comes forward. She carries her papers.

She speaks to Waldorf —

HOSTESS   What is your name?

WALDORF   My name?

HOSTESS   Yes.

Waldorf seems to think: then to guess —

WALDORF   — I was looking for my wife —

HOSTESS   Do you know what plane she's on?

WALDORF   Tall. Grey hair. Small moustache —

He smiles. He has described someone like himself.

The Hostess moves on to Smudger.

HOSTESS   What is your name —

SMUDGER   My name —

HOSTESS   Yes.

He puts the radio down by the footlights. He raises his arms jokingly.

SMUDGER   They usually give you more time, you know. They search you.

Geordie, from the table, left, calls to the Hostess.

GEORDIE   I saw you — !

The Hostess moves over to the table, left. She stands by Geordie and Norbert.

NORBERT   Mummy —

HOSTESS   Yes?

NORBERT   What's that person in the trees?

Bert has gone to the plate-glass and has leaned his head against it. He bangs it with his forehead. He calls —

BERT   Light! Light!

Harry goes to the plate-glass door and opens it. He puts his hand through. His hand cannot be seen through the glass.

He looks at Bert.

Bert murmurs —

              — I'm going to take you to a cell at the bottom of the garden and I'm going to say —

Harry takes his hand from behind the glass. He closes the door. Then he looks at his hands.

Bert holds his head in his hands.

HOSTESS   It's the light of our lives, darlings!

She stands with Geordie and Norbert.

Smudger has lowered his arms.

Bert moves away from the plate-glass, holding his head.

Harry speaks looking at his hands.

HARRY   The problem is, how to live in a very small space: like a head, or a cage on the wall of a municipal building —

He waits. He seems to be listening.

              First find the most comfortable position: on your back, with your knees up. It's an advantage, of course, if you've spent much of your time in bed —

Geordie calls —

GEORDIE   Mummy —

HOSTESS   Yes?

148

GEORDIE   Can I wave?
               Norbert waves at the audience.
NORBERT   Coo-ee!
               Harry turns to the plate-glass window.
HARRY   Then turn on your fingers and toes, with
               your body like the ceiling —
               Bert takes his hands away from his head. He acts
               as if he were holding something in his hands.
               He murmurs —
BERT   Coo-ee.
               He turns to the audience. He opens his hands.
               Now you see it!
               The voice of Sophie comes from behind the
               plate-glass door, right.
SOPHIE   Step back —
               Harry murmurs —
HARRY   — You go over.
               They wait.
               After a time Bert turns his back and acts —
BERT   — Gather around, my children; you can
               brighten your dying sun —
               Geordie speaks to the Hostess —
GEORDIE   They're old?
HOSTESS   Eeeny meeny miney mo —
NORBERT   They go out into the world —
GEORDIE   They die?
               Harry murmurs —
HARRY   They feed it.
               Geordie and Norbert look round the room.
NORBERT   But that depends when you begin —
HOSTESS   Well, where did we —
               The light from behind the window has grown
               brighter.
               Bert has wandered across to the left. He stands by
               the food lift.
               Then he looks at Geordie and Norbert and the
               Hostess by the table, left.
               The voice of Sophie comes from behind the

149

| | plate-glass window — |
| SOPHIE | Can I come in? — |

The Hostess speaks to Geordie and Norbert.

| HOSTESS | So what's the difference — |

Geordie and Norbert look round the room.

| GEORDIE | We go on — |
| NORBERT | We go over — |

Harry looks at Waldorf and Smudger at the front of the stage.

Bert murmurs —

| BERT | And where do you think *he* is? |

The Char is behind the bar.

The older Hostess is with Norbert and Geordie by the table, left.

Bert is by the food lift.

Harry is centre, slightly right.

Waldorf and Smudger, with their backs to the footlights, left, have stepped to the very front of the stage as if to be out of the glare from the plate-glass window.

The gothic door, left, opens. Framed in it is the elegant figure of a Hostess in uniform: she has a hand up to her face as if to shield it from the light. Almost immediately the plate-glass door, right, opens, and Sophie comes in. She wears jeans and a sweater. She begins walking towards the footlights as if to take her bow.

Then she notices, and stops and stares at, the figure of the Hostess framed in the gothic door. It is as if there are now three Hostesses.

Harry yells —

| HARRY | I don't want anyone to see this! |

He waves violently at the wings.

The CURTAIN begins to come down.

It is a dark Curtain, of the same kind as at the beginning of Act I.

When the Curtain is down, Waldorf and Smudger find themselves in front of it.

150

The lights in the auditorium come on.

Waldorf and Smudger seem uncertain what to do. Then they pick up the rifle and the radio which are by the footlights. Then they take their bow, awkwardly, at the front of the stage.

Then they climb down into the auditorium and go off at a side-exit.

CELL

Present-day subjects under taboo — those about which people know but do not talk — are to do with the observation, knowledge, that life seems to maintain itself and evolve only at the cost of enormous waste; that only a small proportion of what is generated is fruitful: together with the conviction — likewise built up over the years of painstaking trial and error — that it seems to be part of a man's special nature to try to prevent this, at least with regard to members of his own species. The observation and the conviction go hand in hand: it is 'advanced' and 'scientific' cultures that insist on the humanitarian need to look after unfruitful members of the species: those that do not, are rightly called barbaric. There is nothing absurd, or incorrect, in this predicament: humanitarianism has become as much part of a scientific man's make-up as are the results of more impersonal observations. And it is perhaps the very mark of something living, evolving, that it should possess such contradictions — to be free to move within. What makes for present-day confusion is the lack of a style, a language, in which to talk about these things — by which a person, in such a predicament, might feel at home. Having no further vantage point from which he might embrace at the same time, as it were, both scientific and ethical attitudes, he is driven to assume that a commitment must be to one or to the other: and because this cannot be done by a person hoping for wholeness and thus for identity (since it involves cutting off part of himself) the result is, even for him, a retreat into scepticism or fantasy — in which he finds enough companions, goodness knows, who feel at home. Men split themselves — between the way they act professionally and the way they act privately; between the ruthlessness of public games and what the players themselves would claim were realities: within the games and the 'realities' themselves — for however much people may try to cut out parts of themselves, these parts exist, and after the cutting they are apt to exist in ways that people have no control over. The result of such splits are vacuums that dreams rush in to fill. But the fact that such a predicament can be glimpsed at all implies that there might be some vantage point from which a viewer might feel at home: that the gap is still not an occasion for despair, but a need for becoming accustomed. It is here that an idea like that of Bateson's categories of learning is relevant — an attempt to evolve a language which will try to deal not just with facts, with units of data, but with the patterns, connections, that such data, together with the minds that observe them, make — in particular a language that can deal at the same time both with the data and with the language that is traditionally used to describe them. By this, apparent contradictions might be held. This language would be elusive, allusive; not didactic. Some such language has been that of poetry, of art: also of love — that seed-bed of self-mocking simplicities! But such complexities, arrogances, are indeed alarming: men are more easily at home, more protected, within the simple and infantile antagonisms of putting one fact against another; of knocking down cases like skittles; of making a fantasy of identity by putting the boot in. To have tenderness involves the acceptance of complexities: growing up involves the recognition of circuits like those of blood — all this within, between and around what are the demands of the internal and what are apparently the facts of the external world.

In the last century efforts were made to embrace contradictions by fusing them into systems — a process known, but seldom with much clarity portrayed, as dialectics. Hegel suggested that the contradictions attendant upon consciousness could be merged into a higher truth: but in trying to describe what sort of thing this truth might be ('the objective world process') he either became aggressively simplistic (the deification of the state) or almost unintelligible. Marx took on Hegel's style: but in his writing, the contradictions and his efforts to deal with them assumed an apocalyptic potency — science and humanitarianism were to join forces for some final struggle, after which there would be peace. Marx's driving energy was a straight materialistic humanitarianism — an outrage that one class of men should be treated like animals by another, and that fantasies of otherworldliness should be used to perpetuate this misery. But in the nineteenth century pleas for humanitarianism had to be backed up by appeals to science: it was thought that men were so rooted in self-interest that appeals to ethics were no use: it could even be held that self-interest was ethical: so fighters against outrage had to call upon 'science' not just because 'science' was the presiding deity of the age, but because only thus could the fighters be given weapons. And so a science had to be made up that had little to do with observation or experiment; but which was, simply, of use in the war against outrage. But such science was no real science. The justifications and the prophesies of Marxism have the same quality, in words, as those of religion — the words can be held to mean different things at different times according to the needs of writers and speakers: there is an impossibility in trying to bring such abstractions or such predictions to the test. It is not clear how much Marx himself believed what came to be seen as the dogmas of Marxism — but this is a common predicament of founders of religions. What seems to have been important for Marx is that he remained a fighter: he could use his 'scientific' reasoning as a weapon for vituperation: but his faith seemed to be less that there should finally emerge a triumphant and rational working class, as that there should be always someone, somewhere, fighting. But although it was the dream of there being a scientific basis for their hopes against outrage that gave Marxists their potency and their victories, it also gave them their curse: for it is in Marxism that the splits and fusions and confusions between scientific and ethical attitudes have become, nowadays, often most observable and ludicrous: words and what they refer to cease to have any connection: the drive for equality is manifested by élitism; the liberation of the working class, to make it work, is paralleled by imprisonment. But in this it is hardly the drive towards humanitarianism or towards science that is at fault: the fault is in the attempt to force them into effect in one logical social system. For if scientific attitudes and ethical convictions are to be brought together this cannot be done, simply, socially: it is just this that has been

157

learned by painful trial and error. What can be done is that such apparently contradictory attitudes can be held in the mind — separately, but together from some further point of vantage — and then, but only then, can they work in harmony socially. The unit, that is, in which such complexities can be held and neither fused nor confused is not a society nor even a person but that which is in interaction between the two: that part of a person which is free, but which survives through society: which enables a society to survive: which in its lively endurance, both is in the form of ideas and is like the genetic material of the outside world: and thus, indeed, is somewhat god-like.

It was Nietzsche who announced that god was dead: who saw all religions (as Marx said he saw them) as shrouds by which truth was obscured: truth being nothing to do with dogmas nor with systems but with a style, an attitude, a process, an activity. Nietzsche's attack was against Christianity: but his enemy would also have been Marxism if he had known of it — Marxism having taken over dreams of simplicity and peace. By dreaming of any perfection — of a future world either in heaven or on earth — Nietzsche saw that men were in fact depriving themselves of chances of coming into working harmony with things as they are — of changing them, through such contact, for the better. Dreams might once have been weapons in the struggle for existence and evolution: dreams were perhaps moves in a general game of what Nietzsche called 'will to power' by which everyone in order to survive had to try to do down everyone else: but in fact those who seemed to 'succeed' in this game were as much trapped within its limited and inhuman processes as anyone else: and in any case such a game, in the modern world and with modern knowledge, was becoming suicidal. The one true chance of human improvement, even evolution, Nietzsche thought, was not for one human being to come out on top of another: not for one set or class of humans to come out on top of another: not to dream, impossibly, of such a struggle one day ceasing through ultimate victory (for then what would be the driving force of life? and what would be improvement?) but for individuals with part of themselves to step out of the continuing trapped and trapping process altogether — it would be to do this that there would be the struggle and this would be the improvement — to reach some point within themselves from which they could observe themselves and those other parts of themselves as well as of others within the predicament: and by this to be truly human — even god-like — being free of the predicament. Also, of course, to be human (and not un-god-like?) and for the predicament to remain. What was necessary was for a man to come into this sort of relationship with himself: to 'overcome' himself not in the sense of dominating, or condescending to himself or indeed others (thus has Nietzsche been traduced): but just in the sense of being able to stand back from the animal-like stimulus-and-response levels of his nature and by understanding them and being kind to them to have a chance to do something about them — and about those of others. This was possible, observably, within an individual: there was little sense in the idea of its being possible — except through the interlocking activities of individuals — in the mass. But it was in this common area of 'standing back' that men could in fact meet: since they would have a chance here of separating themselves and others from their projections, and it would in this sense be that such efforts would be social. Nietzsche saw that a contemporary evolutionary gulf was not so much the one between men and animals, as between men-and-animals on the one hand and some different kind of man on the other — between those, that is, who remain trapped within stimulus-and-response patterns of behaviour and who use only dreams to imagine that they are not; and those who, by virtue of being able to distance themselves within themselves and to look upon such patterns, in some sense and in some part of themselves become free of them — and thus become of a different kind. And such an activity would be open to everyone, however difficult it might be to talk about — too much verbalising being likely to land one back in dreams. Nietzsche's 'other' or 'super' type of man has nothing to do with politics and nothing to do with power (except insofar as such a man has what might be called the power to overcome drives to power

— or at least realise that this way of thinking gives a different use to the exercise of power): it is to do with a man's ability to observe, to question, to test — himself just as much (he is nearer at hand) as others — a tentativeness, a key, a mode, a way of living; not a domination. Nietzsche's language is elusive, allusive, poetic: it is a way of talking about truth by at the same time listening to, judging, what itself is saying: it is a way of defending itself against the comforts of dogma: it is a presentation by which people can, if they keep up in it, find their own truth. Nietzsche's enemies (indeed his so-called friends) were able to make out that he was saying something quite different from what he was because he did sometimes talk as if he were playing in one of their games of cut-throat musical chairs. But perhaps he catered even for this: he saw a function for such friends-enemies. One of the characteristics of his way of thinking was that there can be a function for those who are of a different kind to oneself: enemies can be used: they can be the working parts, perhaps of the grid, the riddle, of personal (social) history: they can supply the shaking from the abrasive action of which there can come sifting and change. Marx, violently, said he wanted to change history: perhaps he did change it: but not (it is still violent) with the result that he had dreamed. Nietzsche tried to see the way that history in fact worked: and by this to look in the sifting for diamonds, as well as for cleaned gravel.

One reason why Nietzsche has made people anxious even when he has not been made out to say the opposite of what he did say (his work was for a time taken up by power-politicians) is that any suggestion that one type of man might be thought different or possibly more suited to evolution than another seems to imply the existence of an élite — and of all the taboo words of the second half of the twentieth century this (perhaps with reason) is one of the most abhorred. 'Élite' has come, historically, to suggest some inborn superiority of class, of race, of intelligence, of aesthetic sensibility: a conjunction between those who have these qualities and those who have power. But in Nietzsche's use of the idea (he did not use the word) there was nothing of this: in fact there was much, precisely, of its opposite. Nietzsche's implication was that there was some special form of activity open to almost anyone who chose; but this was a solitary, not a group, activity; and that on the whole people who liked power did not choose this form of activity simply because their own form of group carry-on seemed more attractive. It was the 'privileged' in the conventional sense, obsessed with power, who found it difficult to stand back from the ensnaring mechanisms of power and see themselves: but it was this standing-back that was the mark of a true élite: so that the members of a true élite were almost necessarily non-privileged. Nietzsche saw as his enemies those who were entrenched in the established worlds of politics and of society and of academic distinction: these were the nonélite. Nietzsche's 'higher' type of man might be bold, intelligent, imaginative; but even in these qualities he would be out of line with powerful society: his one undeniable 'superiority' would be his freedom from other people's slavery-to-power. In this respect other men might envy him and try to do him down: but of this they would be almost unconscious: consciously, they would be able to ignore the standpoint from which he was different. So such a man would find himself working alone, almost in secret: and this was right, because what he knew would be difficult to put into words. Nietzsche saw the raw material of experience going round and round as it were in eternally recurring patterns (there being a finite amount of material energy and possibly an infinity of time for the energy to ring changes) this vision being as if of a treadmill; a hell. But some people, with the part of themselves that saw this, could choose to get out — even if they had to watch other parts of themselves on the treadmill. But what on earth could be said by these people when they saw other people's so powerful preference to stay wholly in? About this, it was true, there seemed to be something of a taboo.

There is enough evidence nowadays, goodness knows, that it is the conventionally powerful people who seem slavish — those politicians, pundits, leaders of the fashionable world who in their uniformity of livery and adherence to strict routines and in their inability to behave as they might like on the spur of any moment not only look like servants and behave like servants but (don't be taken in by this!) actually are public servants — those bewigged and bewildered figures caught sleepless on the steps of aeroplanes; their bags under their eyes like suitcases; always ready to jump to the call of a microphone or a bell; on the trot from dawn to long after dusk; hardly any time to see their loved ones; their engagement books filled for months and even years; and always liable, like soldiers emerging from a wood, to be taken hostage or shot — such vulnerabilities extending to their children and children's children. These are the people who are honoured socially now; who have power; who choose to live like this — this is the point — no one makes them. And the people who choose to try to be able to do as they like, to look for what it is that they like, who discover that this often involves them in difficult (but pleasurable?) rejections of that to which they have been accustomed — these are people held with little social honour in the modern world; who perhaps on some level are envied, but not always enough to stop them making themselves and others happy. For the ability to be in relationship with oneself is the ability to be happy — in this sense to have an area in common with others who are happy — but still, to be often solitary, which is a hard happiness and takes courage. And it is a common misery that is the bond, the reassurance, the comfort, the security, of people who are no more than the parts of themselves in the treadmill that is social. This craving to be a powerful albeit complaining slave to a conventional system — to be as it were a dominant domestic — is due to a fear of freedom: it is within the fellowship of common complaint that resentment, the desire not to let anyone be one up, can be effective: no one, if all are trapped, need feel inferior. Such a fear of a happy relationship within oneself seems to be what a person is born into: a baby is dependent and perhaps confused about what is of other people and what is of itself: and so perhaps a person finds it easier to try to continue to project his own inadequacies and responsibilities on to others rather than to try to grow up, which is the taking of responsibilities within

162

oneself. What has hitherto been objectionable about 'élites' has just been the assumption that such people should have power. But if the word is taken away from the concept of power — if it is recognised that now it is powerful people who seem slavish and who choose to be slavish and the only true concept of an élite would be that of people who are in this sense specifically non-privileged — then, what would be the harm? For everyone — both the non-privileged and the privileged — pays at least lip service to the idea of the overriding value of freedom: and what could be objectionable about an élite which most people who have the choice could not bear to be part of?

Such a picture may seem a bit of a dream, and perhaps it is, if it is imagined that such differentiations between privileged and non-privileged can be seen simply in terms of differing individuals in the outside world. But such patterning is in the mind; and such differentiation takes place, is played with, more (this is the point) within an individual — between parts of him — than outside. In practice most people have one foot at least trapped as it were within the treadmills of routine and power — they have to to stay alive — and most people retain some spark within them by the light of which, at moments at least, they can glimpse a part of themselves that might be able to stand back — until, perhaps, they are too old. Certainly someone trying to hold himself on the side of a non-privileged élite should have no illusions about his involvement with trying to keep in balance differing parts of himself: to feel himself simple would be to fail. He must be handling both aloofness and the social cunning to remain aloof; holding on, not too tightly, to something fluttering, like a bird. As soon as success was grasped it would have to be freed; the mark of success would be something continually changing to stay the same. It would be like a child; to be fostered, to grow; but to live its own life: to be both held, and not held, at once. To learn to love oneself would be like tending a seed, a pearl (as has been said): a matter of skill however much also of luck: the ability to take advantage of luck (and indeed of non-luck): a making the best, and something profitable, of whatever it is that comes one's

163

way: but what comes is usually averaged, and so one has a choice. There is something akin here to processes in psycho-analysis — the painstaking looking after, by making use of whatever turns up, projections; so that they can perhaps become healthy by being taken back; using a language which, by being listened to, can be seen to refer both to its own form and the things it refers to; by these means to undergo a search, a discrimination, an enablement to deal with the riddles that let trapped children out of cages. There is also something here akin to processes of writing plays or novels — that business that begins as the plaything of its creator and then takes off, dis-appears, comes back when it is ailing: takes off again (if it is any good) goes round and round somewhat dementedly and only when you are not looking, but have persevered, it is there! Ah, these plays! on the grid and riddle like happy children! But there is necessarily something secret in all this: people talking about having to be able to choose what they want — how embarrassing! If what they want is life, then this is something that they have to search for, quietly, themselves, and to discover. If they do not — then what one can say is that what they want can indeed be given them on a platter.

It may be of course that dominant domestics, with their inability to have much sense of their own identity except by hurling resentment at others, will sooner or later blow up the world: and then what will it avail the non-privileged élite that they will have, with such tip-toeing difficulty, learned to under-stand complex patterns and to carry their own resentments? They may have come to accept, even, that in the course of evolution all individual organisms have to die: that it is only by throwing cards in and shuffling them and re-dealing them as it were that a continuing strain, a genetic shape, may stay alive. But there is no evolutionary sense in everything dying. A game that can be played with oneself in the middle of the night (those hours when grown-up gentleness needs a little infantile suste-nance) is to try to imagine a circumstance in which a natural or man-made holocaust would destroy preponderantly those whom it might be of evolutionary advantage to destroy — the power-hungry, say (in the game, at least, one has one's own choice of enemies — perhaps those who might carry such infant dreams over into morning) — and would leave alive those whom it might be of evolutionary advantage to preserve — those self-questioners, say, who would in the morning laugh at their dreams. Some Noah's Atoll when the ice-cap comes down from the pole? Some fire to test immortality, like that of Empedocles on Etna? But such games, though exercising the imagination, seem to have no practical relevance: and the qualities of imagination, as Jacques Monod has been quoted as saying earlier, seem to possess no obvious genetic advantage. He also said 'modem molecular genetics offer us *no means whatsoever* for acting on the ancestral heritage so as to improve it with new features'. But none of this need cause dismay. If there is to be a relevant change — if the human species, that is, is to be able to adapt itself enough in order to survive — it is still in the mind that it seems likely that such a change should occur; mind being the latest product of evolution. It is possible, of course, that all minds may be destroyed: but until, and unless, they are, theirs is the ground on which seeds might grow — seeds that are random, of course, but the ground being able to be tended so that certain seeds rather than others might be encouraged to grow — in the hope (there is no other) that if this is done what in time might die would be just that which wants to die (the seeds are so myriad!); and what would live would be just that which does not want to push and pull at its roots and so kill itself but does its work and tills the ground and trusts that forces of life will do the rest for it.

What has been discovered in the science of genetics is that although it is true that the occasion as it were for natural selection is given by chance — mutations in genes happen at random: mutated genes are then 'tested' by environment so that most of them die and only very few prove to be more suited than the usual ones in the line from which they sprang — although this is true and there can be no ordering of chance, yet still it is also true that there are so many possible or latent mutations in humans' genetic make-up that it is still possible for a

165

person (persons) to do things to help, as it were, to bring certain mutations to the fore — by the provision of an environment — perhaps of an 'environment' within personality — by which characteristics which have hitherto been recessive (because unsuitable for survival) might thus be made to seem of advantage — and so not die. The area in which humans might be able to affect themselves, that is, even genetically, is through the environment; and an environment not only, or even mainly, outside; but of heart, soul, mind. It is here that there might be some moving on from the old idea that a human genetically is helpless. There are patterns and styles of thinking that are themselves like genes — could even as it were be genetically selected — and it is over this area that a person has some slight ordering. By the cultivation of a ground for a new style of thinking one might find that seeds suited to it that have been blown there by chance have become established and have grown there because of effort. There are such seeds — how else could one have the idea of such a ground? So — Dig for Circuitry! for Recognition of Complexity! for the Entity worked by the Outside Ground. And beware of Resentment: Helplessness: the Tares of Anti-life. Something like cancer may perhaps be ineradicable: but there is nothing better to do or to try to get established than the encouragement of that which (though it is this that cannot much be talked about) wants, in place of that which simply wants to die, to stay alive.

There are signs, now, as if some part of the social body (some individuals in the social body? some part of the mind of each individual in the social body?) might want to die: as if to try to preserve this part might make the whole body die, as it were from some cancer. It is amongst the denizens of powerful and fashionable worlds that there is the malaise, the will to extinction, that is commonly talked about — the love of seeing and hearing things only violent and appalling; the reassurance from the perpetual round of preying upon others; the passion for titillation, for dope, for the fruitlessness of pornography. But it is these people, nowadays, who are not likely to have children. Or perhaps their children, if they do, will not be likely to have children: children, within such attitudes, are a drag: parents may only render them more impotent. This, even in the mind, is appalling. But it is also here that there is hope. (Can this word be used, if something so appalling can hardly be talked about?) Such people may simply die; may withdraw themselves, modishly, from the area of selection. And it may be just the non-privileged, the unfashionable — who have some drive towards life, some effort towards orderliness, some containment — who might produce at least — children! In the mind at least; or in the flesh; as if they were genes in the body politic — the things which may survive. There does seem to be some force of selection at work here: but at the moment the confusion, the taboos, are such that although a force like this might be respected, it is scarcely encouraged. And although some form of self-destruction may seem inevitable, even justified, it indeed can scarcely be applauded. But what if it were possible to say in some form — to say with that part of one's mind that wants to live while addressing that part of one's mind (as well as that of others) that wants to die — All right, if you want to die, die! but know also that the saying of this is the best way of possibly stopping you. This is the point. This is the sort of thing a father might say to self-destructive children; who would know that it would be his way of stopping them; that a strict injunction would encourage them to be deathly; that his way of making them want to live, and thus of loving them, would be simply to remind them that they had the greatest gift of all for life — that of freedom. For this, still, is the word that can bridge a gulf between, be understood by both those who want to be fruitful and the deathly — it being a commonly acceptable highest moral imperative. One of the fallacies of old ways of thinking has been — if something is bad, stop it! — and it has been observed that this seldom satisfactorily works. But still, it is an attitude that is persisted in, because logical. But as Nietzsche knew, as Popper knows, as any scientist should know, as a proper parent knows with children — it is by your mistakes that you learn: it is by being free to face what is 'bad' that you can learn that it suits you to try to stick with what is 'good': that it is this sort of freedom — trial-and-error, circuitry — that is the only way of becoming something out of reach of the rules of slavery. So, it might be possible to say to people publicly — For goodness' sake, yes, destroy yourselves if you want to! — if this were said with love: this being the hope (the best hope) of preventing them. But this, certainly, needs a difficult sort of language. And some bright understanding. It would have to be seen — half seen — that one was talking about mind; but that this was of direct relevance (the most direct relevance) to the outside world; the outside world being available to patterns of mind; but not in the old bullying type of language; not even in the simple languages in which things are set out dead as on a platter; but in the circuits and secrets and lightning flashes that are the provinces and provenances of life.

CELL

ANDERSON   who played   ARIEL and BERT

HORTENSE   who played   JUDITH and the OLDER
                                   HOSTESS

THE MOOR   who played   ACKERMAN and the BARMAN

DIONYSUS   who played   JASON and HARRY

FLORENCE   who played   HELENA and the CHAR

SIVA   who played   JENNY and the YOUNGER
                                   HOSTESS (SOPHIE)

SCENE: A cellar in a town.

The structure contains two levels. The upper level consists of two rooms separated by a central partition: it is in darkness. The lower level is one long room, with pipes and cables along the back wall as if for telephones, drains, gas, electricity, etc.

This lower level is dimly lit. Left of centre is an old-fashioned stove, which glows. Centre is an elaborate brass bedstead. On the right is an area of junk in semi-darkness. Far left are screens as if in an actor's dressing-room. The flue-pipe of the stove goes up crookedly above the bedstead and into the floor above.

The whole structure is contained within vertical side walls and a flat roof so that it is like a doll's house with the front removed. There are narrow vertical spaces between the side walls and the sides of the stage. In the left vertical space there are ladders descending from what seems to be a manhole at the street-level above: the right vertical space is like a disused ventilation shaft.

A young man, Anderson, is on the bed in the lower level. He sits cross-legged, in his underpants, and has the handpiece of a telephone wedged beneath his ear. The wire from the telephone goes up to a clip on to a cable over his head.

Anderson appears to be listening. After a time he enunciates carefully —

ANDERSON   Get out at Westminster, cross the road, go to the gates, and you'll find a policeman. You'll wear knee-breeches, black waistcoats, and those conical hats, you know, like witches. You'll have the pram, and two

171

barrels of gunpowder like imitation leather suitcases. And when you come to the policeman you will say — Excuse me, mate, where's the team? Excuse me, mate, where's the fucking team —

He seems to listen.

Then he unclips the wire from the cable above his head. He clips it to another cable. He takes from a table by his bed a tuning fork, which he strikes and holds against the bedstead.

There is a high-pitched humming noise; which fades. Then Anderson speaks with the deadpan voice of someone on an intercom radio —

Bert. Two tadpoles. Coming up through the sewers. Tell them what to do, will you?

He stares at the audience.

There is a deep rumbling noise from the pipes; as if from an organ, or faulty plumbing.

Anderson puts his hand over the mouthpiece of the telephone.

The rumbling fades.

Anderson says in an ordinary voice —

Put your hands and feet on the floor. Your body on the ceiling —

He listens.

Then he unclips the wire from the cable: he clips it on to a bar of the brass bedstead. After a time he imitates, rapidly but just intelligibly, the high-pitched gibberish of a voice on a tape being played too quickly —

Whentheycametothebarricadesagainstits softgreywallstheybattered —

He stares at the audience.

Then he imitates ponderously but again just intelligibly, the deep distorted drawl of a voice on a tape being played too slowly —

There-were-not-many-left-to-tell-the-tale.

He listens.

172

Then he takes from the table by his bed a small instrument which makes clicking noises such as is found in children's crackers. With this he makes clicks, in bursts, into the mouthpiece of the telephone; as if establishing a programme in a system by a code.

He listens.

Then he speaks in an ordinary voice —

— The doctor says it must have been agony —

He watches the audience.

After a time a light comes on in the room upstairs, left. This room is piled high at the back with books and old newspapers. There is a stove against the wall of the central partition on the right. (It is into the bottom of this stove that the flue-pipe goes up from Anderson's room below.) The flue-pipe from this stove goes halfway up the central partition and then through into the room which is in darkness, right.

On top of the pile of books against the back wall in the room on the left is perched an elderly man, the Moor, who wears a white robe and has a beard. He reclines on one elbow just under the ceiling — like Michelangelo's God the Father on the roof of the Sistine Chapel; or like Karl Marx, or a gorilla. He has a hand on a light bulb which is on the ceiling. After a time the bulb seems to burn his fingers. He takes his hand away. The light in the room goes out: there is a tinkle as if of glass on the floor, breaking.

Anderson gets off his bed, goes to his stove, takes off the lid, and looks inside.

After a time he drops the lid of the stove as if it has burned his fingers.

He looks at the audience.

Then he goes to his bed, lies on his back underneath the flue-pipe, unscrews an inspection

173

plate in the bend of the pipe above his bed, opens it, and peers up as if the pipe were a telescope. After a time he puts his mouth to the inspection plate and enunciates carefully —

ANDERSON — She will wear a belt, black stockings, and something loose round the top —

He puts his eye to the inspection plate. The light in the Moor's room, upper left, comes on again. The Moor has fitted another bulb into the socket which hangs from his ceiling. (He has beside him a paper bag from which he seems to take his light bulbs as if they were nuts.) He keeps his hand on the bulb. After a time it seems to burn his fingers again. He holds on. It is as if he were in agony.

Anderson takes his eye from the inspection plate. He looks at the audience.

Then he puts his mouth to the inspection plate and enunciates carefully —

The world is on a tortoise. The tortoise is on a bird. The bird is on the sea —

He puts his ear to the inspection plate.

The Moor, upstairs, as if he can hold on no longer, lets go of the light bulb. The light of his room goes out. There is a tinkle as if of glass on the floor, breaking.

Anderson gets up, goes to his stove, and makes as if to lift the lid off. Then he seems to think. The light in the Moor's room comes on again. This time the Moor is holding the bulb with the hem of his white robe.

Anderson looks at the audience. Then he puts a hand in his underpants. He lifts off the lid of his stove using his underpants as protection.

The Moor begins to climb down from his perch of books. He finds this difficult, since he is holding on to the light bulb. But as he pulls on the wire, he finds that this can be drawn down

174

through the ceiling. Then as the wire comes through the ceiling there are cries and gasps from the room, right, which is still in darkness, as if someone were being garotted there.

Anderson looks up.

After a time the lid of the stove which he is holding through his underpants seems to burn his fingers: he drops it.

The Moor has reached the floor. He gives the wire from his light bulb a jerk, and the cries from the room, right, are abruptly silenced.

Downstairs, Anderson looks at his hand.

Upstairs the Moor, still holding the light bulb with the hem of his robe, comes and stands in front of his stove which is against the central partition.

(In this position it might be difficult for some of the audience — in the right half — to see exactly what he is doing, since their view is somewhat obscured by the central partition.)

The Moor lifts the lid off his stove with his other hand using the hem of his robe. He stands with his robe raised as if he is about to pee into the stove.

Anderson leaves his stove. He goes to his bed and lies underneath the flue-pipe and looks through the inspection plate again which is directly under where the Moor is standing. The Moor seems to be having difficulty in peeing.

After a time there is the sound of flute music (a flute sonata by Bach) from the room in darkness, top right.

Anderson takes his eye away from the inspection plate. He looks at the audience.

At this moment the Moor seems to be able to pee.

Anderson closes the inspection plate.

There is a puff of steam from the stove by

Anderson's bed, where the Moor's pee seems to have gone.

Anderson stares at his stove.

After a time, there is a smaller puff of steam from the Moor's stove upstairs.

The Moor puts the lid back on his stove. He looks at the audience.

The flute music stops.

Downstairs, Anderson gets off his bed. He puts the lid back on his stove. Then he comes to the right front of his room and looks up towards the Moor's room, left, as if trying to see (as if from the point of view of half the audience) what the Moor has been doing. He looks at the audience. Then he goes to the front of his room on the left, and looks up towards the room in darkness, right, as if trying to see (from the point of view of the other half of the audience) where the flute music had come from.

After a time there is in this room a flash, as if of a flashlight photograph, or from a small explosion of gas.

Here there can be glimpsed, briefly, the figure of a man hanging by the neck from a wire from the ceiling.

Then the room is in darkness again.

Anderson looks at the audience.

The Moor, on the left, has turned away from his stove. He takes a step towards the left: then he appears to tread on broken glass. He lifts his foot. He holds it as if in agony. He lets the bulb go. It is pulled up, as if by a counterweight, on its wire through the ceiling.

At the same time there is a bumping and groaning noise from the room, right, as if the body were being lowered on its wire.

When the light bulb has reached the Moor's ceiling there is a tinkle, as if of glass breaking.

The Moor's light stays on.
The Moor stays in the position of a statue.
Anderson, who has been watching the audience, goes to his stove and squats down in front of it.
The stove has a door with a glass window in it.
Anderson opens the door into the stove.
He takes from it a small pan which he carries over to a table, right, in the area of junk.
He puts down the pan. He switches on a light which hangs on a wire from the ceiling above the table.
The light in the Moor's room goes out.
Anderson looks up: he seems to listen.
On the table in Anderson's room there are some old-fashioned scientific instruments — a microscope, some slides, some glass retorts and rods.
Anderson sits behind his table and takes a glass rod and dips it into the pan and mimes placing a drop of liquid on one of the slides. He pulls down the light on its wire above the microscope.
At the same time there is raised, on a hinge, the cover to the manhole into the street, top left.
Anderson looks up.
Then there comes from the darkness of the room, right, the sound of a man's voice, as if reciting poetry —

VOICE   — They have left me with no sound, no sight; No taste, no smell —

Anderson listens. Then he puts the slide under the microscope.
The voice continues.

        — My arms so tight;
        The bounds of hell —

Anderson puts his eye to the microscope.
On what seems to be the street-level at the very top of the structure a bright light comes on. (At this level there can be seen what look like the

177

bottoms of buildings.)

On to this level there comes, from the right, a woman, Hortense. She wears shorts and a T-shirt and has a haversack on her back.

She looks over her shoulder apprehensively, as if someone has been following her.

Then she puts her haversack on the ground and stands with her back to the audience as if she were beside a road waiting for a lift.

Anderson looks up from his microscope. As he does this the light at the top of the structure becomes dim.

Hortense looks at the manhole, left.

Anderson stands. He pushes up, on its wire, the light that hangs above the microscope. As he does this, the manhole on the street closes.

Hortense stares at it. Then she comes to the front of the structure and looks over.

Then she goes to the manhole and tries to force her fingers into a crack to lift it up.

Anderson watches the audience.

Hortense goes to her haversack, opens it, and takes from it a frogman's breathing apparatus, which she puts on.

Then she comes to the front edge of the top of the structure and looks over.

The light at street-level becomes watery.

Anderson sits behind his table again and pulls down on its wire the light that hangs above the microscope. The cover of the manhole, behind Hortense, opens.

Hortense, through her frogman's mask, stares at the audience.

After a time, from the darkness of the room, right, there comes the sound of flute music again — the sonata by Bach.

Anderson puts his eye to the microscope.

The light at street-level steadies and becomes

clear.

Hortense goes to the manhole, the cover of which is now open, picks up her haversack, and still wearing her frogman's apparatus, begins to climb down the ladder in the shaft on the left. When she reaches the first-floor level she puts an ear to the outside wall of the Moor's room. From the darkness of the Moor's room, left, there comes the sound of three loud thumps, or bangs, as if of some heavy object being hit against the floor.

The flute music stops.

Then there are three flashes as if of lightning, or gunfire, at the street-level above.

Hortense takes her ear away from the outer wall of the Moor's room. She looks at the audience.

Anderson looks up from his microscope.

The light at street-level becomes watery.

Hortense climbs on down the second ladder in the shaft on the left. When she comes to the lower level she puts down her haversack and rummages inside it.

Anderson gets up from the table and tip-toes to the wall of his room, left. Outside this, Hortense has taken from her haversack what appears to be an electric drill. Then quickly, in mime, she seems to drill four holes in the outside wall of Anderson's room.

Anderson looks at the audience.

Then he tip-toes back to his table. He looks down at it.

Hortense puts down her drill, takes from her haversack what appear to be four sticks of explosive, and pushes these into the holes. Then she turns her back to the wall and puts her fingers in her ears.

Silently, as if the whole thing were happening under water, there seems to be an explosion in

179

the wall on the left — which blasts open, on a hinge, a blocked-up door into Anderson's room. Hortense steps inside. She drags her haversack and equipment after her. Then she tries to shut the door, but it is as if she has to struggle against an inrush of water.

Anderson, who has been staring at the table, paying no attention to what has been happening on the left, pushes up the light on its wire above the table.

The manhole, top left, closes.

As if the inrush of water has ceased, Hortense is able to close the door into Anderson's room. Inside the room, Hortense takes off her breathing apparatus. She mimes taking from her haversack equipment such as putty and a trowel with which she mimes sealing the door. Then, with her haversack, she goes behind the screens in Anderson's room on the left.

After a time Anderson switches off the light above the table.

The light at street-level goes out.

Anderson comes to the front of his room and tries to see over the footlights.

After a time Hortense comes out from behind the screens in Anderson's room. She has put on the clothes of a ballet dancer. She comes to Anderson's table and looks at the table on which he has been doing his experiments.

HORTENSE   Who were you talking to —
ANDERSON   Myself —
HORTENSE   What did you say —
ANDERSON   I love you.

Hortense puts an eye to the microscope.

A faint light comes on in the upper room right. In this room there can be seen, dimly, the figure of the man, previously glimpsed hanging from the ceiling, now sitting on a bed; he is straight-

180

backed, facing front. His arms are wrapped round him. He seems to be in a straitjacket. Hortense takes her eye from the microscope. The light in the upper room right fades.

ANDERSON   It has to be in the dark —
HORTENSE   Why —
ANDERSON   Or how would we find where to go?
HORTENSE   I heard you tapping.
ANDERSON   Wasn't it rats —
HORTENSE   Wasn't it music?

Hortense moves round the room. She seems to act —

        — There were tanks in the street. There were children dying. When they came to the barricades against its soft grey walls they battered —

Anderson has sat on the bed. He speaks as if rehearsing her —

ANDERSON   — I said Jump —
HORTENSE   — I jumped —
ANDERSON   — Jump —
HORTENSE   — I jumped —

Hortense stops by the table, right. She looks down at the instruments. She switches on the light above the table.
The light comes on dimly in the Moor's room, left. He is still standing on one leg. He is leaning forwards, facing left, holding a heavy volume in both hands, as if he were balancing, or were waiting to bang on the floor with the book.
Hortense picks up a glass rod from the table.

HORTENSE   Flat —
ANDERSON   Like that —
HORTENSE   Yes.
ANDERSON   With feeling?

Hortense moves away from the table holding the glass rod as if she were a water diviner. She acts —

181

HORTENSE	— There were tanks in the street. When they reached the Post Office building —
ANDERSON	Wait —
HORTENSE	I waited —

Upstairs the Moor, still on one leg, has opened his book and appears to be reading.

Hortense stops by the table again. She looks up at the ceiling.

HORTENSE	It comes back?
ANDERSON	On the underground river —
HORTENSE	Of pain —
ANDERSON	Of deprivation.

Hortense looks down at the instruments on the table.

HORTENSE	You go out of a —
ANDERSON	Mouth —
HORTENSE	Along a —
ANDERSON	Corridor —
HORTENSE	Into an —
ANDERSON	Anus?

Hortense leaves the table. She goes into the area of junk, back right, and rummages. Then she comes to the front of the structure carrying what seem to be old theatrical props — a radio, a fur coat, a curtain, a gas-mask. She throws these over the edge of the structure, by the footlights. Then she squats down and pokes at them with her rod.

ANDERSON	You can't make a home —
HORTENSE	Why not?
ANDERSON	Till they're ready.

Anderson watches her. He seems to quote —

— Furry friends came to visit me —

HORTENSE	— Dancing girls in red and brown —
ANDERSON	— Till we're all in one room —
HORTENSE	— Like a telephone box.

Hortense is poking about with her glass rod at the props she has put by the footlights. She

	seems to be making them into a nest.
ANDERSON	Come along then —
HORTENSE	Coop, coop —

Upstairs, the Moor has closed his book and placed it carefully on the floor. He straightens, and puts his foot on the book. He balances: as if on a tightrope.

ANDERSON	Hoop —
HORTENSE	Hoopla —
ANDERSON	Upsadaisy —

The Moor turns, quickly, as if on a tightrope, one foot behind the other.

He is now facing his stove again.

Then there is heard again from the room in darkness, right, the flute sonata by Bach.

Anderson looks up. Then he gestures to Hortense, urgently.

Hortense goes to the area of junk, right, and rummages.

The Moor, upstairs left, has taken another book from his pile and is leaning forward with it, facing his stove, balanced on one leg, as if he would place the book in front of him to step on; or bang the ground with it.

Anderson lies on his back on the bed and un-screws the inspection plate of the flue-pipe.

Hortense comes back from the area of junk with a set of plumber's cleaning rods. She hands one to Anderson on the bed.

Anderson pushes it up the flue-pipe.

The Moor, leaning forward, bangs three times on the floor with his book.

The flute music stops.

Anderson becomes still.

Hortense sits on the edge of the bed, as if dejected.

| HORTENSE | It's all in your head — |
| ANDERSON | — Your pretty head — |

HORTENSE	Your tongues like music.

The Moor places his book gently on the ground. After a time Anderson leaves his rod sticking up the flue-pipe and leans back on his bed.

HORTENSE	Can't you —
ANDERSON	What —
HORTENSE	Send out a dove?
ANDERSON	Put it in a bottle?

Hortense comes to the front of the structure and looks down at her nest of props. She seems to quote —

HORTENSE	— On a dark night, just down from the trees —
ANDERSON	— Have you got water and oil? —

The Moor, upstairs, balancing, puts his foot down, carefully, on the book which is between him and the stove.

Hortense tries to see up to the upper level.

HORTENSE	— He said, don't push me dear —
ANDERSON	— I'm peeing.

Hortense looks at the audience.

HORTENSE	Why don't they —
ANDERSON	What —
HORTENSE	Tap.
ANDERSON	They'd rather have music?

Hortense looks down at her nest.

Upstairs, the Moor has taken another book from one of his piles. He stands in front of his stove, holding it.

Hortense and Anderson seem to intone —

HORTENSE	— Is there anything else you can't —
ANDERSON	— Do what you like —
HORTENSE	— Can't —
ANDERSON	— Do you what like —

They wait: then speak in ordinary voices —

HORTENSE	Think of something else —
ANDERSON	What —
HORTENSE	Little wriggly things —

184

ANDERSON   With moustaches?

Upstairs, the music is heard again from the room, right.

Anderson quickly gets himself into position under the flue-pipe. He pushes a rod up.

Hortense hands him a second section of rod: he screws this on to the end of the other.

Upstairs the Moor, facing his stove, has raised the book that he is carrying in both hands.

Anderson pushes the two lengths of rod up the flue-pipe. He probes, delicately, at the underside of the lid of the Moor's stove.

The Moor watches the lid of his stove with his book raised.

Hortense climbs on to the bed and sits straddling Anderson; as if to steady him — or to make love.

The lid of the Moor's stove is raised by the top of Anderson's rods. It wobbles, then falls off. The top of Anderson's rod sticks up through the Moor's stove and moves this way and that like a snake, or a periscope.

Anderson, directly underneath the Moor's stove, appears to have put his eye to the bottom of the rods.

The Moor brings his book down, heavily, on the top of the rods.

It is as if the bottom of the rods were driven through Anderson's eye.

Hortense, on top of him, throws her head back as if in pain — or having an orgasm.

All the lights go out.

The music stops.

After a time, a bright light comes on in the upper room, right.

This room is white-tiled; as if in a hospital, or a madhouse.

There is just a bed, with no sheets or blankets, against the wall at the back.

185

On the bed there is the man previously glimpsed, Dionysus, sitting facing front, wearing a straitjacket.

There is the lamp-wire from the ceiling hanging down in a loop above his head.

High up in the wall, right, there is what seems to be a boarded-up grille, or skylight, to the disused shaft, right.

On the left there is a hole, dirty, half way up the central partition, where the flue-pipe from the Moor's stove comes out.

(This hole, owing to the central partition, some of the audience in the left half have difficulty in seeing; just as the other half have some difficulty in seeing where the Moor's flue-pipe goes into the wall on the right.)

Dionysus gazes out above the audience. Then he smiles.

DIONYSUS   Look!

He stands.

No hands!

Then he prances, in his straitjacket, sideways, to the left, like someone in a ballet; being careful to keep his front to the audience.

When he comes to the central partition, he puts his ear against the wall just behind the opening to the Moor's flue-pipe and purses his lips by the hole as if he were playing a flute.

Then he straightens.

It comes in here —

He looks up at the boarded-up grille, or skylight, top right.

Goes out there —

He looks at the audience.

Or does it.

After a time he prances, still taking care to keep his front to the audience, to the wall, right, where he stands underneath the skylight.

Sometimes they put a pea in it.
He looks up at the boarded-up skylight.
I'm a bird. I'm a camel —
He opens his mouth.
Then he looks at the audience.
I don't want to be forcibly fed.
Then he prances back to his bed, taking care to keep his front turned to the audience.
He stands in front of the bed.

> I've got this method, see, of getting up to the ceiling. I put my head through that noose. Then after a time — Hooray! I see such visions!

He throws his head back as if in ecstasy.
Then he sits on the bed.

> Huts. Watchtowers. Ladies and gentlemen on the grass.

He watches the audience.

> Twinkle, tinkle cow bells.

He waits.

> I think it's something to do with the man next door —

He seems to be searching about amongst the audience.

> Half a lifetime in the Russian Civil Service —

He waits.

> Every time he farts a couple of noughts are knocked off —

He waits.

> Is it you — Is it you —

He waits.

> Da da di dum dum. Da da di da —

He seems to search amongst the audience.

> Like seeds. Like parachutes —

He waits.

> Poor little thing, it hasn't got any arms —

He waits.

> Poor little thing, it's only got two heads —

He stands. He closes his eyes. He acts —

> — I'm going to take you to a cell at the
> bottom of the garden and I'm going to say —

He waits.

> Light! Light!

He faces the audience.

> Let it have — how many?

After a time it becomes apparent that he is not watching the audience, but the vertical plane above the footlights as if it were a wall.

> I know they wanted this baby —

After a time, the voice of the Moor is heard from the darkness of the room next door. It is as if he were reading to himself; and trying to understand, or memorise, the dialogue in a play.

THE MOOR   Bert —

> Yes?
>
> Got the wire?

He waits.

> Got the pincers?
>
> Got the anaesthetic?

Dionysus remains facing the plane above the footlights.

The Moor's voice continues as if reading —

> I was sitting one day when two masked
> men came and tied me to a chair —

Dionysus stands by his bed. He looks up at the wire that hangs from the ceiling.

The Moor's voice continues —

> Act four scene one —
>
> — My lord, what is your will, your plea-
> sure — ?

Dionysus climbs, with difficulty, on to his bed. As he does this it can be seen that there is a flute held within the strings of the straitjacket behind his back.

The Moor's voice continues —

> — They were dressed in a belt, black

stockings, and those conical hats, you
know, like witches —
Dionysus, on his bed, begins to try, with difficulty, to get his head through the loop of the
wire.
— I understand your words but not the
meaning of your words —
Dionysus manages to get his head through the
loop. He faces the audience.
The Moor's voice continues —
We took the child, in its pram, to the
airport —
Dionysus jerks, with his head, on the wire that
goes up through the ceiling.
The light on the ceiling of the Moor's room
comes on. The Moor is sitting on his stove,
facing left, as if it were a lavatory. He is holding
open on his lap a large volume, as if it were from
this that he has been reading.
He looks up.
Dionysus remains with his head through the
loop.
After a time the Moor closes the book, closes his
eyes, and says as if he were trying to learn some-
thing by heart —
Tongue, nose, liver, heart-beat —
He opens the book, seems to read —
Parliament, Church, Army, Civil Service —
He closes the book; closes his eyes again —
Ball, cock, breastplate, anus —
He opens the book; seems to read —
Murder, rape, war, Mummy —
He stares at the book. He seems to think.
Then —
— Keep the palm of the hand flat. The
central finger carefully extended —
He closes his eyes: looks up.
Police, perfection, piles, prostitution —

189

After a time he pulls back his robe where he is
sitting and looks down as if into a lavatory. He
replaces his robe. He stares to his front.
After a time Dionysus jerks on the wire round
his head. Nothing happens.
They wait.
Downstairs Hortense has remained on top of
Anderson on his back on the bed. She pulls at
the rod which seems to be through his eye.

ANDERSON   It's stuck —
HORTENSE   You're boasting —
ANDERSON   What —
HORTENSE   The baby — ?

Hortense climbs, stiffly, off Anderson. She
comes to the front of the stage and looks down
at her nest.

HORTENSE   Can't you think of —
ANDERSON   What —
HORTENSE   Little wriggly things —
ANDERSON   With no moustaches?

Hortense goes to Anderson's stove and takes off
the lid and looks inside.
Upstairs the Moor speaks with his eyes closed.

THE MOOR   Fred —
                  Yes?
                  These old buggers are made of concrete —
He looks down at his book.
Hortense leaves the lid of the stove off. She goes
back to the bed. She takes hold of the rods that
go up through the flue-pipe and tries again to
pull them from Anderson's eye.

HORTENSE   Then it'll go down —
ANDERSON   Up —
HORTENSE   When you're not looking —
ANDERSON   You're joking!

Hortense seems to give up trying to pull the
rods from Anderson's eye. She walks round the
room.

190

HORTENSE	Why did old gods have only one eye?
ANDERSON	So that they needn't see —
	They seem to quote —
HORTENSE	— Death, disease —
ANDERSON	— Get down off your knees —
HORTENSE	— Which?
ANDERSON	— Both.

Upstairs, Dionysus takes his head out of the noose. He climbs down from his bed. He goes and puts his ear against the central partition.

DIONYSUS	Did you say Fred — ?

He waits. He looks at the audience.

Did you hear him?

Hortense speaks walking round the room.

HORTENSE	The left side thinks, gives names —
ANDERSON	Two eyes and a nose, and a room behind —
HORTENSE	The right side knows what things are for —
ANDERSON	Two were too painful.

Hortense goes to the table and looks down at the instruments and slides.

HORTENSE	You too could wear an eye-patch.

Dionysus leaves the central partition and comes to the edge of the first floor. He looks down.

DIONYSUS	Hullo — ?

The voice of a young girl, Siva, is heard off-stage, right —

SIVA	Hullo —

Hortense looks up.

DIONYSUS	— I wondered if you remembered me — ?

He looks towards the right.

Hortense comes to the edge of the structure and looks down at her nest.

Upstairs the Moor has opened his book. He continues as if reading —

THE MOOR	— Down the arteries, up the spine: you've got to give warning —
DIONYSUS	— I loved only you, you see —

The Moor closes his book: closes his eyes.

191

THE MOOR	— Waste from the factories. Jokes. Shit —
DIONYSUS	— I've never loved anyone else — ?

He goes and stands with his back against the central partition, covering the exit to the Moor's flue-pipe. Then he looks up at the boarded-up skylight, right.

HORTENSE	It comes in here: goes out there —
ANDERSON	If it's not in your head —

Hortense goes back to the bed and sits again straddling Anderson. She takes hold of the rods as if to try again to pull them out of his eye.

From above, Dionysus shouts —

DIONYSUS	I saw you!

With a jerk, Hortense seems to manage to get the rods out of Anderson's eye.

The top of them seem to go up into the Moor where he is sitting on his stove, above, as if on a lavatory.

Everything becomes still. It is as if the Moor is transfixed.

Then a faint roaring and shaking begins, as if from the pipes at the back of Anderson's room. Anderson, with the rods out of his eye and up the pipe, closes the inspection plate.

The pipes at the back of Anderson's room and the stove in the Moor's room begin to glow.

The other lights fade.

Hortense gets off Anderson, goes to his stove, opens the lid, and looks inside.

Steam pours out.

Hortense puts the lid back on the stove. She sits on it.

After a time steam begins seeping out as if from the Moor in the room above.

The Moor gets off his stove. He pulls at the rods which are sticking out of the top of the stove.

The voice of a girl, Siva, is heard again off-stage from the right, amplified —

SIVA (off)	Do not leave the building —

The Moor has lifted the rods up out of his stove.
Then he puts the lid on it again and sits on it.
The shaking in the structure gets more violent.
Dionysus, in his room, right, is pressing his back
against the central partition as if to stop the
steam coming out of the exit there from the
Moor's flue-pipe.

SIVA (off)	My men are outside —

There is a small explosion in the Moor's stove. A
hole seems to have been blown in the bend of
the Moor's flue-pipe where it turns to go
through to Dionysus' room. Steam pours out
into the Moor's room from this hole.

The Moor is holding Anderson's rods like a fish-
ing rod. He leaves his stove and comes with the
rods to the front edge of the first floor where
they wave out over the audience. It is as if he
cannot see through the steam: he is about to fall
over.

An elderly woman, Florence, comes on at the
front of the stage, left. It is as if she were a stage-
manager. She looks up. She calls —

FLORENCE	Try it in second —

The Moor swings round, with his rods, until he
is pointing them towards the bend in the flue-
pipe where there is the hole through to
Dionysus' room.

Florence calls —

Now!

The Moor has managed to get the point of his
rods through the hole in the bend of his flue-
pipe.

Dionysus has his back to the exit of the flue-pipe
in the next room. He is staring up at the
boarded-up skylight, top right, as if he were
seeing a vision there.

The Moor lunges forward. The point of his rods

goes through the wall of the central partition and seems to go through the body of Dionysus. Steam drifts through the hole into Dionysus' room. The roaring and shaking begin to fade. Siva's amplified voice can be heard more quietly —

SIVA (off)   Oh let it not have two heads, two arms —

In the room on the left, the Moor seems to be overcome by fumes. He sinks down on to his knees, facing the stove. His rods remain through the wall.

Dionysus, as if transfixed, stares up at the grille at the top of the wall opposite.

Anderson has sat up on the bed. He dabs at his eye.

The roaring and shaking cease. Everything becomes still.

Siva's voice can be heard faintly but clearly —
    Let it have three.

The figure of Siva, a young girl, has appeared at the front of the stage in front of the bottom of the disused ventilation shaft, right. She can be seen putting a microphone down in the wings. She wears mountaineering clothes, and carries climbing equipment. She looks up towards the boarded-up grille into Dionysus' room at the top of the shaft.

Florence remains at the front of the stage, left. She watches Siva.

Hortense gets off Anderson's stove.

She comes to the front of the structure and looks down at her nest.

HORTENSE   I thought it would be more —
ANDERSON   What —
HORTENSE   Two by two —
ANDERSON   In a sack — ?

Hortense looks to the front of the stage, left. It is as if she both does and does not see Florence.

HORTENSE   With bombs —

194

| ANDERSON | Prams — |
| HORTENSE | Imitation leather suitcases — |

Anderson sits up and blinks. It is as if he can now see with both eyes.

ANDERSON	— You know how, you're halfway up the mountain, and there's a bloody great dragon below, and the balcony's a life-time above —
HORTENSE	You can see —
ANDERSON	What —
HORTENSE	Angels?

Siva has stepped inside the structure, at the bottom of the ventilation shaft, right. She seems to begin, quietly, to prepare her climbing equipment.

Upstairs, Dionysus, as if impaled on the rods, has begun to droop.

| ANDERSON | — But she wasn't like that, no — |

Hortense is looking out of the front of the structure towards the left, as if to see where Siva's voice has been coming from. But Siva is out of sight within the ventilation shaft.

HORTENSE	It's a difficult manipulation —
ANDERSON	Behind the nose —
HORTENSE	Throat —
ANDERSON	Eyes.

Hortense looks at the audience.

Then she goes and switches on the light above the table.

There is a small explosion in Dionysus' room above. The explosion seems to blow open the boarded-up grille, or skylight, at the top of the wall, right, at which Dionysus has been staring.

Hortense looks down at the table.

HORTENSE	A sort of piston —
ANDERSON	Pistol?´
HORTENSE	Piston!

She looks up. She seems to quote —

| | — Huts. Watchtowers — |
| ANDERSON | — Ladies and gentlemen on the grass — |

Hortense stares at the audience.

HORTENSE	But if half of it's never used —
ANDERSON	There are seeds —
HORTENSE	Needs?
ANDERSON	Parachutes —

Hortense stamps on the ground. She seems to be testing whether the structure is secure. Then she seems to try another quotation —

HORTENSE	— Two masked men came and tied me to a chair —
ANDERSON	— I climbed —
HORTENSE	— No one's ever climbed —

Hortense moves towards the right.

ANDERSON	It goes round and round —
HORTENSE	Now you see it —
ANDERSON	Then you don't.

She stamps on the ground.

Anderson gets off the bed. He goes to the area of junk, right, and puts on overalls. Then he puts his hand up to the ceiling.

HORTENSE	What prevents it?
ANDERSON	Nothing.
HORTENSE	You have to make it? Go? Grow?

Anderson comes to the front of the stage and looks at Florence, still standing front left.

Florence goes off in the wings and reappears dragging a table, which she sets up in the space between the front of the structure and the foot-lights, left. Then she goes off again and reappears carrying a vase of flowers and a chair. She sets the vase on the table. She puts the chair behind the table. Then she sits, facing right.

ANDERSON	Keep talking —
HORTENSE	You've done it once —
ANDERSON	You've done it twice —

Anderson goes and joins Hortense at the front of

the stage. They look down at the nest at the front of the structure.

HORTENSE   Poor little thing —

ANDERSON   If it only had three heads.

They listen.

Siva, at the bottom of the ventilation shaft, right, having prepared her equipment, now begins to climb up the shaft.

HORTENSE   But it's there —

ANDERSON   Where —

Siva climbs as if the shaft were a 'chimney' — with her legs straddled to either side.

ANDERSON   Step back?

HORTENSE   You go over.

Siva gets half way up the shaft. She rests.

Hortense speaks looking at Florence.

HORTENSE   And the girl — ?

FLORENCE   Which?

HORTENSE   Both.

Anderson speaks looking at Florence —

ANDERSON   Rats, frogs, locusts, honey —

Florence speaks looking down at the table.

FLORENCE   Walls, platforms, pillars, architraves —

Siva has moved on up the shaft. She gets her fingers on the edge of the blown-out grille into Dionysus' room. She rests.

Hortense speaks looking at Florence.

HORTENSE   Huts, wire, chimneys, watchtowers —

FLORENCE   Blood, mucus, liver, heart-beat —

They wait.

ANDERSON   Now you see it —

FLORENCE   Now you don't —

Anderson faces the audience.

ANDERSON   Men with their legs apart, peeing —

He waits.

Then he stamps on the ground.

Siva, in the ventilation shaft, has climbed on till she can see through the grille into Dionysus'

197

room.

Hortense is moving round Anderson's room looking closely at the walls, etc., as if she is trying to find something there.

HORTENSE   There's always a flower-seller outside a Spanish jail —

Anderson faces the audience. He seems to quote —

ANDERSON   — On such a night as this — the fields dirty with snow —

Hortense stops; looking at Florence.

HORTENSE   You need a contralto — ?

Siva has managed to raise herself so that her head and shoulders are through into Dionysus' room. She is thus visible to all the audience.

ANDERSON   But you'd see it when it had —
FLORENCE   What —

Anderson calls, imitating a young girl's voice —

ANDERSON   — The tanks are in the streets! There are people dying! —

Florence speaks in a matter-of-fact voice.

FLORENCE   — The more houses they build, the more places there are in the evenings —

HORTENSE   The smell down there!
FLORENCE   Honestly!

Hortense looks up as if to try to see Siva. She seems to try out —

HORTENSE   — Pretend you are so gentle, so sane —

Florence speaks with her eyes closed.

FLORENCE   With your foot against my face —

Siva, with her head and shoulders through the grille into Dionysus' room, seems to be considering how to get down.

ANDERSON   A cell —
HORTENSE   An egg —
FLORENCE   A liver —
HORTENSE   A heart-beat —

Siva, with her head and shoulders through the

198

grille, watches Dionysus who is against the opposite wall.

Dionysus is staring at her as if he were seeing a vision.

ANDERSON — There's an old man upstairs —

FLORENCE — Can't you get past his milk bottles?

Hortense and Anderson face the audience.

Florence seems to doze.

After a time —

HORTENSE How long have we got?

FLORENCE Fifty minutes.

Siva, in the opening of the grille, top right, is rearranging her mountaineering equipment. She drops a rope down into Dionysus' room. She fastens a rope round herself. She prepares to lower herself down into Dionysus' room.

Hortense is looking at the audience.

ANDERSON They're trying to reach us?

FLORENCE We're trying to reach them.

HORTENSE They hear us? We heard them tapping?

As Siva begins to lower herself into Dionysus' room, Anderson says as if to Florence —

ANDERSON We didn't want anyone to see this?

As Siva lowers herself there is lowered from the flies, centre, in front of the structure, a dummy body like that of Siva's, on a rope. A hook passes through the body. The body is dressed in the same clothes as Siva. It is lowered at the same rate as Siva lowers herself into the room: it pauses when she pauses. When Siva reaches the floor of Dionysus' room the dummy stops at the same level and dangles there, like a bait.

Dionysus watches the real Siva.

Florence remains with her eyes closed.

Hortense and Anderson watch the dummy Siva.

HORTENSE A curtain —

FLORENCE Customs —

ANDERSON Curtain —

Siva unhooks herself from her climbing gear.
She goes and sits on Dionysus' bed. She speaks
to Dionysus.

SIVA	Hullo —
FLORENCE	Hullo —
SIVA	I wondered if you remembered me —

Dionysus has straightened. He seems to be
feeling behind his face where there are the
strings of his straitjacket.

ANDERSON	But if you get used to it —
FLORENCE	What —
HORTENSE	It stays inside?

Dionysus manages to get out of his straitjacket.
It is as if the Moor's rods, that seemed to go
through his body, have succeeded in cutting
the strings of his straitjacket.

He comes to the edge of the first floor and faces
the audience. He raises his hands. In one of his
hands he holds his flute.

Siva watches him.

ANDERSON	To turn —
FLORENCE	Wound —
HORTENSE	Help us ?

In the upper room, left, the Moor, who has been
kneeling with his head down facing his stove,
right, as if overcome by fumes, now straightens.
He sits back on his heels. He watches where the
rods go through the bend of his flue-pipe.

Florence speaks with her eyes still closed.

FLORENCE	Testing. Testing.

Dionysus reaches, with his flute, for the dummy
body of Siva hanging in front of the first-floor
level. He fails to pull it back to him.

The real Siva is sitting on the bed behind him.

HORTENSE	But if they know the code —
FLORENCE	Why don't they know the message?

Dionysus puts his flute down by the edge of the
first-floor level. Then he goes back into his room.

He takes hold of the rods which are sticking through the partition, and pulls them out. He ignores the real Siva.

Siva watches him.

HORTENSE	They were making love —
ANDERSON	They were in the head —
FLORENCE	The Moor? Dionysus?

She looks up. The other side of the partition from Dionysus, the Moor watches where the rods have been pulled through.

ANDERSON	An eye —
HORTENSE	A hook —
FLORENCE	A dead body —
ANDERSON	A heart-beat —

Dionysus comes to the front of the first floor again and reaches with the rods for the dangling body of Siva.

The Moor stands. He goes to the hole in his flue-pipe and tries to see through into Dionysus' room. Then he goes to the front of his floor and watches where Dionysus is trying to pull in with the rods the dummy body of Siva.

HORTENSE	To hurt you? —
FLORENCE	Protect you —

Dionysus cannot get the dummy body of Siva in to the first-floor level. He can only push her sideways towards the Moor's room, left.

HORTENSE	Ladies and gentlemen on the grass —
ANDERSON	Huts. Watchtowers —

Dionysus puts his rods down on the floor.

The Moor stretches for, but fails to reach, the dummy body of Siva.

HORTENSE	But I was with him —
FLORENCE	In that little room?
ANDERSON	Sweet. Pussy pussy. Down boy. Cheep —

Dionysus turns back into his room and looks at the real Siva on his bed.

FLORENCE	What did he do —

HORTENSE	Worked on the farm. Kept animals.
	Upstairs, right, the Moor, having failed to reach the dummy body of Siva, turns and looks at his stove.
ANDERSON	I had this daughter, see, aged fifteen —
	Siva, left, speaks to Dionysus.
SIVA	I climbed —
FLORENCE	No one's ever climbed?
	Dionysus turns and looks at the opening to the flue-pipe in his wall.
	Hortense speaks facing the audience —
HORTENSE	You can hear them at night —
ANDERSON	It's terrible?
	The Moor goes to the opening of his flue-pipe again and tries to see through into Dionysus' room.
FLORENCE	Da da di dum dum —
ANDERSON	Da da di da —
	Dionysus goes to the hole in the wall and tries to see into the Moor's room.
HORTENSE	Little wriggly things —
FLORENCE	With moustaches?
	Dionysus and the Moor turn and stare at the audience.
ANDERSON	It goes on all the time —
HORTENSE	You can't taste it, touch it, smell it —
	Florence says mockingly —
FLORENCE	— Are we gods and goddesses?
	She stands. She leans with her fingers on the table in front of her — as if some session has ended.
	The Moor goes and puts his arms round his stove as if he is trying to pull it from the wall. Dionysus comes to the front of the first floor.
HORTENSE	— And I was left with an only son to bring up — ?
	Siva leaves the bed and goes to the hole in the wall in his room and puts her hands in, trying to

stretch it.

ANDERSON	Birds —
HORTENSE	Love-songs —
ANDERSON	What did we call them —
HORTENSE	Spot? Beauty?

The Moor leaves his stove and comes to the front of the first floor and stretches out his hands to the dummy body of Siva.

Anderson seems to speak to the audience —

ANDERSON   Do you know how often she has to do this?

Siva, having failed to stretch the hole from the Moor's flue-pipe, moves back into Dionysus' room, and begins undressing.

HORTENSE	Steps forwards —
ANDERSON	We go over — ?

Siva has taken off her mountaineering clothes. Underneath she is dressed like a child gymnast.

HORTENSE	To the underground river —
ANDERSON	To the pub!

Dionysus picks up his rods at the front of the first floor and tries to push the dummy body of Siva round towards the left again, as if for the Moor to catch hold of it. But the Moor goes back to the hole in his flue-pipe and peers through it. He seems to see Siva, who is in her gymnast's clothes, as if in a peep-show. He turns to the audience.

Florence, who is standing by her table, left, murmurs —

FLORENCE   — Wild geese are flying from the Arctic —

She sits behind her table again: as if ready for another session.

The Moor takes hold of his stove again. This time he manages, with a bang, to pull it, with its flue-pipe, away from the wall of the central partition. He falls back, embracing the stove.

Dionysus puts his rods down on the ground.

Siva, in her gymnast's clothes, goes to the exit of

the Moor's flue-pipe and puts her hands in it again as if to stretch it.

Hortense and Anderson watch the audience.

HORTENSE   And the people in the valley — ?
FLORENCE   Want —
HORTENSE   What we haven't got —
FLORENCE   So you provide —
ANDERSON   Waste from the factories? Jokes? Shit?

Siva, with the Moor's stove and flue-pipe removed, has succeeded in stretching the hole through the central partition. She puts her head through. She is looking down through the hole through the floor into the flue-pipe of Anderson's stove, which has been exposed by the Moor's pulling his stove away.

SIVA   Hullo —
FLORENCE   Hullo!
SIVA   I was afraid you might not remember me —

Anderson comes to the front of the structure and looks up at the dummy body of Siva.

Dionysus has gone back into his room. It seems that for the first time he is ready to notice the real Siva, who has her back to him and her head through the wall. He stands behind her and lifts her by the hips. He seems to try and help her push through the wall. By wriggling and stretching, she manages to get halfway through. The Moor, facing her, embracing the stove, gazes at her as if he is seeing a vision.

Anderson, looking up, calls —

ANDERSON   Oi! They're getting into government!
FLORENCE   Don't you want your children to see this?

Dionysus leaves Siva and comes to the edge of the first-floor level and looks over. Then he picks up his rods.

The Moor leaves his stove and comes to the edge of the first-floor level and looks at the audience.

204

HORTENSE	A pin —
ANDERSON	A key —
HORTENSE	A lever —
FLORENCE	Liver?
HORTENSE	A heart-beat!

Siva, halfway through the central partition, pushes with her feet. She tries to hold herself up, uncomfortably.

FLORENCE	— Where did they put it —
ANDERSON	— Do you know?
HORTENSE	In a hole, I think, by the lavatory.

Dionysus, with his rods, has succeeded in pushing the dummy body of Siva round to the left so that the Moor can get hold of it. The Moor pulls it in on the left side of the partition. He lays it on the ground. Then he pulls the hook out.

FLORENCE	Your children —
ANDERSON	And your children's children —

The Moor, having pulled the hook out of the dummy body of Siva, pulls out straw. He throws this over the edge of the first floor to the right. It scatters in and around Hortense's nest, in front of the structure by the footlights.

Hortense looks down at her nest.

HORTENSE	— I pulled your hair —
ANDERSON	— I pulled mine —

The Moor stands. He kicks the dummy body of Siva to the edge of the first floor to the left.

SIVA	Quick! It's hurting!

Anderson stares at the audience.

HORTENSE	But if it can see —
FLORENCE	What —
ANDERSON	Huts, watchtowers —
FLORENCE	Ladies and gentlemen on the grass —

The Moor goes and stands by Siva's head where the top half of her body is through the central partition. She holds out her hands to him. She seems to be in pain from the uncomfortable position she is holding.

The Moor does not take her hands.

HORTENSE   Something like a head —

FLORENCE   Or a cage —

ANDERSON   On the wall of a municipal building —

Hortense tidies her nest: then goes and sits on Anderson's bed with her head in her hands.

Anderson looks up at the hook which the Moor has taken out of the dummy body of Siva and which is now swinging free in front of the first-floor level.

FLORENCE   Have you got the pin out?

ANDERSON   Pin in?

HORTENSE   Pin out!

Anderson looks at the audience.

Dionysus unscrews his rods. He lays them by the edge of the first-floor level by his flute. Then he goes to the back half of Siva and holds her by the hips. It is as if he is not sure what to do with Siva. He moves her slightly this way and that.

FLORENCE   How old were you —

HORTENSE   Five or six —

Dionysus leaves Siva. He moves along the central partition towards the back, looking on the ground. He moves the bed to the right; looks on what has been the ground underneath it.

FLORENCE   You had speech —

ANDERSON   Hadn't you —

FLORENCE   Rhyme?

Dionysus feels on the ground at the bottom of the partition at the back. He seems to find what he is looking for. It is as if it were a bolt, which he is withdrawing.

Dionysus comes back to Siva and takes her by the hips and tries to move her towards the back, then the front, as if the partition might swivel on a central vertical hinge.

Hortense speaks with her head in her hands —

HORTENSE	A fog —
ANDERSON	A god —
FLORENCE	A chromosome —
ANDERSON	A heart-beat.

Dionysus lets go of Siva. He seems to give up. He looks at the audience.

FLORENCE	— Did the nuns take you in netball, and dancing? —

Hortense gets up off the bed and gets behind the screens, left. She seems to be changing her clothes.

On the left side of the partition, the Moor bends down and stares into Siva's eyes.

ANDERSON	— They're old —
FLORENCE	Throw them over —
ANDERSON	Is that funny —
FLORENCE	Is it meant to be — ?

Dionysus bends down and stares at Siva's behind.

Hortense comes out from behind the screens, left. She has changed back into her shorts and T-shirt. She waits, with her hands on her hips.

FLORENCE	Try it in third —
ANDERSON	Now?

Anderson goes and puts his arms round his stove in the lower level. He tries to shift it.

The Moor leaves Siva. He moves along the central partition to the front, looking on the ground.

Anderson gives up trying to move his stove. He comes to the front of the structure and looks at the nest.

ANDERSON	It's so soft —
HORTENSE	It breaks off —
ANDERSON	And stays inside — ?

Anderson looks up at the hook.

The Moor seems to find what he is looking for on the ground at the front of the partition.

207

He pulls at it, as if it were a bolt. He looks at the audience.

Then he goes back to Siva. He takes her by the hands.

Dionysus takes Siva by the hips again.

This time they manage to swivel her, together with the whole of the central partition — the Moor on the left to the back, Dionysus on the right to the front — so that the partition pivots on a central vertical hinge. Siva's behind comes round towards the audience with Dionysus: her head goes out of sight towards the back with the Moor. As the partition swivels, the wire with the hook on it in front of the first-floor level is drawn up into the flies.

Anderson watches it.

Florence stands. She rests her fingers on the table in front of her — as if at the end of a session.

Hortense and Anderson look at the audience.

The partition comes to rest against what seems to be the Moor's stove behind it.

The Moor's voice comes from behind the central partition.

| THE MOOR | You moved your bed — |
| DIONYSUS | You haven't moved your books — ? |

Dionysus looks round as if for something to rest Siva's feet on. Then he leaves Siva, with her legs dangling, and moves over into the Moor's room, left.

The Moor appears from behind the partition on the right. He is carrying some books.

DIONYSUS	But if it comes from outside —
THE MOOR	What —
SIVA	Pain —
THE MOOR	Deprivation —

Dionysus has gone out of sight behind the partition in the Moor's room, left.

The Moor puts the books under Siva's feet so

that she has somewhere to rest them.

Florence speaks standing with her hands on the table.

FLORENCE — Either of you two boys coming with me across the park? —

Dionysus reappears from behind the partition on the right. He is carrying some books, which he puts on the bed against the back wall on the right.

The Moor has stepped back and is looking at Siva's behind.

THE MOOR It doesn't break off —

DIONYSUS It stays inside?

Florence sits down behind her table again.

FLORENCE What was the feeling —

DIONYSUS — Get off! There are too many of you! —

THE MOOR One or two get through.

Hortense and Anderson sit on the bed. They put their arms round one another. They look at the audience.

DIONYSUS It's the shape —

THE MOOR Of the head — ?

FLORENCE The head — !

DIONYSUS But if half of it's never used —

Siva's voice comes from behind the partition —

SIVA — Freddie knocks his bowl over and then he can't drink.

The Moor leaves Siva and moves to the left.

FLORENCE You can learn —

THE MOOR Can't you —

DIONYSUS Dance —

Dionysus goes round the back of the partition, left, and reappears on the right carrying more books.

The Moor disappears left and takes hold of his stove which is behind the left-hand end of the partition.

FLORENCE — There's an underground river —

DIONYSUS   — Disgorges its victims.
The Moor gradually drags his stove clear of the
partition on the left. He pulls it to the left side of
his room.
Dionysus circles the partition, clockwise, carrying more books from the Moor's room, which
he piles on the bed in his own.

FLORENCE   — It goes round and round —
THE MOOR   — The same direction at both ends —
Siva's voice comes from behind the partition.

SIVA   — Or in the middle —
Florence looks at the audience.

FLORENCE   — A fate. A weaver of tapestries —
The Moor has succeeded in dragging his stove
clear of the partition on the left. He stands back.
Dionysus seems to have carried sufficient books
from the left to the right.

THE MOOR   If you don't eat it up for dinner —
DIONYSUS   — Repeat it in the coda.
The Moor goes and takes hold of the left-hand
end of the partition. Dionysus goes and takes
hold of the right. They seem to be trying to
swivel the partition further, clockwise. It still
seems stuck. Dionysus looks up at the ceiling.
Now you see it —

THE MOOR   Now you don't —
The Moor goes to the front of the stage and
looks over.
Siva, from the back of the partition, speaks as if
in increasing desperation.

SIVA   — I was put out on a mountain —
DIONYSUS   — Furry friends came to visit me —
THE MOOR   — What have you been eating, toadstools? —
Dionysus and the Moor look at the audience.
They wait.

DIONYSUS   It goes on all the time —
THE MOOR   Like seeds —
DIONYSUS   Like parachutes —

210

After a time Hortense and Anderson look up at the ceiling.

THE MOOR   You had food, hadn't you —
DIONYSUS   Wine?

Anderson looks at his stove, left.

THE MOOR   An itch —
DIONYSUS   A mask —
THE MOOR   A landfall —
DIONYSUS   A skylight?

Dionysus goes and looks up at the grille on the right: then he looks down at the floor underneath it.

THE MOOR   Funny —
DIONYSUS   A sort of breathing?

The Moor goes to the back wall of his room on the extreme left. He feels on the ground behind some books which are still there.

Siva calls out —

SIVA   There! —
FLORENCE   You don't see it?

Dionysus bends down in the extreme right-hand back corner of his room and seems to withdraw a bolt that he finds there.

He and the Moor go to the ends of the partition again. They try to swivel it. It will not move. They look up to where it seems to be caught against the ceiling.

ANDERSON   Begin again —
FLORENCE   Testing. Testing —
HORTENSE   What's the difference — ?

At the lower level, Anderson goes and takes hold of his stove again. He tries to shift it.

Dionysus and the Moor let go of the partition. Dionysus moves to the front of the first floor and tries to see over.

The Moor watches the audience.

DIONYSUS   We've got to do it at the same time —
THE MOOR   When it's ready?

211

Dionysus and the Moor move about, at each end
of the first floor, as if testing it; as if it might be
balanced on a central horizontal back-to-front
axis. They stamp on the ground, as if they might
thus shift it. They also seem to take care to be
balancing each other on either side of the horizontal axis. But the floor seems to be prevented
from moving on this axis by the angle of the
central partition against the ceiling.

Downstairs, Anderson lets go of his stove.

ANDERSON   It's not possible.
FLORENCE   You think you know what you're going to
             find?
ANDERSON   If you do you don't —
HORTENSE   I see!

Dionysus and the Moor take hold of the ends of
the partition again.

Anderson looks at the audience.

ANDERSON   — Ladies and gentlemen on the roads —
HORTENSE   — With little prams, going —

Dionysus and the Moor try to swivel the partition again on its vertical central axis.

Anderson goes and takes hold of his stove again.

FLORENCE   Try it in top —
SIVA   Now!

Anderson seems to shift his stove slightly.

Dionysus and the Moor manage this time — as if
the top of the central partition were now clear
of the ceiling as a result of Anderson's managing
to move his stove-pipe underneath their floor
— to swivel the partition on round: the Moor
towards the back, Dionysus towards the front.

Siva's head appears on the right.

DIONYSUS   Head out —
THE MOOR   Head in —
HORTENSE   You've got to give warning —

Anderson looks up.

Dionysus, coming round with his end of the

212

partition towards the edge of the first floor, looks round apprehensively, as if he might fall over. He kicks the cleaning rods, and his flute, over the edge of the first floor. They fall on, or around, the nest by the footlights.

Anderson shouts —

ANDERSON   — Oi! There's a boy down there on the wire! —

DIONYSUS   Oops!

THE MOOR   Oopla!

SIVA   Upsadaisy!

Anderson pulls at his stove again. He manages to shift it as if the pipe going up from it has been further loosened by the Moor and Dionysus shifting the partition above him. The flue-pipe comes away from the ceiling with a bang.

Then Anderson scrambles, quickly, and goes and stands with his hands up underneath his ceiling on the left.

HORTENSE   What's the advantage —

FLORENCE   It'll survive.

Hortense is sitting on the bed holding her stomach.

Dionysus, holding the front end of the partition, has been nearly pushed over the edge of the first floor. He manages to scramble round to the Moor's side of the partition.

Anderson is holding up, with difficulty, the first floor on the left.

ANDERSON   The baby?

The partition is in place again on its back-to-front axis in the middle of the first floor — but this time with Siva's head towards the right, and both the Moor and Dionysus to the left — the Moor at the back and Dionysus at the front.

Siva speaks looking up at the grille.

SIVA   Hullo —

FLORENCE   Hullo —

SIVA	I was afraid you might not remember me —
THE MOOR	Is that right?
DIONYSUS	No!

Dionysus and the Moor seem to be apprehensive about being on the same side of the partition. They keep close to it, their backs pressed against it, as if to try to stop the floor tilting to the left.

Anderson, with his hands underneath the first floor, left, seems to be holding it up with difficulty. He calls —

ANDERSON	— Oi! They're on the green! They're getting into government! —

Florence says as if amused —

FLORENCE	You didn't want your children to see this?

She stands. She rests with her hands on the table, as if a session is over.

Dionysus stretches out with a foot as if to reach for the dummy body of Siva which is on the ground in front of him, at the left front edge of the first floor. As a result of his doing this, the ground of the first floor suddenly gives way, down on the left, with a bang — the whole of the first floor being on a central back-to-front hinge. The area of the first floor that pivots is just short of what remains of the Moor's stacked books and stove at the back on the left, and of Dionysus' bed at the back on the right: these remain on ledges on the old first floor.

Anderson, with his hands up, just manages to prevent the left end of the first floor coming down further. He calls —

ANDERSON	Help!
SIVA	Push —
THE MOOR	It's begun —
DIONYSUS	— A big 'un —

Hortense puts her head in her hands.

HORTENSE	I can't bear it!

214

Dionysus, on his back, reaches with his foot the dummy body of Siva and pushes it over the edge of the first floor. It falls on Florence's table; Florence brushes at her clothes, as if annoyed. There are two more cracks, or bangs, as if of gunfire, as the first floor comes down on the left a little further.

Florence steps within the structure and stands there looking up.

FLORENCE   *You* can't bear it —
SIVA   I can't bear it!

Siva, with her legs tipping downwards, is trying to find a foothold on the left side of the partition and is pushing with her hands against the right side of the partition which is now facing slightly up.

The Moor is pushing with his back against the left-hand side of the partition towards the right — as if he were trying to balance it to take the weight off Anderson, which he can't do.

Dionysus is pulling himself back to the central partition, as if to help the Moor.

It is as if, in spite of themselves, they are all suddenly laughing.

FLORENCE   Stand back to back —
ANDERSON   Turn —
HORTENSE   Take a step forwards —

Florence puts her hands up against the lower-level ceiling as if to help Anderson hold it. Dionysus turns and tries to reach with an arm round the front end of the partition to his old side on the right.

DIONYSUS   Get a rope —
THE MOOR   Get a curtain —
HORTENSE   Get a doctor —
ANDERSON   Get an engineer —

Florence lowers her hands.

FLORENCE   An explanation?

215

	Siva looks to where Dionysus' arm is coming round the partition.
SIVA	Hullo, hullo, can you hear me?
	At the back, left, the Moor edges along the partition to the front as if he is on a mountain ledge. He gets close to Dionysus.
THE MOOR	— Little green men —
DIONYSUS	— With moustaches —
	Siva stretches a hand towards the front end of the partition as if to try to catch Dionysus' hand and help him round to the right side of the partition.
HORTENSE	— I'll sit on your face —
ANDERSON	— You sit on mine —
	Anderson is trying to lower the left edge of the old first floor. Florence, helping him, is with him underneath it.
FLORENCE	Till we're all in one room —
	With the help of the Moor, behind him, Dionysus manages to edge, precariously, halfway round the front end of the partition.
SIVA	— Where's the wire —
HORTENSE	— In your great big beautiful eyes.
	Dionysus manages, with Siva's help in front of him, to scramble round the partition into his old room on the right. Then he moves up the sloping floor to the right: as he does this, he seems to take the weight off Anderson, who scrambles to the outside, left, of the old first floor.
FLORENCE	Ariel —
ANDERSON	Yes —
FLORENCE	Haven't you got the right man?
DIONYSUS	What a coincidence!
THE MOOR	So where's the difference — ?
	Anderson looks over the top edge of the end of the first floor, which he is holding.
FLORENCE	There were tanks in the streets —
HORTENSE	There were people dying.

They all seem to become serious again.

Dionysus reaches to the centre of his old room, right, and pulls the wire down through the ceiling. The wire from the ceiling of the Moor's room is pulled up. Dionysus pulls the wire right through and coils it. Then he lies on his back, his legs against the partition on either side of Siva, and takes her by the hands. He seems to be trying to pull Siva out of the hole, and over him. The Moor, kneeling, moves slightly back to the left, and pushes against Siva's legs.

Anderson lets go of the left-hand end of the first floor gingerly.

The floor remains balanced.

Anderson calls —

ANDERSON   Oi!
FLORENCE   What —

Hortense, on the bed, looks out over the audience.

HORTENSE   It's only two foot to the bottom!

Florence turns to her.

Dionysus manages to pull Siva out of the hole and on to him. He pushes her up towards the raised edge of the top floor, right. She gets a hand-hold there. Then he passes the coiled wire up to her.

Anderson has had to lean on the top of the left-hand edge of the first floor, to balance it.

ANDERSON   You can sing, can't you —
SIVA   Dance —

Siva has clambered up so she has one leg over the raised end of the first floor, right. She lowers an end of the wire down to Dionysus, who takes it.

DIONYSUS   Next time round —
THE MOOR   Can we kill them?

The Moor has moved backwards, to the left, on his hands and knees, to balance the floor.

217

	Siva seems to be trying to pull Dionysus up to the raised edge of the first floor, right.
FLORENCE	I said — Jump —
HORTENSE	I jumped.
	With Dionysus being pulled to the right, the Moor is moving further to the left of the floor, to balance it.
HORTENSE	What stops it —
FLORENCE	Saves it?
SIVA	Spreads it!
	The Moor suddenly seems to lose his grip. He slides back to the left-hand edge of the first floor.
FLORENCE	Wo!
SIVA	Woa!
HORTENSE	Upsadaisy!
	With the shifting of the Moor's weight, the first floor, on its central back-to-front hinge, has dipped down on the left so that Anderson has to put his hands underneath it again to hold it. Florence, underneath it, ducks.
	At the same time Siva, with the wire, has managed to help Dionysus to scramble up to the top edge of the first floor, right.
	The floor now seems to tip the other way: Anderson has to put his hands on top of the left end of it again to hold it.
ANDERSON	I get these headaches, see —
THE MOOR	Aged fifteen —
	The Moor manages to get his feet down over the left edge of the first floor. He helps Anderson. The floor seems to balance, precariously.
SIVA	Those old buggers —
DIONYSUS	Are made of concrete.
	The first floor is now at an angle of about 30° to the horizontal — up on the right, down on the left.
	Anderson and the Moor and Siva and Dionysus

218

	hold the balance, as if on a see-saw, gingerly.
HORTENSE	They were shot — ?
FLORENCE	There were too many of them.

Florence has gone and stood by Hortense, who is on the bed, looking at the audience.

The Moor and Anderson and Siva and Dionysus speak, holding the balance.

THE MOOR	They were in that trench —
ANDERSON	Then I was in that trench —
DIONYSUS	And the skylight —
SIVA	What about the skylight?

Florence stands looking down at Hortense.

| FLORENCE | Good girl — |
| HORTENSE | Let me see it. |

She stares at the audience.

	Has it got one —
FLORENCE	It's not two?
HORTENSE	Pick it up —
SIVA	Don't hit it!

Hortense stands facing the audience.

HORTENSE	— On a dark night —
FLORENCE	— At the edge of the wood —
SIVA	Oh God!
FLORENCE	And in between?

Hortense leaves the bed and comes to the footlights and stares at the audience. She smiles.

HORTENSE	It looks like the sun.
FLORENCE	What does the sun look like?
HORTENSE	Round, a sort of yellow.

Florence looks up at the see-saw roof above her head.

| FLORENCE | They usually give you more time. |

The Moor and Dionysus speak at opposite ends of the see-saw.

| THE MOOR | — You're my wife — ? |
| DIONYSUS | — You're my child — ? |

Siva, perched on the raised edge of the first floor, right, looks down through the hole of the

old flue-pipe in the central partition as if to try
to see Anderson.

SIVA	Hullo —
ANDERSON	Hullo —
SIVA	I wondered if you remembered me —
ANDERSON	— Oh yes I loved only you, you see —

Siva speaks looking at the audience —

SIVA	— I never loved anyone else in my life —

The Moor looks round the left bottom edge of
the first floor as if to try to find something to
wedge it with. He sees Florence.

THE MOOR	Hullo —
FLORENCE	Hullo —
THE MOOR	I was afraid you might not remember me.

Florence smiles. They seem to quote —

FLORENCE	— You've got the money —
THE MOOR	— You've got the child —
FLORENCE	— Then run —
THE MOOR	— I can't —
FLORENCE	— Why not —
THE MOOR	— Arthritis.

Florence drags Anderson's stove and helps the
Moor to use it to wedge the left-hand edge of
the floor with.

In the meantime Anderson holds down the
edge of the see-saw with difficulty.

SIVA	— Now you see it —
ANDERSON	— Now you don't —

Dionysus is perched with Siva at the top end of
the first floor on the right, facing the audience.

DIONYSUS	Good God, are we talking about —
HORTENSE	The people in the valley?

Hortense, at the front of the stage, and Dionysus
are both staring out over the audience.

HORTENSE	Hullo —
DIONYSUS	Hullo —
HORTENSE	And where were you?
DIONYSUS	In the pub.

220

HORTENSE	And was I left with an only child to bring up —

Siva leans over the right-hand edge of the first floor, trying to see down into the room below.

SIVA	It's a boy.
ANDERSON	It's a girl.
SIVA	Has it really got three heads?

Siva looks at the audience.

The Moor and Anderson, with Florence's help, have succeeded in wedging, with Anderson's stove and bed and so on, the lower end, left, of the first floor. They step back from it gingerly.

THE MOOR	— Huts, watchtowers —
FLORENCE	— Ladies and gentlemen on the grass —

Hortense stands looking out over the audience.

HORTENSE	But if this part of it was never used —
DIONYSUS	Throw it over —
THE MOOR	Is it meant to be?

Anderson has been looking on the ground along the footlights at the front. He seems to quote —

ANDERSON	— Oh you are an old fraud. I'm sure you're frightfully good at it really —

Then he goes and looks along the wall at the back.

The others are all now looking at the audience.

FLORENCE	We go down there —

Anderson speaks from the back.

ANDERSON	Come up here —
SIVA	What happens if I get squashed?
THE MOOR	You won't —
FLORENCE	It's open at both ends —
HORTENSE	And in the middle?

Anderson seems to have found what he is looking for on the ground floor on the right. He bends down.

DIONYSUS	A little room —
ANDERSON	Just behind the eyes —

Anderson looks at the audience.

221

Florence begins looking along the ground at the footlights at the front.

Siva watches her.

SIVA	Oi!
HORTENSE	Oi?
SIVA	— There's a boy down there on the wire!
FLORENCE	— There's a child, in its pram, at the airport —

Hortense speaks, looking at the audience.

HORTENSE	Will you look after it?
ANDERSON	It'll survive?

Anderson comes to the footlights and stands by the Moor looking over.

THE MOOR	It goes down there —

Florence has now moved to the back wall on the left. She gets down on her hands and knees.

FLORENCE	Comes up here —
DIONYSUS	I thought it was a baby —
THE MOOR	No, it's seeds —
SIVA	Isn't that a baby?
HORTENSE	If they look after it.

They all, except Florence, look at the audience.

ANDERSON	But if we go all over them —
SIVA	They'll kill us?

Florence seems to have found what she is looking for at the ground floor at the back. She seems to draw a bolt. Then she turns to the audience, crouching.

DIONYSUS	Say it's a tomb —
THE MOOR	It's a laboratory.

Florence comes to the front of the structure, treading carefully. She stamps on the ground.

ANDERSON	Huts, watchtowers —
HORTENSE	Ladies and gentlemen on the grass.

Siva speaks from her perch on the top right of the old first floor.

SIVA	What's holding it?
ANDERSON	You'd better jump.

	Florence speaks to Anderson.
FLORENCE	You took the pin out?
	The Moor watches the audience.
THE MOOR	Your hands and feet on the ground. Your body on the ceiling —
	They wait.
	After a time Hortense looks up at Dionysus.
DIONYSUS	Did you stay with me, for ever, in that monastery — ?
HORTENSE	We were married —
	The Moor speaks to Florence —
THE MOOR	Weren't we?
	Florence is looking over the footlights.
FLORENCE	Children see by what they learn —
	Anderson goes to the back wall again and feels on the floor on the right.
SIVA	One or two —
DIONYSUS	Get through —
HORTENSE	And the rest?
FLORENCE	The people in the valley?
THE MOOR	Are buried —
DIONYSUS	Beneath the tree —
HORTENSE	And grow —
SIVA	One or two —
	Anderson straightens and comes forward on the right, gingerly.
FLORENCE	Now you see it —
ANDERSON	Don't you?
	Anderson stamps with his foot at the front of the stage. They wait.
FLORENCE	You got it?
	Florence and Anderson seem to be making slight forward-and-back movements as if to test, facing the audience, whether the stage might be balanced on a left-to-right axis at the very front of the stage — against the counterweight of the auditorium.
HORTENSE	How will I recognise you —

SIVA	In that great big room?
ANDERSON	With your head in your hands —
FLORENCE	And just behind your eyes —
THE MOOR	No curtain!
DIONYSUS	Customs —
HORTENSE	An avalanche!

The to-and-fro movements that Florence and Anderson are making seem to be having no effect.

SIVA	Hold it in your arms —
HORTENSE	Is it crying?

Siva moves along to the front edge of the raised first floor. She stretches her hands down as if to Anderson. The Moor looks up at her.

ANDERSON	But if we don't hurt them —
FLORENCE	You think they'll keep us?

She and Anderson go again to the wall at the back, left and right. They look on the ground there.

SIVA	Look —
DIONYSUS	Isn't it sweet —
THE MOOR	It can fly then?

Siva straightens. She and the Moor look out over the audience.

Anderson comes from the back, right. He stops halfway between the back wall and the footlights and he rocks, one foot in front of the other, as if to see whether there might be any movement in the stage.

Florence is watching him from the back, left.

FLORENCE	Try it now —
ANDERSON	One over the top —
HORTENSE	They go down —
SIVA	We go over.

Dionysus has edged forwards, with Siva, to the very front of the top left of the old first floor. He looks down at Hortense.

DIONYSUS	Oh my darling —

THE MOOR	Oopsadaisy!
	Anderson speaks facing the audience.
ANDERSON	Do they see —
	Hortense speaks in a matter-of-fact voice facing the front —
HORTENSE	— You didn't really sleep with her —
DIONYSUS	Didn't you?
	Florence straightens, back left, and stands there gingerly.
SIVA	— Was that really a bomb in your pocket —
ANDERSON	Wasn't it?

Hortense and the Moor, at the footlights, are now making slight forward-and-back movements, facing the audience, as if to see whether the stage-and-auditorium might pivot on the axis along the footlights.

FLORENCE	Didn't we have children —
THE MOOR	There are enough, God knows.

The Moor is looking at the audience.

They all suddenly become still — as if the stage-and-auditorium might have moved slightly on its pivot. They balance; or hold on to whatever they can get a hold of.

ANDERSON	We go out into the world —
THE MOOR	It's working.

They wait. They watch the audience.

After a time —

FLORENCE	Who's a pretty boy then —
HORTENSE	Girl —
SIVA	And one makes —

They wait. It is as if they are apprehensive of making a decisive move.

They watch the audience. They make slight movements as if to counterbalance any movement they see in the audience.

Then Siva stands, balancing on the very front edge of the raised first floor, facing front. Dionysus helps her, carefully.

225

THE MOOR	It can walk —
DIONYSUS	It can talk —
FLORENCE	It can —
ANDERSON	— Look!
HORTENSE	It's smiling!

Florence, back left, begins to walk forward towards the footlights.

Dionysus and Siva are on the top front edge of the raised first floor. Siva stands with her arms out as if ready to dive — or to jump or to fly. Hortense and the Moor are side-by-side at the footlights; they smile apprehensively at the audience.

When Florence is parallel with Anderson, half-way between the back and the footlights, he joins her in walking forwards towards the footlights purposefully. When they reach the front of the stage they put their hands up as if to lean or push against a vertical plane there.

There is a bang — as if something has given way and the whole theatre is about to pivot on its left-to-right axis at the front of the stage; the stage coming up and the auditorium going down.

The CURTAIN comes down.

It would be unusual for these plays to be performed. What actors are practised at is the portrayal of characters at once formidable and yet helpless — like pornography, or Macbeth, or muscles on an artist's drawing-board. One of the most touching of modern plays is Beckett's *Happy Days;* in which the heroine — buried at first up to her waist and then up to her neck — can give — oh! — such magnificent performances! trapped and indomitable, just like ourselves. And so we get comfort. Almost no grown-up plays (or novels for that matter) show anything of life as a successfully going concern: this is reserved for children's books and fantasies. To suggest working optimism in a sophisticated world is to be thought presumptuous: sophistication is held to involve seeing difficulties but not skills: what actors and audiences like to be reassured by are reminders of our common cheeky awfulness. In this predicament we are one of a crowd — in a sort of gay Darwinian tumbril. An attempt to get out — to show imagination or intelligence as a means for satisfaction or happiness — is to suggest — Look you too can do it! but only if you work at it, if you think and even then you may fail: there is always bad luck — for you or for others. And it is this that is taboo: the point of a taboo being to protect against misfortune and difficulty. Conventional acting has come to be concerned with the entrapment, comic or tragic, of a person at odds with his environment or himself; with failures of connection within families and societies; with inabilities between friends and lovers. From the webs of such predicaments such consoling beauties can be snatched! like sad, exotic insects. And it is with such images that people feel at home; publicly and privately. And the areas in which chances of success have any meaning — within an individual; between one part of him and another; through these connections to the chance of an effective relationship with the outside world — these are channels that have to remain almost secret: as if the forces running through them have to be insulated from earth.

227

And perhaps they do, with so much prevalence of entropy. But not at some conjunctions, possibly, where minds like ends if open can be lively. But to portray such a network would be to do not just with acting but with what acting is not — non-acting being that which is guarded by but which also can sometimes be conveyed by acting — that liveliness, current, that can be glimpsed just behind the eyes and then the glimpser and that which is glimpsed have to look away; but not perhaps before they have recognised and been recognised: still with not much spoken: speech having to do with the guarding, not the secret. On the stage and in films directors have sometimes used non-actors to try to show something of this reality behind words and behind eyes: but this has usually been done for the purpose of portraying innocence, and not for the demonstration of intelligence and cunning. But it is for such careful balancing, connecting, creating, that a human being seems to be for: this is what his consciousness seems to consist of: the creating of conjunctions that can, like any other form of procreation, give not only energy but pleasure. What is missing at the moment in even the most brilliant films and plays is any sense of what all the brilliance is about: a framework a glimpse even, which will explain (and thus give joy to) what knowingness is up to: a sense of its efficacy and profit. Such an understanding could, as has been said, probably not be much spoken of: the third 'eye' (the 'eye' of Siva) that is said to lie behind the other two can be a judge, and destructive. But still, this could be shown, even harmlessly, in a play, non-acting being with difficulty acted. For only some would see it. And so, who would be imposed on? An actor, not acting, by being conscious of himself would appear slightly above himself: being conscious of this, he would be able to move as it were between his two: it would take someone else, conscious of this, to see it. So who would envy it? An actor might be able to show to a member of an audience what it might be like to be truly oneself — a condition of 'truth' being a situation in which an observer can both observe and get some assessment of his observation — and this would be just an exercise in the ability of choice; of being chosen.

[I once wrote a screenplay from one of my novels in which I tried to say something of all this: the film was made: there had been interest in the ideas. Then when the wheels began to turn, the actors to act, I was told — Look when it comes to it, acting is not about the question of what is acting and what is not, what is truth and what is not, what is testing: acting is about people who are recognisably simple and all-of-a-piece; we cannot act characters who are tormented and yet succeeding — people are either one thing or the other — and if they are seen to be struggling, then they are distraught! Again, I once wrote a novel in which my hero, a politician, made out that he was distraught deliberately in order to satisfy the needs of people around him: he had a delicate mission to perform and needed protection from the simple demands and intrusions of others. But in keeping the effective and hopeful part of my hero somewhat secret I succeeded in deceiving not only the people round him (and sometimes even parts of himself) but also my readers: for it was insisted, again — Look! it must be that this man is simply distraught! how can there be a successful end to a mission (for the mission was successful) by a man who you say is skilful but appears distraught? If distraction is what is being acted then there can be no such thing as success in the not-acting: things are necessarily all-of-a-piece: if we do not know just where we are, then are we not distraught?]

In the attempt of an actor to move between what acting is and what it is not — and by doing so to demonstrate 'truth' — there would have to be something of the self-questioning of Brecht's Chinese actor who 'expresses his awareness of being observed . . . observes himself . . . will occasionally look at the audience and say "Isn't it just like that?" ': a question not of — What will happen next? — but of — What is happening now? — the former question involving helplessness (though perhaps comfort in helplessness) because the answer is unknowable; the latter involving pleasure in prospects, because the facts for hypotheses and testing are there. There would be a going-round, a sifting, a searching — on the part of actors and audience alike — to see what in the end, as in a riddle, is left. This

229

is something of the way in which the mind does work: consisting of connections, eliminations, selections: such processes being reflected in, and by, the world. How else could consciousness work? What would it be able to be conscious of? And the 'waste' that there would be as a result of all this would be — in the world, in a person (in a play?) — most useful: for what can be searched for, found, with no rejection? and so, what is wasted? Liveliness can often only be described, circumscribed, in terms of what it is not: of what is around it: of what it comes up against: in life, in language. And so what a function for waste — a seed-bed for children! Or for gold, diamonds: which require much hard work: the processes of which are not obviously dramatic. They are a persevering, a waiting, a labouring, a dedication — and then the seeing, the discovery, of what, as a by-product, is there. Not a fabrication with the roots out of the earth like barriers in the mind or a cancer: but the something glimpsed behind the eyes as if with a third eye, or like love. But not, as has been said, for those who do not have it. But then, again, they would not want it. And so there is this freedom. And by not being envious, people might also not want to kill it: not even (the mind so quiet) if they see it. It is on some such stage as this that there might be being enacted, as Nietzsche said, 'the great hundred-act play reserved for the next two centuries in Europe . . . the most terrible, the most questionable, and the most hopeful of all plays' — the play of putting to the test not just this truth versus that truth but the question of truth itself: its style, its substance, its patterning. It is for this that there would have to be a code — in so violent and occupied a country! Such a language has been poetry: but poetry often protects itself in music. And music comes in so separately: through little pipes in the ceiling. This code, to create, would have to invade, connect, grapple with — not just others, but with this danger of separateness in mind, itself. Its message — to stand back, to coincide with, to go between, to be re-born — would be — a bright day on a mountain: people under watchtowers in the night; a skill, an encirclement, a cell, a conception. If this cannot be stated explicitly it can be grasped, let go, sought out again: as happens to anything that is loved; that wants, in what way it can, to perpetuate itself — a bird, a seed, a play, a three-headed baby —

These plays go round and round — for diamonds or stones; for corn or chaff; a grid, a riddle — both for characters and actors, trying things out, and for audience or readers, seeing what is there. This happens wholly neither on the stage nor on the page nor in the mind of watcher or reader but in between: in the sifting of 'what is going on' and 'who is it who sees this': with the imagination, perhaps, that these questions are the same. But what is left will be in the mind; and of the people who make it so. Works of art, of literature, have been like this — resonances depending on those who work for them, giving and getting. Or on the luck which makes some give and get. But if there is liveliness beyond luck there has to be imagery to deal with it — this is what consciousness is like — an imagery not static but teeming, burgeoning, bursting; referring to, responding to, simultaneously different faces of itself; by these reverberations influencing that which is similar in the world. It would be something not analysable nor ultimately penetrable but palpably working; in violent harmony, in itself, alive, against the listlessness of entropy. And there will be those who see this and those who do not: depending on — a preference? for life rather than death? for cheerfulness rather than ease? for discomfort rather than despair? It may be that there is simply some randomness of selection in this coming of consciousness to terms with itself: but the fact that the substance of people is the same as that of the things around them might imply (though it is this again that cannot be much talked about) not only the ability by knowing oneself to know the outside world, but the ability of the outside world as it were to know oneself; to know its own kind, that is; to recognise those who are fitted to it, perhaps, by being conscious of it — 'recognise' in the sense that by fitting they may survive. Or those parts of one that are thus fitted may survive. And those that are not, will not. There is amongst people, it seems, an ordering force (or there is not) that can make them (or some parts or products of them) in relation to the outside world like their genetic equipment in

231

relation to themselves — cells, genes, chromosomes, DNA — things forming, proliferating, interlocking, being sent out into the world — by which there is decided — however much unseen, even in such a public area as their bodies — not just what will be formed but what will be passed on — the to-and-fro, the patterning, the activity, the liveliness. These processes are random in that the fate of an individual is not known: they are not random in that the knowledge of an ordering is there. And the skill of a human being, perhaps, is simply to see this; and to try to prepare — not for what he cannot change, which is the burgeoning which comes from outside — but the ground which is himself; on which thus he can choose that some seeds (there are myriads) rather than others might grow. Which choice, learning, indeed is his — between death and life. There is in everything living something quite passive, and active; passive, and active: that folds in on itself, lets itself go; folds in on itself, lets itself go: thereby picking up — what? — an old love? a girl at an airport? a baby? both itself, and its complement; one or two, but they get through: and produce — all the building, exploding, increasing, being cared for: the baby not just for itself but for others; and these, too, the same: and so — for anyone seeing or reading these plays — hold on — there is, yes, the grid, the riddle: it goes round, in the mind, where there are these reconciling totems: and fold in here — there will be chaff, gravel — and here — for corn! diamonds! — all so that life may go on; anthropologists explain

But if there is a code —
The message would also be a story?

CYPHER
A Novel

Cipher, cypher . . . . . A manner of writing
intelligible to those
possessing the key . . .
also . . . the key to
such a system

1

The Professor walked to the steps of the Old Science Buildings. A tomato hit him on his coat. Watching a seed run down he thought — Take it apart, and hold it, and throw it back at you, children: would you become no more than shadows, and it would be your sun.

There were students each side of the steps to the Old Science Theatre. They were raising their fists and shouting. People with the Professor were trying to speak into his ear. He thought — I am Caesar, entering the senate, beneath the portico where starlings sat. He went up the steps between angry fists and the shouting. He thought — What if the conspirators knew they were playing only to themselves?

The theatre was a lecture hall with the seats going up so steeply that the people at the top seemed to be on a seige machine. Most of the seats were filled; there were desks in front of each row; the audience appeared cut off at the waist like busts. The Professor thought — I am in a mausoleum, trapped by these our memorials. The small rostrum, with its lectern, seemed to be underneath the seats. He thought — It is in our heads that we can get out, with one great jump.

The Professor stood at the lectern and laid out his notes. The people who had come in with him were settling down in chairs at the front of the auditorium. The students who had been shouting remained outside. The notes for his lecture were headed *Selection: Natural or Unnatural.* He thought — the adjectives, following the noun, are the baying of hounds outside. The doors of the theatre were being closed: men with long poles wound up windows. The shouting had turned into a chanting: the eroding of wind and rain. The people on chairs in front were crossing and uncrossing their legs. The Professor thought — It was his colleagues who killed Caesar: the crowd, with its tomatoes, only wanted his sacred heart.

The Professor was a brown-faced, thick-set man with grey hair like a laurel wreath. When he began his lecture he spoke in the flat, quiet voice by which he hoped sometimes that his words might fly: an almost hesitant voice, but which could dip its wings down into the wind and then up, floating: neither too little nor too much or it might stall: himself at the controls but hardly touching them: the wind carrying him.

I have called this lecture *Selection: Natural or Unnatural* and the noun is first because this is the fact and the adjectives are to some extent fiction. Evolution through selection is a scientific fact: there is a sense in which this process can no longer be said to be natural. Men can, and do — at least they think they do — tamper with processes of selection. This ability has come about as a result of one of the products of natural selection — man's consciousness.

The chanting from outside had grown quieter. The Professor thought — If it dies, will there be enough wind for my words to fly? A dark-haired girl in the second row was staring at him intently. He thought — She is not with her lover?

Consciousness occurred as a result of innumerable small mutations and selections. Such mutant structures as were fitted to their environment lived, those which were not did not. The mutations were by chance: the processes of selection were inevitable. By environment I mean not just the outside circumstances in which an organism might live, but the circumstances in which a piece of information within an organism might find itself encouraged or not to live. There is in this sense an environment inside as well as outside —

The girl in the second row was remarkable not only, he thought, because he knew her well — and she was intelligent, pretty — but because with her air of outward-turned reflection

240

she reminded him, strikingly, of someone at the centre of his past life; in her student's role listening to him so intently; someone who, he thought, should also be in this audience; who had been as pretty once: a line thus going between the two of them in his mind. And then in fact he did find her, this other one, sitting at the back of the auditorium now and smiling down; an elderly lady with a pudding-basin hair-cut: he thought — Like Cleopatra. And these connections between the three — himself, the old woman, and the young girl in the second row — in his mind, in the lecture theatre — all seemed to be taking place in some system of recognition; not belonging either to one or to the other but in between them, the inside and the outside worlds.

I am not speaking here of the possibilities of tinkering with the genetic code. As members of the audience will well know, there has in recent years been some genetic manipulation in order to produce, in laboratory conditions, substances that are difficult to come by naturally. This has been useful for the purpose of experiment. But I do not think that molecular genetic engineering, however useful in such fields, will in the foreseeable future be able to play the part that is sometimes imagined for it — that of being able to alter, or to improve, the patterns of our species. There are technical reasons for this; as well as the commonplace difficulty of deciding what might, or might not, be an improvement —

The chanting outside had ceased. But now there had begun a shuffling, a turning of heads, within the hall itself; as if the audience might be a school of fishes; this in response to a tapping, a scraping noise, from one of the high-up windows. Something like the head of a dinosaur seemed to be trying to poke through. There was a bang; then a slight tinkle. The window was being forced. What came through, after a time, was the nozzle of a loudspeaker.

Man evolved through chance mutations in the genetic

code; also through the fact that certain mutant structures occasionally had advantage in a changing environment over others that had previously been more fitted. All evolution depends on the juxtaposition of these two factors — the operation of chance, and the operation of environment so that some results of chance rather than others live. It is in this latter area that men in theory at least might now possess some organising ability —

The Professor was smiling: the head of the loudspeaker leaned so drunkenly! The old woman at the back, like Cleopatra, was smiling too. He thought — I have been so lucky with those I love! The young girl in the second row still frowned intently. He thought — She will learn that connections, for their advantage, are often witty.

The qualities of imagination and intelligence in a modern society — those qualities which might be thought necessary for the survival of such a society — while being admittedly factors of personal success are still in no way factors of genetic success: the imaginative and self-reflective, that is, are not those, statistically, who do most to reproduce. In fact, the opposite is the case; and it is modern science, with the help that it offers to the genetically unfortunate, that has helped to bring this about. This is not to say that this is not correct —

The loudspeaker was making a crackling noise. The Professor had gone on talking because, he thought, there was a better chance now that his words might fly: the disturbance in the audience was growing like a wind. There was a man with a long pole stretching up towards the window: the Professor thought — Like St George: but is not the dragon, like a woman, now on top?

But just as there is nothing that can be done about improvement of the species by genetic engineering, so, I believe, is there little more that can be done, in direct

242

ways at least, by social engineering. This has been attempted, up to now, so far as it can be, by good and efficient people. But the benefit, the learning, that has accrued socially does not of course transfer itself to the genetic code —

He had been leafing ahead through the pages of his notes. He thought — I am stalling: I must hang on: I want it to be over: they must hurry. Then — It is right, of course, that they should object to what I say?

But since it is man's genetic equipment that seems to contain, whatever the social conditions, some — I should not say flaw — but some piece of information or lack of it that does not allow a person to be as it were in a good and harmonious working relationship with himself —

He thought — Please God, let them start. Then — But some will hear what I say?

— which seems to result not just in his capacity to blunder but in his feeling at home as it were in his blundering —

The loudspeaker began to play Beethoven. The Professor thought — Now at last I can fly — cry — a piece of the Third Symphony, was it? dropping down, climbing — da da di dum dum, di dum dum — a formulation of — what — beauty? violence? order? knocking out thought. The students had pushed the loudspeaker through the window. They were trying to drown him: to prevent anyone hearing what he had to say. He thought — But of course, this is what I am saying: that what I say should be permitted to grow, or not, in secret.

In the past an infirm species, ill-fitted to itself or to its environment, has died. Such a catastrophe may, indeed, happen to us humans as a species. And there may then be a chance for a more fitted strain to grow. On the other hand it has been suggested that man's consciousness might be used for the planned control or sterilisation even of the genetically unfortunate — so that we can make of ourselves a strain more fitted. But here — apart again from the difficulties, impossibilities even, of deciding what should be encouraged — it is a fact that our modern humanitarian ethic would prevent any such possibility, and of course rightly; for humanitarian ethic is as much the product of human evolution as is scientific understanding; and it can no more be jettisoned in the name of science than can the process of scientific method itself —

Nothing of what he was saying was getting through. The music banged on beautifully: like a flood, a fire: enabling men to die, he thought, grandly: as if on an ice-cap coming down from the Pole. The unity that there had been in the room — the audience's heads turning from himself towards the window like fishes — was now broken: people were standing, sitting, facing this way and that: they were like random molecules of gas, he thought: but broken up by — what? — the power, the orderliness, of music? He thought — Men played Beethoven, Mozart, before and after putting others into gas ovens.

Humans cannot tinker with the genetic code. They cannot hope for genetic improvement directly through social effort. They cannot, being sensible, plan for social or ethical catastrophe. Yet it seems necessary to have some hope of genetic adaptation for our species at a time when the split between what we know and what we can handle seems likely to destroy us —

There were people pushing to get out of the door of the hall. The door seemed blocked. St George, with his lance, was making little headway against the dragon. The Professor looked up at the old woman like Cleopatra. She had a hand over her mouth and was rocking to and fro. He remembered — Sometimes she seemed to laugh so much that her face was pulled into different patterns. He looked at the girl in the second row.

244

But there is still something we can do —

A boy had appeared at the very top of the auditorium. He was tall, with fair hair. He was at the top of one of the gangways near the old woman like Cleopatra. He did not seem particularly interested in the music — or the lecture. He seemed to be looking for someone in the audience.

There might be encouraged some environment in the mind by which the results of one chance mutation rather than those of others might live —

The boy was coming down the steps. The Professor thought — He is looking for the girl: between the random molecules of gas and the noise like a sun-shaft: between angels and pillars, for that fond non-virgin —

I say 'in the mind' because it is here that evolution has most recently taken place and it is here it would seem most likely to take place further —

The loudspeaker was being pulled away from the window from outside. The audience seemed in danger of settling down. He thought — It is I who must hurry.

An environment that would encourage a new type of thinking, person, piece of DNA: that would look on not only the world but the way we look on the world, and thus affect this —

The scene in front of him did indeed seem to be some model in reality of what he was saying: about himself, the boy, the girl, the old woman like Cleopatra: to do both with himself and with what was happening to the others: the boy searching for the girl; the girl still trying to catch his, the Professor's words; the old woman laughing: all forming some exact brightness within the uproar —
The music stopped.

He began to collect up his papers.

The boy with fair hair had reached the front of the auditorium. He was looking at the girl in the second row. The girl was staring at the Professor. The old woman at the back seemed to be picking up her bag.

He thought — Of course, all this would be in code —

Then — But who will get the message?

With the ceasing of the music, the audience was settling down as if to continue to listen to his lecture.

One sheet of his notes had slipped off the lectern and had flown over the edge of the stage like a bird.

The window was closing. There were faint cries from outside. The space in the front of the auditorium was being occupied by large men with blue suits and ties.

Someone had stepped on to the rostrum and was wiping at the tomato on the Professor's coat. He thought — My sacred heart!

The girl in the second row was picking up the page of his notes which had landed close to her.

The boy with fair hair had turned and was making a gesture to the Professor, as if he were telling him that he wanted to speak to him.

The old lady had gone.

The Professor, with his notes, stepped down from the rostrum. He walked towards the door into the courtyard.

Someone plucked at his sleeve.

He thought he would say — But I've said everything I wanted to say!

Then — I need not even say that.

2

The girl with dark hair, who was called Judith, had left the lecture theatre and had walked across the courtyard. She was followed by the boy with fair hair who was called Bert Anderson. She decided to ignore him. Then as she went into the street she feared that she had lost him. She thought she might pretend she had left something in the theatre, and go back.

She rummaged in her bag for — comb, notebook, mirror. Then he appeared. He was wearing his old jersey which hung like a cow bell. She walked on briskly. He came up beside her; jogging. They were moving along a street each side of which were grey stone buildings. He began to roll his head and mutter. He seemed to be acting as if he were tiring. Then he slowed, and looked at his hand as if it held a stop watch.

He said 'Not bad. See if we can get it down to — what — ten — fifteen minutes?'

She said 'What —'

He said 'Our quarrel.'

The crowd that had come out of the lecture hall was dispersing. The street ahead was empty. There was a blood-red sky above the rooftops. Anderson (Judith thought of him as Anderson because she did not, at that time, like the name Bert) was running beside her again, panting and staggering. Then he seemed to give up, and leaned with his head against a doorway.

She went a little way past him and stopped and turned.

He said 'We'll get it better.'

She looked up at the pediment of the doorway above his head. There was a coat-of-arms of a man with a breastplate and a short skirt leaning on a sword like an umbrella.

Anderson said, as if declaiming, 'Judith, Juliet, I know I don't get on with your parents! —'

She walked on. She thought — He will now do his funny walk of the drunk man with one foot in the gutter.

He called '— Juliet, is it because they think I've got one leg shorter than the other? —'

She stopped and leaned with her head against a lamp-post. She thought — Why doesn't he grab me: is it because I could then escape him, and he is too clever?

Anderson came up beside her and said quietly 'Do you really have to go?'

'Yes.'

'Why?'

'I said I would.'

He moved slightly away. Then he raised both fists to the sky and declaimed '— I will have such revenge on you both — that all the world shall — I will do such things —'

She walked on. She thought — I like him because he is as strong as me? He knows I do not want to get away from him?

He came up beside her. He said 'What does he want?'

'To hear me. In his play.'

She thought he might say — At this time of night?

She looked up at the sun, which was settling above rooftops.

He said 'Do you know why people go to plays? Because they get comfort from seeing old men being humiliated and tortured, like King Lear.'

She said 'Where did you get that?'

He said 'From the old woman I go to.'

She thought — How extraordinary to say — From the old woman I go to!

As she watched, the sun moved behind the chimneys of buildings. The sky became translucent as a stage set.

He said 'And they like to see Judith, Juliet, being so adoring; nipping a chap's balls off.'

She said 'Is that why you like me then?'

He said 'Because you don't want to?'

They were coming towards a corner where the grey stone buildings gave way to a demolished area on which there were huge advertisements: there were men with guns hanging down like breasts: women with their legs apart like explosions.

248

She said 'You say so exactly the same sort of things as he says!'

'What does he say?'

'About people liking being humiliated. About them then knowing where they are.'

'And what does he do about it?'

'He writes plays.'

A gang of boys were running towards them across the wasteland. They were mostly black; they wore white shirts and black trousers. They were smiling. There were blue and yellow lights as if from police cars flashing in the distance behind them. She thought — They are like fishes, being driven out of the sea.

Anderson said 'Doesn't he try to make things better?'

He had taken out of his pocket what appeared to be a hand grenade. As the gang of boys approached, he pulled out the pin and held the grenade outstretched between finger and thumb. With his other hand he held his nose as if he were about to jump into water. The boys made a small detour round him. One of the boys at the back, watching Anderson, suddenly doubled up with laughter: then he acted as if he had been shot, holding his stomach. Then he went on. Anderson smiled.

Judith shouted 'I do hate it when you do that!'

Anderson put the pin back in the grenade. He put the grenade in his pocket.

He said 'Does he make things better?'

They walked past the wasteland towards the bridge across a river. There were the sounds of bells, and sirens, in the distance.

He said 'You can't act goodness. You can't act intelligence, or authority, or happiness.'

She said 'You can act —'

'What —'

She thought — But he, the other one, would say: You can't talk about that.

They were going over the bridge across the river. The water moved sluggishly.

She said 'Well what do you do.'

He put an arm around her.

249

She thought — Was that a body, or a whirlpool, going past in the river?

He said 'Oh, if you show that you know that you are acting —'

She thought — But that's what he says. Then — You make things better?

She put her head against Anderson's shoulder.

She thought — There is something so hard about him; like a visor.

She said 'You show what —'

He said 'Creation? Procreation?'

They had crossed the bridge. They were moving towards an avenue with cherry trees.

She looked up at him. She thought — The visor lets through half the light; the other half is reflected back into himself.

He stopped and let go of her. He said 'But when you know all this —'

She thought again — What —

He said 'How are you going to get back tonight?'

She thought — Is he, or is he not, acting?

Then — I mean, does he or does he not want me? want to stop me?

They were facing one another. They were at the edge of the avenue with cherry trees.

She thought — But what is he protecting himself against?

He said 'Or aren't you going to get back tonight?'

She put a hand against his face, not hard, as if she were acting hitting him.

He put a hand up to his cheek. He seemed to be feeling for something inside his mouth with his tongue.

He said 'My God —!'

'What —'

She thought — I must not laugh.

'It's that tooth I had, filled with cyanide!'

She began to laugh. She put her head against his shoulder.

He put his hand on his heart.

He said 'Judith! Juliet!'

'Yes?'

He said 'I love you.'

250

She said 'I love you too.'

They walked on.

She thought — Do I, or do I not, want him to come in with me?

He said 'It all lives such a life of its own!'

She said 'Then let it.'

Across the entrance to the avenue they had come to was a rope, which sagged. In the middle of the rope there was a sign with a diagonal bar across it. Beyond were rows of detached houses with gardens and cherry trees.

Anderson said 'How much did you hear of that lecture?'

She said 'He didn't want us to hear much, did he?'

Anderson said 'Then he's lucky.'

They had stepped over the rope. In the avenue there were houses with corrugated iron over windows. She thought — Like matchsticks across eyes.

Anderson said, as if quoting '— The tanks are in the streets —'

She thought — There are people dying —

She remembered how he — the other one — had said: Language is useful not for saying what things are, but for saying what things are not.

He said 'You have to do it then?'

She said 'I think so, don't you?'

He said 'I mean now: you.'

They were coming towards a cross-roads. She had slowed. She took her head from his shoulder.

She said 'Here we are.'

She thought — But of course I don't want him to come in with me.

She put her hand across her eyes. She thought — There is a fog, sometimes, in the brain, like a curtain coming down.

He said 'Of course I can't say — What about me.'

She said 'I'm sorry.'

He was standing slightly apart from her. He began to walk in a circle.

She said 'Will you come in?'

A police car had appeared at the cross-roads. It had a blue light going round and flashing. There were four policemen in the car. They sat like toys. She thought — Like those toys with spikes up their arses.

Anderson took her by the shoulders and put her with her back against a tree. Then he leaned with his arms on either side of her.

He shook his head.

She thought — Now at last he will kiss me?

The policemen were looking at them out of the window of the car. One was speaking into a walkie-talkie radio.

Anderson looked up towards the rooftops. He seemed to be observing some event there.

A door in the police car opened. A policeman got out.

She remembered, suddenly, that Anderson had in his pocket what might, or might not, be a hand grenade.

She wanted to hit him with her fists and cry — Oh fool! fool! you want to destroy yourself!

She put her face up to be kissed.

They, and the policemen, seemed to be the only people in the street. There were leaves like broken glass between them.

The policeman who had got out of the car was coming towards them. Then he stopped. He looked up at the rooftops in the direction in which Anderson was looking.

Anderson said, quietly but distinctly, 'Go away!'

The policeman looked at Anderson.

Then the radio in the policeman's breast pocket began to make a crackling noise. He took it out and held it to his ear.

Then there was a crack in the air as if of a rifle bullet: then from far away, the report as if of a rifle.

The policeman hesitated: then began to move at a run back towards the car.

Anderson put his face down to Judith's and kissed her.

She was trying to bang her fists against his chest.

The engine of the police car roared.

She wanted to shout — You can't get away with things like that!

The policeman had clambered back in the car: the car skidded and drove away.

Anderson took his face away from hers. He said 'That was a

lucky one!'

He looked up again to above the rooftops. There was a glow in the sky, as if part of the town were burning.

She said 'It was nowhere near us!'

He took his arms away from her.

She walked across the pavement. She put her hand on a garden gate.

She thought — It is strange I was not frightened!

She said 'Will you come and get me? I mean, afterwards.'

He said 'No.'

He was still looking above the rooftops.

Beyond the gate, there was a path to a detached house on the corner.

She said 'Why not?'

He said 'I don't know.' Then — 'I've got to do something about my film.'

She pushed on the garden gate and went through.

She said 'Goodbye then.'

'Goodbye.'

She thought — We are children: trying to build something like coral inside us —

He had turned and was walking back the way they had come.

She thought — Or in the streets outside, like a honeycomb.

3

The Professor stood outside the door of his flat in the corridor of a modern apartment building. He felt in his pockets for his keys. He found — wallet, pencil, wall-nails, notebook. The doors in the row were almost identical with just a different number on each. He thought — In memory there are these corridors: you search; turn away; then a door is opened for you. He felt in the lining of his jacket. Sometimes his keys fell through a hole in the pocket and hung there: he thought — Like Gandhi, his balls above the dust.

The door in front of him was being unlocked quietly. First there was a noise of a chain, then of the mortise lock, then of the Yale lock above. He thought — I will stand with my hands through my pockets and try to dominate the world. The door was being opened slowly. He had once seen Gandhi like this; his legs apart as if he were peeing.

A woman's face appeared through the crack in the doorway. She was carrying something large and round and white beside her neck. He thought — Atlas was a woman?

He said 'I told you not to open the door!'

The round thing at the side of the woman's neck was a baby. It was facing backwards over her shoulder, wearing nappies.

The woman said 'Are you all right?'

She turned and went ahead of him into the flat. The head of the baby came round and beamed at him. He thought — If you are the sun and moon, and I am gravity —

He said 'Of course I'm all right!'

The Professor closed the door behind him. He put the chain back in the slot. Then he followed the woman and the baby into the sitting-room.

She said 'I thought they might be trying to break up your

lecture.'

He said 'They were.'

The baby stretched out its arms to him.

The Professor tickled it under the chin.

The baby said 'Awa, awa, goo goos.'

In the sitting-room there were books on the floor, on chairs, in bookcases. Along one wall was a window that looked out on to a garden.

The woman said 'We were anxious, we thought you —'

When she turned to him again there was pale hair, brown face, dark eyes; a slight bruise at the side of one eye as if she were an apple.

He said '— might have been murdered.'

She said 'Yes.'

He thought — When she doesn't finish her sentences she is like a fisherman; or like God, in thigh-length boots, with a hook —

He said 'I might have been.'

The baby's behind was now towards him: its head, at her back, seemed to struggle to get round.

He sat down on the sofa and held out his arms to it.

He thought — If the baby were a god it would be like Janus; two-faced; seeing both in and out —

He said 'Nobody loves me!'

He thought — Or with herself at the centre, a pivot, like Atlas, they would be three —

He took the baby. He threw it up and down. It held its arms out like a bird.

She said 'He loves you.'

He said 'I'm old.'

He thought — A baby is like an earth, breaking away, but being held, by its sun —

She said 'What happened?'

He said 'They played Beethoven at my lecture.'

Each time he caught the baby, and held it, the baby crowed, and beamed.

'Why?'

'They didn't like what I said.'

255

'But did they hear what you said —'

'Exactly.'

The baby had leaned down and was trying to put its fingers into his ears, his eyes.

He said 'Awa. Awa. Goo goos.'

He put the baby down. He held it by the hands, as it stood on the floor, as if to see if it would walk.

He said 'You can't fly?'

The baby held out its arms to its mother.

He said 'I told you not to open that door.'

She said 'I heard you outside.'

He thought he could say — You heard someone.

She took the baby. She undid her blouse. She sat on the sofa behind him. She took out a breast, and gave it to the baby.

He thought — From that breast, like a planet, I used to hang.

They were in a group, side by side, with the baby between them. He thought — Like a piece of sculpture; or in someone's mind.

He said 'You two had a fight —'

'Yes.'

'What about?'

She was holding her breast and pulling it to help the baby. He thought — A breast is like a penis?

She said 'Oh well he had that girl, you know, coming for a sort of audition —'

He said 'What girl?'

'Judith. Juliet.'

He thought — Do I say: But she was at my lecture!?

She said 'But it wasn't really that.'

'What was it?'

'I was horrid.'

'How?'

The baby was pulling at her breast. He thought — Do women now have everything — breasts, penises, truth?

She said 'I wanted to hurt him. I said — You think you can do everything! You think you're God!'

He said 'Ah, and that was horrid?'

She said 'Yes. And so he hit me.'

The woman, who was called Lilia, was some thirty years younger than the Professor: with her pale hair, brown face, dark eyes, she was something hot, looking out, like a squirrel.

The Professor got up and went through into a bedroom, where there was a four-poster bed. The curtains of a small window were drawn. The room was slightly airless, as if people had been sleeping there.

He picked up off the floor a rattle, a toy hammer, a woollen sock, some plastic pants. He sat on the edge of the bed. He thought — These fragments she takes with her into each of her different worlds —

He called — 'What shall we do to your mum to keep her? tie her to a bedpost?'

Lilia had come to the bedroom door. She said 'I know it might have been him outside in the passage.'

She came and stood close to the Professor. He put his arms round her. He put his head against her skirt.

She said 'Thank you.'

'For what?'

'For putting us up.'

He said 'For not putting it up.'

She said 'Do you want to?'

He thought — Is there a Madonna like this; at a deposition, with a breast out?

She said 'You know I know how to make him angry.' Then — 'Perhaps I wanted to see you: it was awful when you weren't here.'

He said 'Your baby will look after you.'

She stroked his head.

Looking up, past her, but still holding her tightly, he said 'Where is your baby?'

'On the floor.'

'Well, look out for the window.'

As he said this there was a slight pressure, going in and out, as if from a distant explosion.

He said to himself as if quoting — A sort of terror, breaking —

Lilia left him and went into the sitting-room.

Lying on his back, and looking up at the canopy of the four-

257

poster bed which was like a baldacchino above an altar, he thought — But am I not godfather, if not god, to both the girl and the child?

Lilia called — 'There's a fire.'

'Where?'

'Come and see. It's in the direction of the Old Science Buildings.'

He sat up. He said 'Well it's nothing to do with my lecture.'

He went through into the sitting-room where Lilia had drawn back a corner of a curtain. She was looking out into the night. She had picked up her baby.

She said 'Who is it then?'

He said 'The Liberation Army.'

He held a finger out to the baby; who took hold of it, and beamed.

She said 'What do they want?'

He said as if he were quoting '— The destruction of everything: or that something new may grow —'

He thought — What will the baby learn then?

She said 'I'd better go back.'

He thought — Coloured lights, shapes, music.

He said 'No, stay here.'

He thought — Cherubs: gods and goddesses on the ceiling.

He went round the flat opening windows. Then he came back into the sitting-room and drew the curtain shut. Then he went round closing doors.

He said 'Go into the bedroom and get under the bed if there are any more explosions.'

She said 'What will you do?'

He thought — Oh these enormous events elsewhere! like eels, like turtles, breeding.

She had sat down on the sofa. It was as if she were about to cry.

He said, tickling the baby again, 'What goes on in that huge head!'

There was another explosion; from closer; the curtain blowing in and out.

The Professor had the impression — he was tired — of some

258

presence, or presences, entering the room; taking up their position round the walls; saying to himself, to Lilia, to the baby — Look, if you feel yourselves prisoners, with one great jump —

Lilia said 'I hope they all kill themselves!'

He thought — Perhaps mothers can say this.

He sat down again beside Lilia. The baby was lying across their laps.

He said — 'Promise —'

'What.'

He thought — To be here when I get back?

Then — Promises are not true!

He put a hand up and touched the bruise on her cheek. He said 'Did it hurt?'

She said 'No.'

He thought — We should be out in the streets like hostages — myself, the boy with fair hair, the girl, the one who is like Cleopatra —

He said 'That girl was at my lecture.'

She said 'What girl?' Then — 'Oh.'

The baby, with its dark intelligent eyes, looked up at him.

He thought — Turn with that bright eye on them, and your enemies will fall dead.

He put a finger on the centre of the baby's forehead.

He said 'Get it out, get it out, don't be frightened.'

She said 'Get out what —'

He said 'That little eye, the third one, with which you see inwards: with which you look down on yourself from the ceiling.'

He stood up. He went to the door. He turned and smiled at her and her baby.

She said 'If you throw him up, he always knows there's someone there to catch him!'

He said 'I'll be at the Old Science Buildings.'

4

A man in a high-necked sweater and corduroy trousers sat on top of a radiator with his hands under his thighs and his toes pointing inwards. Occasionally he lifted himself as if he were over a slow fire. He looked down at Judith, who sat cross-legged on a carpet in front of him. He said 'Just murmured —'
  'Yes.'
  '— Go away —'
  'Yes.'
  Judith was taking puffs from a cigarette and was backing away as if the smoke were coming after her.
  'Then there was a shot —'
  'Yes.'
  'And then —'
  'It was terrifying.'
  The man, who was called Jason, pushed himself up off the radiator and hung there as if on parallel bars.
  He said 'You don't seem terrified.'
  Judith beat in the air at the smoke coming after her.
  Jason thought — I am pretending that I am on fire from the heat of the radiator; as if I so much desired her?
  He climbed off the radiator. He picked up a typescript from the floor. The room was furnished with just carpet, lamp-stand, curtains and cushions.
  He said 'Well, you've got to speak as if you know that you are acting.'
  Judith stood. She took the typescript in one hand. She held out her other with the cigarette in it as if she were on a tight-rope.
  She said 'Why can't I play the girl?'
  'Because I want you to be an older woman.'

260

'Why.'

'Because you're so powerful.'

She held the typescript out in front of her. After a while she seemed to read —

'— Ariel, will you tell your father, I've done his socks and they're in the oven —'

She flicked the ash from her cigarette on to the carpet. She looked down at it.

She said 'She's trying to get him —'

'Who.'

'Jason. Ariel.'

Putting a toe out to the ash on the carpet, she began to giggle.

He thought — This fire in my head, heart, balls. Then — Lilia, have I hurt you?

He came and took the typescript from Judith. He wrote with a pencil in the margin.

She said 'Who plays the girl?'

He said 'You want to?'

'Not Lilia?'

'I can't write about Lilia!'

He handed the typescript back to her. He had written in the margin — They know they are embarrassed.

Judith said 'Why can't you write about Lilia?'

'She's good. She's not trying to be powerful.'

Judith said 'So Lilia could play —' Then — 'And I'm not good?'

'I don't know.'

She held the typescript. He stood watching her. He thought — Get it out, get it out: on the carpet —

He said 'But you may make good things happen.'

'How.'

He thought — Lilia, Lilia, it is myself I am hurting!

She said 'And Lilia may make bad things happen?'

'If one lets them be bad.'

She looked at the typescript. He stood watching her.

After a time she seemed to read '— And would he never, never, do this to anyone again —'

Then she said 'Where is she?'

'Who?'

'Lilia.'

'With her older lover.'

'You had a quarrel.'

'Yes.'

Judith lowered the typescript. She seemed to be blushing. He thought — With her mind running down into her jeans —

He said 'And you had a quarrel with your boyfriend?'

She giggled.

He went to the window. There was a tree, a road, a red glow above the rooftops.

After a time he said 'You go to and fro; between yourself, and what is going on elsewhere.'

She said 'What is going on?'

He thought — A mountain, an airport, a cellar in a town; a tree —

He said 'You find out —'

'What?'

He thought — If I make things worse, will it be better? because I can then cry out —

He murmured, as if quoting 'I love only you, you see —'

She seemed to shout 'All right!'

He turned to her. She was in the middle of the carpet. She seemed to be on the edge of tears.

He held out his hand. He said 'I wanted to hurt myself. Not Lilia.'

She said 'Do it then!'

She took his hand.

He said as if quoting '— I've loved other people in my life —'

She said 'Dear God, you make it easy or difficult, don't you!'

The room in which they were standing was on the ground floor of the detached house on the corner of the avenue with cherry trees. Leading her by the hand, they went out of a door and up a staircase.

The stairs were in the half dark. There was a glow from the night sky outside.

He thought — I think you protect yourself from pain by inoculating yourself with pain?

Lilia had stood here at the top of the stairs. She had said —
All you ever care about is your fucking work! It's pathetic, you
think you are God! He had hit her.

He led Judith through into a bedroom. He took some
nappies from the bed. He turned back the bedclothes.

Judith was standing by the door. She said 'I'm sorry —'

He said 'Never mind.'

She said 'It's a sort of fog —' She put a hand to her head.

He sat on the edge of the bed. She came and sat beside him.
He put an arm round her.

She said 'These people in the plays, they all know each other
so well!'

'Yes.'

'What else?'

'They want to change: to be changed.'

There was a slight pressure, in and out, as if from a distant
explosion.

She said 'I don't want to act. I want you to help me.'

He stood up. He began to take off his clothes.

He thought — But if there's that crack in the rocks; the roof
or the floor coming down —

She had taken off her jeans. She lay on the bed with her legs
sideways.

He thought — This is a geological problem; like that of a
mountain, or the surface of a brain —

He lay on the bed next to her.

There was another explosion, much closer, in and out: the
sound of glass breaking.

He thought — Now if I cover her body with my body, my
arms in a cross, the glass will not hurt her —

After a time, in which he had put an arm across her, there
was cold air coming in; and light; and the feel of passages and
tunnels.

She said 'What was that?'

He thought — The miles and miles of rubble: the aeroplane
flying away into the distance.

She said 'Never mind.'

He was looking down past her rock-forms; her strange hair,

her ear.

He said 'A bomb.'

'But it was close!'

He thought, as if quoting — A big one.

He rolled sideways and put his feet to the floor.

She said 'The window's broken!'

He was trying to arrange stepping-stones with his clothes to avoid glass on the floor.

Walking on tip-toe, as if on a tightrope, he went out on to the landing. He was naked.

She said 'Where's the baby?'

Looking back at her, where she had followed him, naked, with an arm across her breasts, like Eve —

He said 'Lilia took the baby.'

In a smaller bedroom, at the side of the house, there was a cot, and the window blown in, and jagged splinters of glass all over the mattress.

Judith said 'It's there that it would have been sleeping?'

He thought — But if you got back, into that Garden, you would never tell what you knew —

Judith was standing beside him in the small bedroom.

There was a light like a sword from the street outside.

He thought — Nor would you stay there?

5

Anderson felt his way up a stone staircase in the dark. At the top, beyond a door, there was a whirring sound. He thought — Do blind people construct a world outside? or do they see that their fingers and ears send messages just to themselves in the dark?

Pushing with his feet, and finding a landing, he saw a flickering light beneath the door. He felt for the handle, knocked, and went in. Inside, there were images flashing against a wall; a baby was being held in huge hands. In the centre of the room there was a cinema projector, whirring.

Closing the door, and groping for a chair, he sat down behind the projector. The image on the wall had changed to that of a mediaeval horseman with a lance through a dragon's throat: then to a marble statue of an old man wrestling with snakes. Beside the projector, slightly in front of him and with her back to him, was the seated figure of a woman with a pudding-basin hair-cut.

The image on the wall changed to a portrait of a head fragmented like glass: then back to the baby, where it rested, the huge hands like those of a god.

The area on which the images were thrown was cut into at one corner by a vase of flowers which stood on a bookshelf. It was as if the baby were being attacked, or tickled, by the shapes of flowers or snakes from outside.

Anderson thought — I can explain that I could get another camera that would include the frame, the flowers, the bookcase: so that it would be clear that the baby is being attacked from outside —

The image on the wall changed to an archaic statue of a man, or a god, walking forwards with his hands by his sides; his blind eyes smiling. The flowers from outside, like flames, were almost at his genitals.

Anderson thought — Then will these be figures who will be able to try to get away from the attacks of the flowers, the bookcase —

The light suddenly faded and went out, the whirring noise ran down.

In the darkness the woman said 'Damn.'

Anderson thought — But if they were not blind, would they be smiling?

The woman stood up. She went to the window. The town was in the dark; except a part that seemed to be burning.

She said 'Those flowers —'

He said 'Yes!' Then '— Come in from outside.'

He thought — But if you had the framework in which they would be framed, you could be smiling?

She said 'And then the lights go off!'

He thought — A fog comes down over the heart, the mind —

The woman came back from the window. She sat in the chair, and looked at the blank wall.

She said 'The baby looks very well.'

He said 'He is.'

In the dark, Anderson felt around on the projector and pushed up the lever which released the film. He took the film out of its sprockets.

The old woman, who was called Eleanor, said 'You think people want to get rid of those flowers which are, what is it, tickling them?'

He said 'Wouldn't they?'

She said 'Those mad, archaic people?'

He was winding the film back on to the top reel. He spun the wheel, flicking it.

He said 'You mean, the flowers got them moving?'

He thought — But if you held such an idea in your head, like those hands round the baby —

She said 'But when you do stand back and see yourselves —'

'What —'

'You think you're horrid?'

266

'That's what happened —'

'When.'

'About five hundred B.C.'

She said 'And do you?'

He took the reel off its holder. He put it in a can.

He thought — Of course, what she sees as her job, is talking about me.

She said 'Before that, people hadn't been able to see themselves? You think they might want to now?'

He said 'Perhaps if you see yourselves seeing yourselves —'

He thought she might say again — And do you?

She said 'What was it they didn't like —'

He said 'Well, those images.'

'Inside the baby's head —'

'Yes.'

'So —'

'They had to make things outside horrible in order to feel at home.'

They were, the two of them, sitting staring at the blank wall. He thought — Any moment now the light may come on and the projector whirr busily.

She said 'And now, what is it that we see if we see ourselves seeing ourselves?'

He thought — We see ourselves staring at a blank wall?

He said 'We don't like the images. But we like the fact that we can see.'

'So —'

He thought — So can we make a light come on?

He said 'Well, we can try to find out what's happening if we know we're in the dark.'

It seemed that the back of her head, somewhere in front of him, was staring out as if over some valley of the Nile.

He thought — Those people in the cave, when they knew that it was only shadows they were seeing on the wall, might have welcomed darkness —

She said 'Did you hear that lecture?'

He said 'I thought you couldn't hear it.'

He thought — They would have been afraid of the sun outside?

She said 'What happens next?'

He said 'When?' Then — 'After five hundred B.C.?'

She said 'In your film.'

He said 'Oh. Well. The things they still do to babies. Push a stick up its nose; put a finger in its mouth, as if to pull out a hook there.'

He thought — If they saw this, and were able to talk about it —

She said 'You know about babies?'

He said 'I saw it being born.'

He thought — Was the sun too bright?

She said 'But they didn't do those things to this baby.'

He said 'They tried to.'

She said 'They do those things to keep it alive.'

He thought — Don't we keep it alive then?

The light in the projector suddenly started up again and the motor whirred busily.

Anderson picked up the flowers and moved them away from the light on the wall.

She said 'What made you think of the baby?'

He said 'Oh well, you, I suppose.'

She said 'And those huge hands —'

He thought — You don't like to think, even now, that we hurt babies?

She said 'They're his? They're mine?'

The light in the projector went out again. Anderson went to the window. He looked out. There was the part of the town burning.

He thought — Or you mean it's this that you can't say?

A fog, like a curtain, coming down, up, down.

He said 'When did they invent handwriting?'

She said 'Oh good heavens, handwriting!' Then after a time — 'About seven hundred B.C. I think. At first they wrote from right to left. Then they wrote one line from right to left and the next from left to right. Then they started writing from left to right about five hundred, I think, yes.'

He said 'Good heavens.'

She said 'And music, what about music?'

There was a slight explosion from somewhere beyond the rooftops, which made the windows, the walls, seem to go in and out.

He said 'Music?'

She said 'I'm trying to think what stopped them seeing themselves.'

He said 'Seeing themselves seeing themselves?'

She said 'Yes.' Then — 'Stopped them not liking what they saw.'

He frowned. He said 'But it didn't.'

She said 'But you said they came to feel at home.'

A few sparks, like inverse rain, were rising above the rooftops.

He thought — To be not at home, one would have to be an orphan?

She came and stood by him at the window. They looked out.

She said 'I'm married to him, you know?'

He said 'Yes.'

She said 'Frau Professor Ackerman.'

He thought — I had it a moment ago: they are connections, those huge hands —

He said 'What went wrong?'

She said 'Nothing.'

He thought — Who are my parents then?

She said 'It was those flowers, those beautiful flowers, or sticks, do you think, coming in from outside —'

There was the curtain coming down again over his mind, his heart —

Then she said 'So what about your girl —'

He said 'What girl?'

She said 'Judith. Juliet. Why do you sometimes call her Juliet?'

He thought — It is what you know but can't say that is passed on? Like genes: like chromosomes —

After a time she said 'What are you thinking?'

He said — 'It's the connections, not just the images, that might be passed on.'

She said 'And they're not horrible.'

He said 'No.'

He wanted to explain — By this window: now: looking out into the night: the sparks coming up above the rooftops —

She said 'He and I adored each other.'

He said 'Yes.'

He thought — And so we are all happy now?

He left the window. He walked around the room.

He said 'There are such coincidences!'

She said 'Yes.'

He said 'In the inside or outside worlds —'

Then she said 'You said that defensively.'

'Shouldn't I?'

'Why?'

He thought — In those huge hands —

There was another bang, in and out, from beyond the frame of the window.

He wanted to say — That is in the outside world!

Then he said 'Perhaps one could say things as though one were saying them in inverted commas —'

She said 'You're a very clever young man. So yes, people want to shove a stick up your nose, your throat, your arse —'

He thought — Exactly.

Then he smiled. He thought — Did she say 'very'?

She said 'Language is mostly negative. Not communicating love.'

He said 'What does communicate love?'

She said something like 'Awa, awa, goo goos.'

He thought — I could get an image of that baby being carried through streets pursued by Herod: then sparks, or broken glass, coming in like angels from outside the frame to rescue it —

She said 'You have to trust.'

He thought — Of course, all this would have to be kept somewhat secret.

Then she said 'You don't want to get rid of Judith?'

He said 'What do you mean? Of course I trust!'

Eleanor laughed. She said '— What do you mean, of course I don't want to get rid of Judith —'

He thought, suddenly — I could get them moving through
streets, like seeds, like sperms through corridors —
   He said 'I must go and rescue the rest of my film!'
   She said 'She's quite like me.'
   He said 'It's in the Old Science Buildings.'

6

Lilia walked through streets with her baby on her back. The baby was in a carrier so that it faced the same way as herself. Its head was just above the level of her shoulder; so that it was as if she were a tank and the baby were her driver. She thought — We are on a road with refugees coming past: if we had remained in the building, by windows, we would have been more vulnerable.

Two bombs seemed to have gone off in the town. There was a column of smoke rising like a funeral procession above each.

Some of the people in the streets seemed to be hurrying towards where the bombs had gone off; some seemed to be hurrying away. Lilia thought — Who, would you say, will be survivors? Most of the people appeared to be purposeful and smiling. It was as if (would the Professor say?) the bombs had given them identity and location: they had something to pull against now, like goats that are tethered.

He (the Professor? Jason?) had said — The reason why good stories have so far not been happy is a technical one: shape requires delimitation: delimitation requires death.

The baby was pointing over her shoulder and was exclaiming as if at sights of interest.

She said to it cheerfully ' — Coloured lights! Shapes! Music! — '

She had said to Jason — Then is not what you are writing good?

They were coming to a green, at the far side of which was a grey stone building. The front of this was cordoned off. The fire seemed to be in a block beyond. There were police, and firemen, inside the cordon. The crowd that had been moving with her in the street seemed to have jammed at the cordon and spread sideways like foam: then settled on the edge of the green.

Jason had said — It is of people knowing that they are telling stories.

When Lilia stopped, the baby on her back seemed to kick and struggle for her to go on.

She shouted 'For goodness' sake we can't go farther!'

He had said — she could not remember — It is something that forms, turns in on itself, breaks, re-forms its shape: instead of violence —

Some of the women in the crowd were looking at her disapprovingly. She was out too late at night: had she not been told the streets were dangerous. The women might reach out with claws, to take her baby.

She and Jason had been standing at the top of the stairs. She had been shouting — what — to get it out? Then — It was to get me out of the house, he hit me?

Somewhere in front, across the green, she thought she saw, for a moment, Jason. He was going down an alleyway at the side of the Old Science Buildings.

She thought — I was trying to make him drive me out?

The old women were talking amongst themselves. They were like priestesses on the steps of a temple; attendant on the sacrifice of a child.

The figure of what might have been Jason had disappeared. There was a glow, and what was like a fog, above the rooftops.

A fire engine had arrived on the green. It had flashing lights and brass like trumpets. There were hoses, and men in helmets and raincoats. And a taste, and smell, like something bitter, from childhood.

Lilia was trying to pull the baby out of its carrier and hold it to her front. She said 'Look! Fire engines!'

The baby stared into her face. It smiled. It pulled at her mouth, her ear.

One of the women — grey-haired and with steel spectacles — touched her on the arm. Lilia thought — I can jerk away; cry out; hold my baby in the air, to be caught up by angels.

She had said — You think you're God!

He had said — You're a devil!

— Get it out: help me —

273

The baby, hanging on to her hair, was reaching down to get rid of the hand of the woman with steel spectacles.

Lilia thought — Perhaps the woman, if she touches my baby, will be struck dead by a hand coming down through the fog above the Old Science Buildings.

The scene in front of her — the men round the fire engines chatting amicably a block away from the fire — was like, she thought, a gathering on one of those plains in Portugal or Spain where children had seen a vision of God or the Virgin Mary; the grown-ups collected as if for a scientific experiment; and because of this nothing further could happen, except for the millions of bottles of fruit juice and cameras and trinkets.

And the message that had been given to the children was —

There was the sudden blast of a loudspeaker.

A girl was coming towards her across the green. She was wearing a jacket long enough to be an overcoat. Lilia recognised it as one of Jason's.

The words from the loudspeaker were giving some warning about danger that was unintelligible.

Lilia wanted to shout at the people round her — If you loved enough, cared enough, you would take your baby through streets no matter what visions —

The girl said 'Hullo.'

Lilia thought she might say — I wondered if you might not remember me.

'Jason asked me to say —'

'Where is he?'

The baby had turned. It was stretching out its arms to the girl.

She said 'He asked me to find you.'

Lilia said to the baby 'It's all right, my darling.'

'Then I saw you here.'

The woman with steel spectacles had taken her hand away from Lilia's arm.

Lilia said 'But what's he doing?'

Lilia and Judith, together with the baby, began to walk round the back of the crowd at the edge of the green. It was as if they were in some dark landscape with burning towers.

274

Judith said 'Oh I forgot! Don't go home!'

'Why not?'

'There was a bomb; it blew in the windows. Gas is everywhere. Water.'

Lilia thought — A pressure going in and out. Across a plain. A ruined city.

Judith said 'And glass was all over the cot.'

Lilia said 'Glass was all over the cot.'

Judith said 'Where he would have been sleeping.' Then — 'How can I tell you.'

Lilia thought — Yes how can you tell me.

She said 'Thank you.'

They had moved away from the green. They were walking, with careful steps, between grey stone buildings.

Judith said 'Jason went to look for you.'

Lilia said 'I see.'

She thought — But what do I see? My life: and a crowd with its arms up, rushing towards a river —

— And I, with my baby —

They had come, in their walk, to the entrance of a courtyard where a wrought-iron staircase went up on the outside of what seemed to have been a warehouse. Judith stopped. Lilia began taking the baby in its carrier off her back. Judith said 'I've got to go in here for a moment.'

'Right.'

'Then we'll look for somewhere for you to stay. Would you like to stay with me?'

Lilia said nothing.

'Can I get you a cup of tea?'

Lilia sat on the bottom step of the staircase. She said 'No thank you.'

She held her baby close to her.

She thought — I want to be somewhere where I am not trapped when all this terrifying music stops —

There were bits of the night sky flying around her.

Judith went up the steps.

Lilia thought — Perhaps it is my own breast that is pouring out stars —

Then — Do you think he slept with her?

The baby was looking up to one of the large windows which were like those of a warehouse.

There were people moving in and out of the courtyard. Lilia thought — They are like those boring people going on a ladder to what they think is heaven from hell.

After a time, because she was cold, and because her baby was restless, and because she wanted to look at what might be reality instead of her visions, she stood, and walked a few steps up the staircase, and held the baby so that it could see through the first-floor window. She thought — Now, if it amuses you, see something like earth!

When she looked through the window herself it seemed that the large high room like a warehouse was some sort of newspaper office: it was brightly lit; it had posters and notices on the walls. Men and women were sitting on or leaning against desks with an air of bright expectancy; as if they were waiting to be fed at some zoo. A poster depicted a Chinese soldier with a rifle raised like a fist: an American flag had blood running down it. Behind the desk nearest to Lilia a man with a cigarette in his mouth seemed to be trying both to suck smoke in and to blow it out at the same time; it was as if he had a cloth over his face and were being tortured: a woman, leaning towards him, held her smile in front of his face. Lilia thought — But this is a vision of what we like being fed by: before we rush out to the fire.

There were packages of newspapers piled around the walls: she had a vision — Like packets of explosives.

Taking her baby down from the window she thought — We fight for our lives: but at what cost for survival —

A boy with a loud-hailer had come out onto the iron landing outside the first floor of the warehouse. He put the speaker to his mouth as if he might address the crowd in the courtyard. Lilia thought — Or down his throat molten lead might be poured.

The baby had turned towards her and was playing with her necklace.

The boy with the loud-hailer was also carrying a banner

which he seemed to be trying to unfurl. He moved the loud-hailer and the banner from hand to hand; as if he were doing a trick on a tightrope.

Lilia, with her baby, went up a few steps.

People in the newspaper office suddenly began shouting and screaming.

Lilia was close to the boy on the landing. She thought — Stand still. Hold your hands by your sides.

The boy looked at her and the baby.

A bundle of newspapers landed on the iron landing between them. It had been thrown out of the room like a warehouse.

The boy on the landing stepped back: he seemed to get a leg caught on the stick of his banner: then he half fell, at the last moment half seemed to jump, over.

Lilia thought — Turn away: wait till they have gone past you.

Then — This is ridiculous: people thought the bundle of newspapers was a bomb?

The boy had seemed to land head first on the cobbles.

Some people in the room were still screaming.

Lilia turned with the baby and walked down the steps.

She thought — Perhaps it might have been a bomb. Then — I cannot help it if it is so boring.

Some people had run into the courtyard to the boy. They were bending over him.

Lilia remembered that Jason had said — When leaves disappear from the bottoms of trees, it is not that some giraffes grow longer necks —

She clung on to her baby.

The bright glass coming into his cot like daggers —

— It is that the giraffe that happens to have a longer neck —

There were the lights, and bells, of ambulances, far away, coming closer.

She had said — Survives?

He had said — If it's lucky.

She wondered if she should go and spread tears like oil over the fallen boy.

She had to keep moving.

She said to her baby which she held in front of her — 'It's all right, my darling, it is only your adversary the devil that is walking about like a hungry lion —'

She had said — What is a longer neck?

She went out of the courtyard and into the street.

He had said — Living as if nothing else mattered at any moment more than —

She had thought — Why do we leave so many of our sentences unfinished?

— A hook; a line; a heartbeat; a baby?

7

Jason, having seen the Professor go down the alleyway at the side of the Old Science Buildings, had said to Judith — Go back home, will you, and if Lilia comes there, will you explain —. He had thought later — Explain what? He had followed the Professor down the alleyway. — Why I am not at home? why Judith was at home? why I am going to ask the Professor if he has seen Lilia? Or just — There are no explanations to these questions. He had had little trouble with the police going through the cordon. He had pointed to the Professor somewhat ahead; had looked confident, and nodded and smiled. Then he had walked forwards with his arms by his sides: he thought — Like a mad archaic statue. Or — Explain that if you move as if you were slightly mad or off the ground then they may think you are not real, and so not shoot you.

The alleyway seemed to lead in a line parallel to the fire. The Professor was not in sight. There was a door in the wall on one side of the alleyway with no handle and a smooth surface. He thought — As if desperate hands might have scratched there. The door was ajar. Then — There are these stories in fairy books: you push in your mind, and enter a strange corridor.

The corridor had no light: there was a faint smell of burning. By holding the door open he could see by the light from the alleyway a short distance in front. He thought — You hold the light with one hand and are tied to what you remember: go ahead with the other, but then are you in the dark. Letting the door go behind him, he moved down the corridor. He thought — Do blind people construct a world outside them: or do they see that their fingers and ears send messages just to themselves in the dark?

At the end of the corridor there appeared shadows, lights, monsters. He thought — The Professor has a torch.

He could go up to the Professor and say — Bang! I have shot you!

So — We are in a film: real or unreal like cowboys?

At the end of the corridor there was a T-junction and he turned left. A torch shone into his eyes. He raised his hands and murmured 'Light!'

The Professor said 'Just what we want: an electrician.'

Jason thought — It is, isn't it, as if we were here for the sake of something being mended?

When the Professor turned the torch away Jason saw that the space that they were in was a small hallway which contained a door to a lift-shaft. The Professor, as he flashed his torch around, became visible himself from its reflections.

Jason said 'Have you got Lilia?'

'She's at my flat.'

'And the baby?'

'He seems to be fine.'

The Professor, with his torch, seemed to be examining the entrance to the lift-shaft. There were double doors, smooth, with a crack in the middle.

Jason said 'Will she stay with you then?'

He realised — This is ambiguous: it could mean either that I want her to stay, for safety; or that I don't want her to stay, because of you.

The Professor said 'I told her to.'

At the top left-hand corner of the right-hand door to the lift-shaft there was a small slot in the shape of a mouth, or a smile. It was on this that the Professor's torch shone. He was feeling in his pockets as if for keys.

The Professor said 'The power's off.'

'Yes.'

'And the stairs are blocked.'

The Professor took from what seemed to be the lining of his pocket a bunch of keys. He tried uselessly to shove one or two into the slot that was shaped like a smile.

Jason said '— And somewhere downstairs, is there that little bottle, which, if it falls into the wrong hands, will blow up the world —?'

He thought — This might be true?

The Professor said 'I've got to get my notes, which are in the basement.'

The Professor tried another key. Then he gave up. He pulled with his hands at the crack between the doors.

Jason said 'I used to know about lifts.'

The Professor had put the torch between his legs. He said 'The things you know.'

Jason said 'I once translated a manual about lifts into Italian, to earn some money.'

The Professor pulled at the doors. He said 'Did you have an Italian girlfriend?'

Jason thought — That's witty.

Then — Perhaps it is what is witty that, like what is in that little bottle, either will blow up or will save the world.

The Professor gave up pulling at the doors. He took from the lining of his jacket what seemed to be a half bottle of whisky.

Jason murmured 'What a big bottle!'

The Professor took a drink. He said 'That's witty.'

Jason took the torch from between the Professor's legs. He moved with it around the hallway.

On a wall at one corner of the hall was a small box with a glass cover. Inside it was an instrument like a key. The end of the key was curved into something like the shape of a smile.

Jason said 'It's if the lift is here, that you won't be able to get down the shaft.'

The Professor seemed to think about this. Then he said 'A metaphysical problem.'

Jason gave a bang on the glass door of the box, which opened. He took the key out.

He said 'From one of the explosions, which was near our home, the window of the baby's room blew in, and the glass went all over his cot. So if Lilia had not taken him away, I mean if she and I had not quarrelled and she had not gone to you, that is where the baby would have been, and he could have been injured or even killed.'

The Professor handed Jason the bottle. He said 'Here.'

Jason drank. He said 'Thanks.'

The Professor said as if quoting '— Radioactive waste: cancer-carrying bacteria —'

Jason said '— What is in that little bottle?'

The Professor took the bottle of whisky back. He said 'And I thought that she walked out because of me!'

Jason went to the doors of the lift-shaft and held the key up to the small opening like a smile. The key went in. He turned it, and pushed. Then he tried to pull the doors sideways. The doors opened a crack.

The Professor said 'Can you get your fingers in?'

Jason thought — This is absurd.

He said 'There's another catch inside.'

The Professor said 'I'll pull. You try to get at it.'

The Professor went in front of him, almost underneath him; Jason thought — Are we lovers; keeping an eye on each other for our mutual girlfriend? The Professor pulled at the doors: Jason reached up into the lift-shaft.

Looking round for somewhere to put the torch, he thought — I could put it in my mouth —

The Professor said 'This is absurd.'

Jason found the catch on the inside of the lift-shaft. It was above the doorway, in the dirt and darkness.

The Professor pushed sideways; the doors opened further.

When Jason shone the torch into the shaft there appeared to be a drop of about six feet to the top of the lift, which was at the bottom.

Jason thought he might say — Do you really want to get down? Or are you doing this because you think you have to —

The Professor said 'It is possible?'

'Yes.'

'There's a trapdoor —'

'In the top of the lift.'

The Professor sat with his legs over the edge of the lift-shaft. He took the bottle from his pocket again. He drank. Then he handed it to Jason.

Jason drank.

He said 'The problem now is not how to get in, but how to get out when at the bottom.'

'Because people usually get out at the top?'

'When they're stuck. Exactly.'

Jason handed the bottle back to the Professor.

They sat, side by side, with their feet hanging down the lift-shaft.

Jason said 'Supposing you had the chance to do away with a third of the people in the world — would you take it?'

The Professor said 'At random?'

'Yes.'

'If you were God?'

'Yourself included.'

The Professor took another drink from the bottle.

He said 'And your loved ones included?'

Jason, looking down the lift-shaft, thought — Ah, those arms out, flying, that know they will always be caught —

The Professor said 'It wouldn't work, no.'

'Why not?'

'Because the occasion's got to be fitting.'

Jason said 'I see.'

He thought — What do I see?

The Professor said 'I mean, if the occasion is contrived, not at random, then what are you being fitted for?'

Jason said 'And what are you being fitted by —'

The Professor said '— Even if you think you are a god.'

Jason thought — You mean, if you are a god, you are still just what happens?

They sat at the edge of the lift-shaft, drinking whisky.

There was a cluster of cables that went down the centre of the lift-shaft.

After a time Jason said 'I could go down.'

The Professor said 'Why should you?'

Jason thought — Perhaps I'm grateful.

He said — 'I'm younger.'

The Professor said 'I'm not so old!'

Jason said 'All right, I'm grateful.'

'What for?'

'For your looking after Lilia.'

The Professor said 'Dear God!'

Jason thought — But she should not have walked out!

The bundle of nerves, down the lift-shaft, trembled slightly.

The Professor said 'There's an electrical system, with emergency batteries, which, when the power's cut, needs to be turned on.' Then — 'I'll explain when you've got down.'

Jason thought — So it is not your notes! Then — So it may be true about the little bottle?

The Professor said 'There are also my notes.'

Jason took off his jacket. He leaned forwards to touch the cables, which were greasy.

He thought — Should I take the rest of my clothes off, like a cross-channel swimmer?

The Professor said 'And I'll buy you a new pair of trousers.'

Putting a hand on to the cables, Jason thought — It is true that symbols exist in the outside world: there are forces like angels with flaming swords above rooftops —

Then the Professor said 'In order to get money, you have to say you're enquiring into the nature of disease.'

Jason thought — Did he really say that? Then — You mean this is what he really is or is not doing?

The Professor said 'Turn left. Go along the corridor —'

Holding on to the cables, Jason leaned out over the drop.

He thought — You mean, annihilation might in fact be about to be loosed on the world?

Then — Only a few feet to the bottom.

He stretched out a foot over the chasm.

— Oh where is that backdrop! those wings —

— That old man in the sky — A middle-aged man who can rise again and take his bow at the end of the third act —

— That bird for which they stay alive —?

He kicked off with his other foot; launched himself down the lift-shaft.

8

Eleanor entered a long low room lined with bookcases in which were gathered men mostly middle-aged, some dressed in outdoor clothes and some in overcoats over what looked like pyjamas and some in dressing-gowns. They seemed knobbly and slightly out of shape, like rejects of seed potatoes. They were peering out of windows; as if in a hall of comic mirrors. A few turned to look at Eleanor as she came in: then turned away, as if she might be normal. The talk and the excitement blew in gusts: there were cries and exclamations. Eleanor thought — Is it this fire, which is in the jungle, that is drawing human beings up out of the sea? There was a police officer holding his hat which was like his head underneath his arm: there was what seemed to be a dwarf propped up in gum boots.

Eleanor went to the window and looked out. There was her own head, then a lawn, then a chandelier behind her: then the fire above rooftops.

She thought — This comedy — we call it comedy — is the bustle of things coming up through the earth: the opening and shutting of mouths like penises: if it stopped, we would die.

Beyond the window — in her head — containing the chandelier, the fire, the lawn — she thought — I will sit in the dust and with my finger will draw patterns of this strange tribe.

There were these substances or planes, depending upon what degree of accuracy or activity you required: the framework of the building; the men talking in the room behind; the figures moving on the lawn carrying boxes. She wondered — What will they choose to rescue from the fire? not what will survive: that will work for itself. These members of the tribe — in the common-room behind her or in the burning night —

from these would be rescued — who? — she began to laugh —
she had just seemed to pick up, with her smile in the window,
an old man with a bald head and a body like a genie in the room
behind her; and deposit him, closer to the fire, at her elbow —

He was saying — with his long bald head, his neck, his mouth
opening and shutting like a penis —

She thought she might explain — I am slightly drunk: I have
not been eating toadstools.

She tried to take a handkerchief from her skirt to put to her
face to hide her laughter. She found she had got hold of —
underwear, nightdress, holy shroud. She thought she might
explain — I am not laughing at you: it is myself: why should I
not move, sometimes, like a genie in and out of a bottle?

Or — I have sat so long at nights in countries where the only
company is myself —

A pillar of smoke had risen above the rooftops.

She thought — The column, drawn by six white horses, rose
to a height of several thousand feet —

The people in the room behind — the fellows and guests of
her college — were talking, excitedly, about the fire beyond
the lawn: as if it were about food; their mouths opening and
shutting; the food being this excitement which gave them
placement; identity —

The man like a genie was talking to her.

She could say —

— We've introduced a strain into a culture —

He was talking past her, as if through the window, into the
night. She could not hear what he was saying.

— To test whether or not in laboratory conditions —

— You do it yourself it hurts you —

— You do it to yourself it kills them —

She thought — Supposing all the sound were shut off on a
stage?

When she had been in her room in college earlier that
evening and had switched on Anderson's film which he had
set up, she had sat in the dark and watched the images
flickering against the wall and there had been sirens and bells
outside and she had thought — But if there is a connecting

principle — beyond placement, beyond identity — It would be something with which our instruments, which are to do with placement, could not deal —

Anderson had said — Words themselves are the enemy?

In the room behind her, the policeman who seemed to have his head tucked under his arm was standing directly underneath a chandelier. The chandelier had a sharp glass point hanging down.

She thought — If I concentrate, can I make that chandelier fall on to the space that would have been his head so that his whole contraption will light up and play a tune like a juke box?

Her husband Max, the Professor, had said — One of these days there may be the escape of some substance into the atmosphere —

She had said — Or the escape of some substance from the atmosphere into oneself —

He had said — That's witty.

On the lawn outside there was a body being carried past on a stretcher. The stretcher seemed to be a furled banner. Some boys and girls were following it, as if in mourning.

She had said to Max — What exactly are the experiments that you are doing?

He had said — Do you want me to use the jargon? or to say nothing about it instead.

She had thought — All words are a protection then?

In the room in the quiet night, with the pillars of the university coming down like those of the Philistines, she thought — But if there is some message — like lightning; like music; like the result of football pools in Andromeda — we could put ourselves in the way of it — that huge head — the glass in front of me containing the fire, the room behind, my own features —

The chandelier that had been hanging so pointedly above the policeman's neck had not fallen: she thought — This is a sign: perhaps I should go out.

She found she had moved away from the window towards the door. The man who was like a genie was watching her. She thought — If he comes after me I will pounce, turn him inside

287

out, him and his bottle, like an octopus.

She was out in the night.

She seemed to remember — Derivative strains from components of human intestinal flora —

Then she thought — I will make my mind a blank: throw seeds up into the air to see which way the wind is blowing.

She had wanted to ask — If they got out, they could destroy — who? — some, or everyone — ?

Or — There is no creation without destruction.

She thought — But can you think this, let alone say it!

Then — I am tired. I have not eaten much today. When I was in West Africa, in Borneo —

— Things happened just outside the limits of consciousness. People dressed up and came in from the jungle: they pretended; and it became real. There were figures that waved above rooftops like Petrouchka. You held on, and watched, till they went away.

There were bits of broken glass on the pavement.

She thought — I will follow it; like arrows; like bits and pieces of DNA —

— There is no such thing as human cancer virus: there is only the failure of mechanisms which prevent it —

She was moving towards a bridge. The current in the river seemed to be moving sluggishly both ways.

— Something like a map —

— In the mind —

— A needle turning.

There was a woman on the bridge. She was carrying a baby. Eleanor put a hand to her head.

— Hullo —

— Hullo —

— I wondered if you remembered me —

There had been a time when she and Max Ackerman had first been married and no young girls had yet come in —

In making her mind a blank, what she had hoped would come in would be —

The woman was coming towards her.

'Hullo —'

'Hullo —'

'I wondered if it was you.'

Eleanor put a hand out to the baby.

Had she never wanted to kill such a girl as this: to take her by the hair; to hit her; to drag her on to a landing —

'Hullo, my lovely —'

'I can't get in to my house. The windows have been blown out.'

Eleanor said to the baby 'And how are you getting on, my angel?'

She thought — I last saw you in those huge hands —

She said 'Where's Jason?'

'I don't know.'

She had said to Max — And what do you know of the mechanisms that prevent it?

He had said — Prevent what?

She had thought — You don't want to prevent sickness?

She had not wanted to drag her —

She said 'Would you like to come to my place?'

Lilia said 'That would be terribly kind.'

— Something open —

— Like a hook —

— That goes both ways —

He had said — People would find, if it was necessary, their own ways of survival.

She said to Lilia 'How old is he now?'

'Nearly a year.'

'Hullo, sunshine!'

She had said — Some people. Then — And what is it that would be necessary?

Lilia said 'He thinks everything's lovely. He thinks everything exists for him, and he is good.'

Eleanor thought — Then it is you, as his environment, that has made him good.

They had turned down to a towpath by the river. The water moved sluggishly.

Eleanor said 'Can I carry him?'

The baby held out his arms to her.

She said 'That huge head!'

The baby had bright dark eyes. When she held it, it seemed to search for something within her forehead.

Lilia said 'On my way here, I thought I heard someone shouting above rooftops.'

Eleanor said 'I thought I saw something like a body floating in the river.'

9

Anderson had moved through streets with the can of film that he had been showing under his arm; had seen the fire above the rooftops with its arms up like Petrouchka; had waved and called as if in sympathy; had crossed some cobbles, past a clock-tower, to the edge of the green by the Old Science Buildings; had seen, in the entrance, the rubble like roots and concrete earth; had thought — Or like a cancer, O my children and my children's children. He had come to the rope of the cordon: had seen a policeman turning to send him back.

By standing still, and by peering into the half light as if to try to recognise the policeman personally; then by straightening, pleased, as if the recognition had delighted him; he thought he might make the policeman come towards him as if on the end of a piece of elastic and then fire him off, like a stone from a catapult, on his way round the universe —

He said 'Ackerman: Professor Ackerman' quietly, as if it were a password; while the policeman was still almost out of earshot.

He thought — Perhaps I have got my can of film under my arm just so that I can say —

When the policeman was close to him he patted the can under his arm and said 'I've been sent to get this. Or we're all in trouble!'

The policeman watched him with no interest or understanding behind his eyes.

Anderson stepped over the rope. Going past the policeman, towards the entrance to the basement with its iron roots and rubble, he thought — Do they shoot you in the back? Or am I covered by that figure flying above rooftops —

When he came to the edge of the rubble, he had to climb

over it to get to the entrance. He thought—Have I been clever? or am I now like Napoleon at Moscow. There were some firemen with crowbars and torches. He thought — The stage has collapsed; the orchestra is buried. He had to put his can of film down on the ground to get a hand-hold: he thought — Perhaps they will think it is a bomb. Or — I am preparing to be lowered down a cliff-face?

It was beyond the building that there had been the bells and lights flashing. He thought — Is it true, it is luck, that the scene of the fire is just elsewhere?

He climbed down steps, over rubble. No one stopped him. He thought — You act: no one jumps up on a stage —

— We know each other so well in this small world: but what of the audience?

He was climbing with difficulty down through a hole in the rubble. There were lights from the engines outside. He wondered — Perhaps acting is with one half of one's brain to the other, which is watching.

Bits of the ceiling had come down and were festooned like cobwebs. He was now on the level of the basement. The firemen with torches had moved away. He thought — You go along a corridor, in the dark, with your hands out; like one of those mad, confident statues —

There was a door, and a smooth surface, then another door, on his right. Somewhere, in his memory, was the door, at the end of the corridor, to the room where he had been keeping the main part of his film. The film at the moment was hanging in strips from the ceiling like cobwebs. Or like chromosomes, he imagined, waiting to be joined —

There was a faint light playing as if through a peep-hole somewhere along the passage.

He thought — But there would be no discovery, if you knew what you would find?

A quiet voice said 'I can't.'

A voice from far away said 'Why not?'

— The first voice from the tomb —

— The second voice from a mountain-top —

Anderson thought — Or seeds that fall, like an apple, or like droppings from a bird, in a laboratory.

The light from behind the pinhole elongated and faded and disappeared. From this, Anderson constructed — I am in the small hallway in the basement which, I remember, contains the door to the lift.

'You've got —'

'What —'

'The inner —'

'But not the outer —'

The voices were, again — far away, and then quietly: far away, then quietly. Anderson thought — If you laugh, does it make the whole network light up?

He made his way to the outer door to the lift-shaft. There was what seemed to be a crack in a rock. He put his ear against it. He thought — Or it is a woman, and I am listening for a baby.

'Can you get back?'

'No.'

'Dear God —'

Anderson said in a sepulchral voice 'You've got to go on.'

He thought — Or you are carried away, screaming, in a strait-jacket.

The voice from far away said 'Who's that?'

'It seems unlikely —'

'Can he get you out?'

Anderson thought he might say — Some grandson, I think, in Australia —

Then the voice which came from within the lift-shaft said 'There should be a little key, in a glass case, somewhere on the wall, I think, to the left.'

Anderson thought — But did I not, a short time ago, want to kill you?

He said 'I haven't got a torch.'

Jason's voice from within the lift-shaft said 'Well I'd lend you mine, if you had one to get me out with.'

Anderson thought — That's witty.

Then — It is just men, and not women, who get themselves stuck in a lift-shaft?

He began groping round the hallway.

The voice from within the lift-shaft said 'You put it into a little slot, that is shaped like a smile, at the top left-hand corner of the right-hand door.'

Anderson thought he might say — Doesn't putting into a slot mean some other thing?

Then — But did he sleep with her?

The voice from far away said 'Is it really him?'

Anderson said 'It depends, right or left, which way you're facing.'

Jason said 'Well which way are you facing?'

Anderson's hand touched a small box on the wall of the hallway.

The voice from above said 'What's he doing here?'

'Looking for a key.'

'Can he find it?'

'I think so.'

Anderson thought — Should not God on a mountain-top speak to me directly?

— Is that not the orthodox position?

He opened the glass door of the box. He took out the key. He came to the door of the lift with it.

Jason said 'There's a little opening —'

'I know —'

The Professor said 'How did he get in?'

Anderson said 'I climbed.'

He thought — No one's ever climbed —

Jason said 'I thought it was blocked up.'

'Perhaps it was. But now there's an opening.'

He was feeling for the keyhole on the top of the door on the right.

He thought — So with one great jump —

'Can he —'

'What —'

'Pull sideways —'

Anderson thought — Ah, I could leave you both trapped!

He banged with the key against the slot and tried to pull the door sideways.

He thought — You go out of a door, along a corridor, in through the same door —

— You can tell the difference?

294

The door opened slightly.

There was Jason, with the torch between his teeth, pushing the door sideways.

The torch shone into Anderson's eyes. He backed away, with his hands up.

He thought — But he would not have wanted to kill me?

Jason stepped out of the lift.

Anderson said 'You said I could borrow your torch.'

Jason made a noise that was unintelligible.

Anderson followed Jason along the passage. There were lights, and shadows, like cobwebs.

Jason, having taken the torch out of his mouth, said 'Didn't miners have a bird, or something, that they sent ahead of them along a passage?'

He handed the torch to Anderson, who went in front.

At the end of the passage there was the room with his film hanging in strips like chromosomes.

Anderson thought — But wasn't in fact one of the firemen, in the rubble, wearing a gas-mask?

Jason said 'How's it going?'

'What?'

'The film.'

'Oh, all right.'

He thought — Wife and kids?

He put the torch down on a table. He began unclipping strips from the ceiling and putting them in a cardboard box.

Jason sat on a table. He said 'I don't think the fire's anywhere near here really.'

Anderson said 'Then what are you here for?'

There was a bellowing noise, as if from someone trapped in a red-hot iron bull, from the direction of the lift-shaft.

Jason said 'He wants me to switch something on —'

'Oh yes —'

'Do you know what?'

'Yes. In a moment, I'll do it.'

Jason had picked up the torch. There was a door on rollers to the next room. He pushed on it.

Anderson said 'It's a film about people being able to look at

295

themselves and like it.'

Jason said 'Like being able to?'

'Yes.'

'Still, would they like what they saw?'

Jason had got the door open. He went through. The next room was a laboratory with glass pipes and retorts and dials and wires. Jason shone the torch around.

Anderson said 'It's not dangerous.'

'But people might think it is —'

'Right.'

Jason shone his torch on a tray containing liquid. There were wires going into the tray: a plate like something cooking.

Jason said 'Little green men —'

— With moustaches —

Anderson, from the next room, could see Jason looking round the walls of the laboratory as if they were the walls of a cell.

Jason said '— Radioactive waste. Cancer-carrying bacteria —'

Anderson said 'They'd think they liked it?'

There was the bellowing noise from down the passage again; as if from a god, or the man in the red-hot bull.

Jason said 'Oh, and his notes.'

Anderson thought — But after all, what did you do with Judith?

He went through into the laboratory where Jason was shining his torch.

He said 'But they'd have to get back to the truth sometime, wouldn't they?'

Jason said 'Who?'

Anderson said 'Ah, that's the question.'

Jason went back into the room where Anderson had been packing up his film.

He said 'I've got to go now.'

Anderson said 'Does everyone get what they want?'

Jason said 'I think so: don't you?'

Anderson said 'Can I keep your torch?'

Jason said 'It's his anyway.'

10

When the crowd had panicked in the newspaper office because someone had shouted that a packet of newspapers might be a bomb, Judith was by a tea machine watching a nozzle pouring out liquid and a light going off and on; then she went out on to the landing of the outside staircase holding a cup of tea in either hand as if she were on a tightrope: but Lilia had gone. There was just the boy who had fallen into the courtyard. She thought — So why was it him; while we, and others, go on?

The crowd was dispersing to other doors and exits. People were kneeling by the boy on the cobbles. His head seemed to be underneath his arm.

Judith put down her cups of tea on the platform. She went down the iron steps and across the courtyard and out into the street. There were the bells and sirens of ambulances. She thought — It is by such ghostly music that an audience is drawn in, then rolled over, in the aisles?

The street of grey stone buildings down which she had walked some hours before with Anderson was to her right; it was cordoned off; it led to the area of wasteland and the bridge over the river. Beyond, there was the avenue of broken glass and plane trees. It is necessary, she thought, to keep some map in my mind: then I will have a picture at least of leaves blowing to the bonfire. He, Jason, had said — The reason why travellers came across each other so often in eighteenth-century novels was because there were so few travellers. And he, Anderson, had said — Or because they were writing novels. The fire-engines seemed to be concentrated round a corner on the green in front of the Old Science Buildings. There was a seventeenth-century façade with people talking in twos and threes: she thought — Or in conical hats, like conspirators. A policeman was carrying something round and flat like a bomb: she thought — Or a reel of film.

There were soldiers sitting in trucks with rifles sticking up; or, if they had been toys, with spikes up their arses.

Some of the crowd from the newspaper office had made their way to the green. There was another boy with a loud-hailer as if he was carrying his head underneath his arm. Occasionally he put it to his mouth: then took it away: she thought — It is as if he were being tortured. A fireman on a ladder seemed to have been overcome by fumes: he drooped, the pee flopping from his hose lethargically. She thought — Old people become incontinent: our life-support system needs to be switched off: we are an experiment that has taken a wrong turning. Sparks seemed to be flying above the rooftops: she thought — Petrouchka, with his arms out flailing: or a column, drawn by six white horses, rising to a height of several thousand feet. Ambulances had come on to the green. They were spreading their lights like a net, as if to catch victims.

She had the almost physical impression of her body, as if on a hook, being raised or lowered to or from — where? — the sky? the flies of a theatre? her elbows to her sides and her toes turned inwards to lessen the pain: the line held by an old man like God, dressed in thigh-length boots like a woman —

People were carrying a body on a stretcher. The water was being turned off in the hoses. The doors of an ambulance were open. The façade of the Old Science Buildings was lit like the backdrop of a stage. The fireman on top of the ladder was hanging from a harness. The Old Science Buildings seemed to be like a person who had had molten lead poured down his throat. Some of the firemen were wearing gas-masks. She thought — Do firemen usually wear gas-masks?

There was a stinging in her eyes: a tightness in her throat. People around her were pulling out handkerchiefs and coughing.

Within the façade of the grey stone building she imagined she could see — the backdrop of the building dissolving as the lights came on as it were behind the stage — the rooms, cells, cages, as if of a mind; the puppets in their boxes; the actors in their rooms making up, dressing and undressing; like wasps in a nest; a brain; an organism with the skin torn off; but still with herself watching. She thought — Do I make it with my mind, this honeycomb?

Two trucks with soldiers in them suddenly started up and drove away. They ran straight over the rope of the cordon, dragging it after them.

The policeman who had come from the entrance to the grey stone building had put down on the ground not far in front of her the round object that was like a bomb or a reel of film. She looked at it. She thought — But that is Anderson's film! I know it! It has his name on it.

Policemen were walking, in twos and threes, towards the doors of houses round the perimeter of the green. They were eighteenth-century houses with lights coming on.

The fireman on the ladder was hanging from his harness.

Judith picked up the reel of film. She thought — Under a sky at night: in a brain: there are these coincidences; connections.

She walked down the edge of the green towards the river. The river, with a shadow that might be a body in it, ran down towards the sea; with whirlpools, underneath willows.

She thought she would kneel, and dip in the hem of her skirt, and hold it to her face, and make a pattern of her face there. The body seemed to have been a log. The stuff of her skirt against her face would be as if she were being immortalised on a shroud; or tortured.

She thought — I could pretend I am sick; have fallen; I will be picked up by hands that are there to catch me.

The log — if it was a log: she was on the bank of the river — seemed to be moving in the opposite direction to the current. When she had been on the bridge, looking over, it had not seemed that this was the way to the sea. She thought — The map was in my mind: what is the reality?

She began to walk along a path by the river. The path, she thought, would make a long curve and come out by the bridge between the area of rubble and the avenue of cherry trees. There, on one side, would be the advertisements of guns hanging down and legs being blown open like wounds: on the other, of bits of broken glass like sunlight on a cot.

She thought — Children see by what they learn: what was it I have seen? a sort of wonder, breaking.

The stars in the night sky were so beautiful! There was a gate, to a footbridge, over the river. It went to an island, where there was a willow tree and an allotment. She thought — But I have been here before! there was a caravan, and an old woman digging.

— I can explain: Do you remember me?

Or — I am ill, can you help me?

He, Anderson, had said — Why should one want to become ill? To be protected?

She had said — At least, you could pray for me!

She put a foot over the gate. There were spikes underneath her. She thought — At least they will not go up me as if I were a policeman.

When she had come here before, she had thought he, Anderson, was going to make love to her —

She had said — Who lives here? He had said — She is our good godmother in the fairy tale.

She was climbing over the gate. The footbridge went over a branch of the river.

What we are trying to get rid of, she thought — in our practice: our acting: in the Old Science Buildings — is the image of ourselves as dolls, painted cheeks, stiff movements: only coming alive when wounded. — Turn my head, put my hair behind my ear, wait while I am picked up. Trapped in this form — Help me! Putting one foot over the edge of the footbridge she said quietly, 'Help me!'

Beyond the bridge, over the river, was the allotment. Beyond the allotment was the caravan; and what looked like, yes again, an old woman digging. But in the dark. There were an oil lamp, a table, a bottle of wine, a fire: there were shadows thrown upwards on trees.

Judith thought — Something waiting to be born; here and now; as it once was from that crack in the rocks in Africa —

Quietly, her skirt outspread like Ophelia, she stepped, or fell, into the river.

She was in fact wearing jeans. She thought — How far is it to the bottom?

By pressing outwards with her legs she could stand on mud, which went up between her legs quietly —

— Should she not rest for a while in any wild struggling, which only made her sink down deeper and deeper —

The old woman appeared above her. She was like a finger pointing down. She said 'What happened?'

Judith said 'I slipped and fell in.'

'Why?'

'I don't know.'

'Well can you get out?'

'I think so.'

The old woman sat down on the footbridge.

The mud, which Judith had stepped in up to her thighs, was cold.

The old woman said 'Do you want me to make it difficult for you to get out, or something?'

Judith thought — I could pull you in on top of me!

The old woman said 'Or would it be better for you if you pulled me in, and then climbed out on top of me?'

She held a foot out to her over the river.

Judith, with the help of the foot, pulled herself towards the footbridge.

The old woman said 'Would you like some hot soup?'

Judith said 'Yes please.'

The woman turned and went back to the encampment.

Judith dragged herself out on to the bridge. There was mud clinging to her legs and thighs. She thought — Like an afterbirth?

Then — We do this to stay alive?

She walked towards the caravan.

The old woman, Eleanor, was sitting by the fire stirring a cauldron. By the fire was a clothes line with a nappy.

Eleanor said 'Leeks and potatoes.'

Judith said 'Is Lilia here?'

Eleanor said 'Yes, and the baby.'

Judith thought — Well, am I not becoming used to this sort

of thing?

Eleanor said 'You can take off your clothes.' She stirred her soup.

Judith went to the back of the caravan where there was a small tent. She sat on the grass. She began to take off her jeans.

She thought — Do you know how often I have to do this? Then — It's funny?

She sat with her hands round her knees, looking at the moon.

She thought — Are we not moving into the influence of some new constellation?

Eleanor came with a bowl of soup. She stood over Judith, watching her eat.

Judith said 'Do things really work like this?'

Eleanor said 'I think so.'

Judith said 'What is the difference between being in the age of Pisces, and moving into the age of Aquarius?'

Eleanor said 'The one is to do with fishes; the other is to do with the carriers of the water in which fishes swim.'

11

The Professor, having launched himself into space with a hand-kerchief round his hands and his hands round the cables at the centre of the lift-shaft, uttered a shout as if of terror as he went down: he thought — I am too old for this: I am dead: I will retire. He landed on top of the lift-cage. Jason, before him, had removed a panel in the roof. He thought — Or is it the cells in my body that require rejuvenation: the ache, the longing in my balls, heart, mind. He had to get down on his stomach to scrape through the trap-door into the lift-cage.

He groaned; made bumping noises. He thought — Thus are thunderbolts cast down: babies are born: lions walk the streets. The edge of the trap-door seemed to make a screaming noise as he went past. He thought — And so are we made bearable? unbearable? His hands and clothes were filthy. He picked at the grease, as if it were afterbirth.

He was standing in the lift-cage. There was a slight glow beyond the open door into the hallway.

Stepping out, and shaking, he thought he might appear like some old god — hairy arms, staring eyes, long top lip like a gorilla. He would go along the corridor to the door of his room; there then would be the man and the boy: they would leap to their feet knocking over a bottle of whisky, a torch, a lighted candle; the shapes of them going up in flames like those from the neighbouring buildings above. In his room he found Anderson sitting at his, the Professor's, desk; he was alone; on the desk was the half bottle of whisky. The torch, on its end, shone upwards. Anderson was reading a typescript. The Professor thought — Note the especially fine modelling round the mouth, the eyes —

He said 'Where's that fellow —'

'Gone.'

'Where to?'

'I expect to get more copy.'

The Professor stretched out and took the bottle of whisky. He tipped it to his mouth, and emptied it.

He said 'He took my whisky.'

Anderson said 'He seemed to think you had some notes.'

The Professor took the torch and went through into the laboratory. He shone the light around glass pipes, wires, dials. He went to the tray of liquid and shone the torch in it. Then he took from a shelf above a small bottle of colourless liquid which was sealed: he shone the torch on it; he shone the torch on the seal. Then he carried the bottle back to his office, put it on the desk, and sat facing Anderson.

Anderson said 'Why did you come down?'

The Professor said 'Another metaphysical question!'

The room in which they were sitting had just a desk, two filing cabinets, a hatstand, a table, and two chairs. There were the torch and the two bottles on the desk. There were pipes and wires along the back.

The Professor took the typescript from Anderson's hands and leafed through it briefly and then threw it into a cardboard box on the desk which contained the strips of Anderson's film.

Anderson exclaimed 'My film!'

He went to the box and lifted out the typescript. He re-arranged his strips of film delicately. Then he put back the typescript.

The Professor said 'How can that script work —'

Anderson said 'I don't know.'

The Professor said 'In what way are we like genes; like chromosomes.'

Anderson said 'Well we have to go out into the world —'

The Professor picked up the bottle of colourless liquid and turned it round in his hands.

Anderson seemed to be listening as if for a noise along the passage.

He said 'We could always write our own stories.'

The Professor said 'Well here's to yours!' He held the

empty bottle of whisky up, as if he would drink a toast.

Anderson said 'Thanks.'

From along the passage, somewhere by the hallway by the lift-shaft, there was the sound of picking and clinking.

Anderson said 'If they come in here —'

The Professor said 'Yes?'

'All you have to say is —'

'I'm not saying anything —'

'— That something terrible is happening.'

'They won't believe me.'

'Right. Then don't say anything.'

The Professor stared at him.

He said 'You sound like one of his characters.'

Anderson took the bottle of colourless liquid from the Professor. He sniffed it. He said 'Gin?'

The Professor said 'Good heavens!'

From along the passage, past the hallway by the lift-shaft, the sound of clinking had become louder.

The Professor leaned back and put his feet up on the desk. He said 'I thought that fellow had your girl.'

Anderson said 'I thought he had yours.'

The Professor said 'She isn't mine.'

Anderson said 'Well she isn't mine either.'

Then Anderson took the torch and began to look round on the floor underneath the table.

The Professor said 'What are you looking for?'

Anderson said 'My film.'

The Professor said 'Your film is in that box.'

Anderson said 'No, the reel I was carrying. This is real. Reel! I've lost it.' Then, as if quoting '— With an air of intense anxiety —'

He went out into the passage.

The Professor said 'So something terrible has happened?'

The Professor thought — He really does look like someone who has lost or dropped something that may blow up the world.

Anderson said 'I can't bear it!'

The Professor said 'You'll find it.'

He thought, watching Anderson —

305

— We were on a hill, with fir trees, once, Eleanor and I: and I said — Why don't we have children? And she said — We have got children —

— He would have been like this, so bright and troubled, if we had had a child?

Out in the passage there seemed to be a flash, travelling both ways, towards the rubble by the stairs and back from it, creating a light both in front and behind the eyes; like a backdrop or nerve-ends burning; leaving a taste on the tongue like something from childhood —

The Professor said 'Wait here.' He put the bottle of colourless liquid in his pocket, and went out past Anderson and along the corridor.

When he came to the hallway there was the door to the liftshaft and three men in gas-masks. One was held up by two others: he thought — Some sort of devil's deposition. The Professor shone his torch in their faces. One seemed to reach for — a gun? a Geiger counter? bat's piss? The Professor thought — I am so bored of these people! He swung his torch to and fro, as if he were making an erasure.

Anderson had come up behind him. He was saying 'Oh damn! damn!' He was searching about in the rubble.

The Professor shouted 'Get them out of here!' Then he sat down, heavily, on some rubble.

He thought — I am drunk.

Then — Have I, or have I not, sat down on that little bottle of liquid that will destroy the world!

He put his hands to his throat and coughed. He thought he might say — No need to panic!

Or — Gather around my children: you can brighten your dying sun —

There was water pouring through the roof and down the rubble.

Anderson was saying to the men in gas-masks 'Don't you know what this place is?'

The Professor thought he might say — I should do; I run it.

He sat with his elbows on his knees. Anderson came up and squatted beside him. Anderson said 'Are you all right?' The

306

Professor wondered — Is he acting?

The Professor said 'Yes.'

Anderson said loudly as if he were acting '— There's no need to panic. People will destroy themselves if they want to! —'

Looking at the men in gas-masks, the Professor wondered — What if there were something — in the mind, in the outside world — that would destroy only men in gas-masks?

Anderson was making as if to help him up through the rubble. He thought — Like Aeneas, after the fall of Troy.

Anderson had his cardboard box under his arm. He was still looking around on the rubble.

When they were out in the night sky, it was so beautiful! There were fire-engines like old space-craft, landed.

The Professor thought — So this is what the world looks like after so many plagues and prophets —

Anderson was saying 'I know I did have it!'

The Professor wanted to pray — There could still be some Noah's Ark in this flood?

One of the men in gas-masks was coming up out of the rubble. He was putting a finger under his chin as if to take off his face.

The Professor thought — What terrible words might be loosed in the world from behind it!

Then he thought — Yes, it might work if I say: I have nothing to say about any of this.

12

Eleanor sat on the branch of a willow over the river. Her feet hung down. She began to see, as the sun came up, a pattern of birds, in the water, in the sky above; they were sitting on five lines of telephone wire, like notes of music. She tried to sing them — one long; one down, two going up; the first two of these quickly; the last one a long one; two down; up; down. She thought — The last theme from *Götterdämmerung*? Another bird appeared. She herself had been doing her breathing exercises — in, one two; hold it, three four; out, five to eight — with which she meditated; like someone having a baby. This was in counterpoint to the birds on the wire. Then there was the she that was both above and slightly ahead of the music, like a conductor. She thought — Perhaps in such a way, at dawn, witch-doctors thought they could affect the universe.

The light, under the water, behind the curve of the world, created a slight transparency; the sun and the trees like the head and arms of a drunk man coming up over the edge of a table —

She thought — Sometimes life itself is as if you had eaten toadstools.

Lilia and the baby were asleep in the caravan.

Judith was in the camp bed by the fire.

Her head was clear; like the sky; like the fire and water of the night before.

There was some sort of test, she remembered, in which you had to draw — a tree, a house, a river, a snake, a road: and depending where you put them — the snake going into the house; the river cutting off the tree; the road a guide-line or a barrier — something could be known about the person doing the drawing: who he was, what she required, what were his or her defences.

There was something like a lion moving on the far side of the river: it was under the trees, going in and out of the darkness: or was becoming striped like a zebra.

There had been times in Africa when she had sat like this and had watched the sun come up and there had been the animals by the pools like a pre-laid breakfast —

She thought — What does the world require? we are here with one another: we do not want to eat and be eaten?

There was a figure squatting beneath the trees at the far side of the river. It was holding something clasped to its middle — like entrails, she thought; or like those pipes that had once played music —

There was the story of a dark god who had sat like this and had charmed lions and zebras —

The figure from the other side of the river called — 'I'm coming over!'

She thought she might say — There's a footbridge at the back, for heaven's sake, on the other branch of the river.

The figure called 'Do you think I can walk?' Then — 'I need to do this. I feel so guilty.'

She had recognised the figure as Jason. He stood, and stepped into the water. He held high above his head, as if to keep it dry, a plastic bag — or organ-pipes, or entrails.

She said 'It's too deep to walk!'

He said 'How did you get your caravan over?'

Eleanor thought — This is ridiculous.

Jason climbed back out of the water. He seemed to be looking for something on the far bank.

He called 'Can I borrow your clothes-line?'

Going back to the caravan, along a short path through a wood, she thought — Perhaps you have to go through fire and water, do you, like a pilgrim, to reach the holy city?

By her caravan there was a clothes-line. She took it down. Judith was still sleeping.

Going back to the river she thought — We have the fire and water: this is the holy city?

In the river Jason was standing up to his waist again. He held his plastic bag above his head with one hand.

Looping the clothes-line, and keeping hold of one end, Eleanor tried to throw the other end across the river.

Plunging sideways, at the third throw, Jason managed to catch it.

Then he climbed out again on his side by the river and tied it to the branch of a tree.

Eleanor began, self-consciously, to tie her end of the clothes-line to one of the branches of her willow.

She thought — But of course it is true that peace comes down when we are doing busily the odd things that we are doing: then violence climbs mountains; desolation crosses rivers —

She wondered if she should say — The girl's here too!

Jason had stretched the clothes-line tight across the river. Then he took off his belt, made a loop with it round the clothes-line, put it through the handles of the plastic bag, and hung the plastic bag from the clothes-line.

Eleanor thought — Well we can never say anything sensible, can we, about the holy city.

Wading into the river, and holding on to the rope, Jason managed to get the bag some way across without it touching the water.

She remembered a quotation — I would believe only in a god who could dance —

Jason seemed to be getting out of his depth. He could no longer hang onto the clothes-line without the bag touching the water.

Eleanor said 'Let it go.'

He said 'How can I pull it if I let go?'

'You can swim with one hand and hold the bag with the other hand out of the water.'

Jason said 'That's difficult.'

Eleanor thought — Then I won't watch: if it would be easier for you.

She looked up to the leaves, the shadows.

She thought — Was that really a lion?

— And how did Jason know that Lilia was here?

There was a sound of gasping and splashing. Jason was

climbing out on her side of the river. He was holding the plastic bag still clear of the water. He had some weeds hanging from him. She thought — A god: or the man with sausages in a pantomime.

— Or has he come to see the girl?

Then — That lion must have escaped from some zoo.

He said 'I've got milk, and rusks, and nappies, and that sort of thing.'

He had undone his belt, and was taking the plastic bag from the clothes-line.

He said 'The stuff that she keeps in a basket, like witches; that sort of thing.'

Eleanor said 'Do you feel better?'

He said 'Yes.'

Jason began making his way along the path through the wood.

She thought — There are these circuits, yes, through mountains, rivers; in the body, in the mind —

He said 'Why do we behave as we do?'

Eleanor said 'I hear that the baby might have been killed or injured.'

He said 'Yes.' Then — 'Perhaps I'll die of cold.'

Eleanor was following him. She said 'How did you know she was here?'

When Jason came to the caravan he saw Judith asleep outside the tent. He put a hand to his eyes, his throat; he crept closer; peered down; then turned to Eleanor with sad, reproachful eyes.

Eleanor said 'They're in the caravan.'

He said 'I didn't know anyone was here. All I saw was a nappy on your clothes-line.'

Eleanor got down on her hands and knees by the fire.

Jason went round towards the entrance to the caravan.

Eleanor blew on the fire. The fire glowed.

Eleanor thought — The nappy was like a flag: or like one of those birds singing on the wire.

Jason came back without the bag he had been carrying. Looking down at Eleanor, he said 'I don't want to be here when

311

they wake.'

She said 'Neither do I.'

He said 'Why?'

She said 'Because I'm tired and hungry. And I think they should be on their own.'

He looked away over the tree-tops. He seemed to hum.

She thought — Shall we say we've lost our keys, and can't get in before morning?

He said 'Would you like to come to my place?'

She said 'I thought your windows were blown out.'

He said 'They are. But there's food and a bed on the floor, in the kitchen.'

Looking up at the pink sky, Eleanor thought — Can we be so happy, when bombs come down?

Jason said '— Tuck you up. Make you feel safe —'

She said 'Well I'm not going to swim that river.'

She picked up a handbag, a blanket. She poked at the fire.

She thought — But is it not true that I want to re-affirm some sort of baptism?

Jason said 'There are plenty of women who've swum the Channel.'

She said 'Yes. Both ways.'

They walked back along the path towards the river.

He said 'Do you think it's women who push men to extremes? I mean, both good and bad? Like Faust? Mephistopheles?'

She said 'Oh I don't know, do you?'

When she came to the river she took off a gum boot and put a toe in the water, which was cold.

He said 'I thought you weren't going to swim the river.'

She took off her other gum boot and handed the two of them to him.

She said 'I think women know more than men, but they won't take the responsibility.'

He said 'For what?' Then — 'Shall I carry your gum boots?'

She said 'For what to do when they know they're ridiculous.'

When she was halfway across the river she became very cold; she thought she might say — Are you sure you felt better?

Or — With one great leap —

312

When they reached the far bank she sat and looked at the clothes-line. She said 'Shouldn't we be able to take that down?'

He said 'You mean, people then might think we had walked on the water?'

Going up on the far side of the river, she felt her feet so numb that there might be bits of glass cutting into them; an ache that was like an ecstasy in her heart, arms, mind. She remembered a time in Africa when she had been carrying — what — a sick baby? they had done something to it to make it a member of the tribe: and she had thought she could save it: she had felt she could say to it just — Get up! You can walk!

She said to Jason 'Did you see a lion?'

Jason said 'It must have escaped from some zoo.'

Then — 'But they'll be all right, won't they, on that island?'

13

Anderson approached Eleanor's caravan by the footbridge over the river. To one side, by the island, was an area of trampled reeds as if a body had fallen in there. Beyond it, on the stump of a tree by the footbridge, was what looked like the reel of his film. He thought — But I left it on the rubble: you mean, after all, there are angels?

He sat down on the edge of the footbridge. He thought — Dear God, thank you, thank you.

Then — Will I one day have to suffer?

The entrance to Eleanor's caravan was facing him. On the far side was the tent where Eleanor sometimes slept. He thought — She, or someone, takes up my reel of film, like a holy house, and whirls it through the sky, and dumps it by the river —

There was a faint singing or gurgling noise coming from inside the caravan. It was like someone blowing rainbows.

He picked up his reel of film.

A voice from inside the caravan said — 'Hullo, darling!'

He thought he might say — Hullo!

The voice from inside the caravan, or as if from a cloud, said 'And how are you this morning?'

He thought he might say — Very well, thank you.

He went toward the caravan. On the steps, as if delivered — by a milkman? more fairies? — were placed, neatly, a carton of milk, a packet of cereal, a tin of biscuits, and a bag of nappies.

Anderson stood with the cardboard box with his film in it clutched against his middle.

Lilia's voice said 'Isn't this a pretty place! With such nice curtains!'

Anderson put one foot on the steps of the caravan. He knocked. He thought — Will I appear to be an angel?

After a time the door of the caravan opened and Lilia looked
out: with her pale hair, and bright black eyes. She carried her
baby, who was like the moon, over her shoulder.

Then, looking down at the steps, she said 'How terribly
kind!'

Anderson said 'But it wasn't me!'

She said 'Who was it then?'

As Lilia bent down to pick the things up off the steps, the
baby's head swung forwards and upside down and gazed at
him intently as if it were the sun.

Anderson said 'Awa, awa, goo goos.'

Lilia heaved the baby up so that its behind was towards him
again. Then she turned with the provisions and went into the
caravan.

Anderson put out a hand and tickled the baby under its chin.

Lilia said 'Look who's here!'

Anderson said 'Your prophetic soul, your uncle.'

Inside the small caravan, which reminded him of a shrine, or
of childhood, there were flowers, and cushions, and rugs, and
wooden and metal images. He thought — Lilia and I used to
play in a room like this; as if on a raft, on the bedroom floor.

He said 'Does he talk yet?'

'Talk!'

'Da da di dum dum. Da da di da.'

He sat on the bed and took the baby. He raised it and
lowered it several times.

He said 'I don't think he should ever talk. He should have a
different system of communication.'

Lilia said 'He has.'

Anderson said 'He can fly —'

He held the baby up in the air. The baby held its arms out.

Anderson said as if quoting '— Language is useful for saying
what things are not, not for saying what they are —'

Lilia said 'Where's Eleanor?'

'I don't know.'

'She was here last night.'

'Did she find my film?'

'Your film?'

'I lost it.'

'I don't know.'

The baby seemed to blow a bubble: then looked up in wonder at where it might have gone.

Lilia came and stood by them. Anderson put an arm around her.

Lilia said 'How did you know I was here?'

Anderson said 'I didn't. I came to see Eleanor.'

Lilia said 'Then who brought the milk and biscuits?'

Anderson said 'Angels.'

The baby looked at Anderson sideways; then put its head against his shoulder, as if shy.

Anderson said to the baby 'Perhaps you did. Perhaps you found my film. Perhaps you'll lift your family out of the mud and slime —'

He raised and lowered the baby.

Lilia moved away. She said 'Someone must have been here.'

Anderson said 'Listen!'

He rolled his eyes at the baby. The baby crowed, and put a finger in his mouth.

Anderson said 'A lion!'

Lilia was wearing an old dressing-gown of Eleanor's. She undid it, and held her arms out for the baby.

Anderson said 'Can I have a bit?'

Lilia said 'You are disgusting.'

There was the sound of someone moving, as if surreptitiously, behind the caravan.

Anderson raised a finger.

Then he said loudly — 'After all, I am your brother!'

Lilia sat on the bed and fed her baby from her breast.

Anderson, watching her said 'On my way here I met a man who was looking for a lion escaped from a circus.'

He had a memory, suddenly, of when he had been present when the baby had been born; Lilia's face had been flushed and sweating; her legs had been so far apart that they seemed to be splitting her; the baby's head was like an oak from an acorn; he had thought — Thank you, my sister, for letting me see this sun.

Lilia said 'What about Judith?'

316

He said 'What about Judith?'

She said 'When did you last see her?'

The noises from outside had ceased.

He said 'People were always overhearing things in nineteenth-century novels.'

He thought — Why did I say that?

Getting up and leaving Lilia, and going out of the caravan, he went round to the back where there were the tent, the camp bed, the sleeping bag, the still smouldering fire. Someone seemed to have been sleeping there: no one was there now.

He thought — Well, who did rescue my film?

Then — But it is impossible to think about coincidences.

Lilia called — 'I thought that was because they wanted to get away from each other.'

He said 'Who wanted to get away from each other?'

She said 'People in nineteenth-century novels.'

He thought — One gets what one wants: does one?

— Or one gets into the sun, coming up from behind the trees like the head of a drunk man from behind a table —

He said '— Shove one's head in its mouth, that old lion —'

Going back into the caravan, he found Lilia transferring the baby from one breast to the other.

He thought — I can put into film some events like these —

He said 'Eleanor's not there.'

'Who was it then?'

He thought — People moving, yes, like genes, like chromosomes; making a head, a hand, here, there; from the inside world; out into the universe —

He said 'They're expecting us this morning, aren't they?'

Lilia said 'Shall we go?'

He thought — Those baby's hands are like sea-shells, trying to shape Lilia's breast, which is the sea.

14

Judith bent down at the door of the Professor's flat and tried to see through the letter-box. Pushing with a finger and thumb against the flap, she made the door swing open. She thought — And so you fall on your face; as when the train is left by the railway station —

It was still very early. She held in her hand the page from the Professor's notes that she had picked up at his lecture. She had been going to push it through the letter-box. She thought — Now I will go inside and leave it even more mysteriously; like a reel of film in a landscape —

She went into the hall. The door into the Professor's bed-room was open. She thought — He is waiting for someone to come into his dreams?

She stood with one foot in front of the other as if she did not want to be caught moving.

As she went into the bedroom — stepping, stopping, stepping — she thought: In grandmother's steps, is it Red Riding Hood who in fact wants to jump on her poor old grand-mother?

The inside of the bedroom was dark. She had the impression of being watched from elsewhere. She thought — Through a two-way mirror: or through the fourth wall that actors pretend either is or is not there —

The Professor was lying on his bed. He was on his back, with his hands folded across his chest. She thought — Or I am the dog at his feet; or the third eye that looks inwards, like the eye of Siva —

She stood still, her hands by her sides, one foot in front of the other.

The Professor turned and looked at her.

She thought — Will he say nothing: or will he send me back to the beginning?

The Professor said 'I was lying here dreaming —'

She took a step forward. She thought — He can imagine it is not exactly me who is here?

He said 'And what I was dreaming of was you —'

She remained still.

'— Would I, or wouldn't I, prefer the reality to the dream?'

She reached for the bed with a jump. She said 'Got you!'

He said 'Because what I was doing in my dream was —'

He put his arms around her.

She said 'Well, here I am.'

He said, quoting '— I will do such things — what they are yet I know not —'

Judith got off the bed and went into the passage and closed the front door. Then she came back into the bedroom.

He said 'Where's Lilia?'

She said 'With Eleanor.'

He said 'And that other girl. What's her name —'

'Who?'

'Judith. Juliet.' Then — 'Why does he sometimes call you Juliet?'

He propped himself on an elbow, watching her.

She thought — You mean, something kinky?

She said 'Because I can be part of sometimes this dream, do you think, and sometimes that?'

He lay on the bed and looked at the ceiling. He said — 'Or what would be the difference?'

She sat on the edge of the bed. She said 'They were taking samples of soil from in front of the Old Science Buildings.'

He said 'And getting people out of the surrounding houses?'

She thought — I could put a finger on your forehead and say — Get it out! Get it out!

He said 'You go on for so long, and then you go crazy.'

He held out a hand to her.

She said 'What do you think it is?'

He said 'Nothing.' Then — 'You think there was something in that basement?'

She said 'But what do other people think was in that basement!'

He said 'They'll think they can't talk about it.'

She said 'And will you talk about it?'

He said 'No.'

She said 'That's all right then.'

She began undressing.

She thought — But on a stage, you could try to say something about it?

When she was undressed, she climbed on to the bed.

He said, watching her, 'What do old men do?'

She said 'Lie on their backs, don't they, and look at the ceiling.'

He said 'You take away some sort of death, some sort of protection, from me.'

She wondered — Do old men need to be hit, as well as want soft lights and sweet music, like a baby?

She lay on her front. He sat up and began to stroke and caress her.

She thought — Oh I am a queen bee, with all my workers, hanging from the ceiling!

Then — What we are now doing, that is a metaphor —

— A sieve, a riddle —

— Oh I am a nugget of gold —

— Is it you? Is it you? —

— That baby.

He said 'There!'

Then — 'Upsadaisy!'

He had put his head down against her and was laughing.

She thought — But if making love is between the two parts of the brain —

— Yes?

He said 'An old man wanted to die within the dream of his young mistress —'

She thought — One part thinks and gives names: the other part doesn't speak much but knows what things are for —

He said '— But as his life was passing in front of his eyes —'

She said 'Yes?'

She had rolled over and was looking at the ceiling.

He said '— He saw her, waved, and said — Coo-ee!'

She jumped up and went through into the bathroom.

She thought — Well that was fine: wasn't it?

He called after her 'Do you still want to be an actress?'

She thought she might say — Can you smell something burning?

When she came back into the bedroom she said 'Are you often lonely?'

He said 'I'm what I want.'

'So am I.'

She began dressing.

She said 'But you've done it. I mean, your life —'

He said 'You can send me postcards.'

When she was dressed she said 'What is that bundle of nerves called between the two parts of the brain?'

He said 'The corpus callosum?'

She said 'Do you think that is like making love?'

He said 'Oh good heavens!' He jumped off the bed, and began dressing.

She was standing by the door of the bedroom.

She said 'I mean, I've brought you that page of notes from your lecture.'

She watched him dressing.

He said 'Bet I'm first into the passage.'

She said 'You can't possibly be first into the passage.'

He said 'Why not?'

She said 'You're still dressing and I'm halfway there.'

He finished dressing.

She said 'How?'

They went out of the bedroom and moved towards the door into the passage.

She said 'Is that what you're working on now?'

He said 'How to make love with two parts of the brain?'

She said 'Lucky old you!'

They were at the door. He opened it.

She stepped aside to let him go through.

He ushered her ahead of him into the passage.

15

Lilia and Jason walked at the edge of a ploughed field beneath a cold sky and trees as if reflected in water. Jason was carrying the baby on his hip. Sometimes it looked out on the world as if it would tell it what to do; sometimes it studied its parents as though they were legs, lungs, livers, heart-beats. Lilia walked on a furrow balancing with her arms out like a swan. She said 'You didn't sleep with her, did you?'

Jason shouted 'Of course I didn't!'

The baby clapped with one hand against his chest.

He said 'And you didn't sleep with him?'

She said 'No!'

She thought — He shouted too loud? Or need I believe him, when it comes back on the curve of the universe?

The ground they were walking on was strewn with flints. Some of them might have been chipped with axes thousands of years ago.

Jason said 'Did he talk about the experiments he is doing?'

She said 'I think, you look through a peephole, into what seems to be a room of walls, tables, chairs — then you look at it from above and it's just lines.'

He said 'Perhaps something to do with the anatomical structure of the brain.'

She said 'Or recessive genes: or chemical warfare —'

He said 'Or some such.'

They were coming to an edge of the ploughed field. There was a wood, with beech trees.

He said 'You know that thing called Catastrophe Theory'

She said 'Do I?'

He said 'Things are apt to change without your seeing just how or why, in jumps.'

She said 'Like the opening of a flower —'

He said 'Or the breaking of a strain —'

She said 'What about Catastrophe Practice?'

There was a wire, which he held up for her. She climbed under. Then she held her arms out for the baby.

He said 'I did bring you milk!'

She said 'I thought it was the fairies.'

She took the baby. He put a leg over the wire. Watching him she thought — It is in no-man's-land, of course, that men are so vulnerable.

He said 'That's a good title!' Then — 'Like genes, we are and are not so vulnerable.'

In the wood there was a path with leaves dropping. They walked quietly.

He said 'I was so miserable.'

She said 'I suppose it was my fault.'

He said 'Of course it wasn't!'

Somewhere in front, through the trees, there was the sound of an engine roaring.

Lilia said to the baby 'Tell it to go away.'

Jason said 'Go away.'

The baby, which Lilia was now holding, put a finger out, pointing.

She thought — Like God: that old man on the ceiling —

There were some figures in front of them through the trees. They were gathered round what seemed to be a lorry.

He said 'Keep moving.' He put his hands out for the baby.

She thought — You hold your hands by your sides: put one foot in front of the other —

The lorry seemed to be stuck in some mud. Its engine roared and faded.

She said 'I do wish they would hurry up and die.'

He thought — Mothers can say that? Then — That is one of the gifts given to grown-ups by babies.

Some of the men round the lorry had stopped trying to push it and were watching them.

The baby turned its head away: looked up at the leaves, the shadows.

323

Lilia and Jason turned off down a side-path at right angles to the lorry. They looked at the ground as if they were careful of where they were treading.

Lilia said 'Isn't the place near here where they go underground if there's a war or something?'

Jason said 'And dream of breeding like rabbits.'

The baby held a finger up as if he were listening.

Lilia thought — You could wish them dead if they were rabbits —

Jason thought — Cannot one say that?

They walked on.

They had come to a part of the wood that was cut off by iron railings. There was a mound, covered with undergrowth; a blocked-up entrance to something like a womb.

She thought — Womb? Tomb?

— Laboratory?

Then — If it would stop them, one could say that.

They stood looking at the mound. Jason was holding the baby.

She said 'I want to stop thinking.'

She thought — What was it: to get back to the garden, you've got to go right round the world and in at the back way —

There was the sound of shouting behind them.

They walked on through the wood.

Jason said 'I once asked the Professor: If the solar system were an atom, what it would be an atom of.'

She said 'And what did he say?'

'Nothing.'

She thought — Nothing?

He said 'I mean, he said that there is nothing, except the solar system itself, which could be such an atom.'

She thought — A cypher then?

There was a large puddle across the path in front of them. They looked for a way round.

She said 'Do you think there are trip wires?'

They turned back the way they had come.

He said 'On Saturday morning; in a quiet walk through the wood —'

There was the sound of something crashing through the

324

undergrowth to one side of them.

The baby seemed to have gone to sleep.

She said 'We'll stand still: shall we?'

He stood with his arms through hers; the baby between them.

She thought — A cipher, cypher; what goes between —

Then — We might be on that journey across a desert?

There was a man in a woollen cap plunging through the undergrowth.

When he was close to them he stopped. He seemed to look in his pocket for — a handkerchief? a gun? a hand-grenade? Then he smiled: he went on.

She thought — Breaking down the fences: leaping up the waterfalls —

The baby opened one eye and looked at them.

Lilia said 'You won't die, will you?'

There was the sound of a backfire, or a gunshot, from the direction of the lorry.

Jason said 'No.'

They came again to the railed-off mound like a tomb. Its door had been forced open. It hung on one hinge.

After a time Jason bent down carefully as if to see inside.

She thought — Dials; switches; ladies and gentlemen on the grass —

He said 'There's no one there.'

She said to her baby 'There's no one there.'

Her baby pointed with his finger the way on through the wood.

He said 'Walk normally. The way back to the car.'

They were moving down the path which went past where they had seen the lorry.

She said 'Do you pray?'

He said 'Sometimes.' Then — 'Do you?'

They stopped. There was the lorry. There was no one round it. The baby began to struggle to get out of his arms.

Lilia held her arms out for the baby. She said 'It's all right, my darling —'

There was what seemed to be a body lying in the mud by the lorry.

Lilia said 'Don't go!'

She thought — We are goats, tethered, in a clearing in the jungle.

The baby was studying her face.

Men were coming down the path from the direction of the ploughed field and the road. They were wearing woollen caps and gum boots.

Lilia said 'What shall we do?'

The baby began struggling to get out of her arms down to the ground.

Jason said to the baby 'Do you want to walk then?'

The men who were coming towards them were carrying a stretcher. One of them had a rifle over his shoulder.

Jason put the baby down. He said 'Look! He can walk!'

Lilia thought — Can he fly then?

The men with the stretcher were going past them. They were watching them curiously; or incuriously.

Jason said 'Did you see?'

Lilia was watching the tops of trees.

The men with the stretcher were going away from them.

Jason said 'Isn't he clever!'

She said 'Yes.'

Jason picked up the baby.

When they got to the edge of the wood he held the wires apart for her. She went through. Across the ploughed field, they could see their car.

She said 'I can't go on.'

'Of course you can.'

She said 'Did he really —?'

'He took two steps!'

Jason put the baby down in the ploughed field.

The car was some way above them on an embankment.

Lilia said to the baby 'Aren't they silly people, my darling!'

Jason said 'I'll just check there isn't a bomb under the car.'

Lilia said 'Let me see!'

Jason said 'He didn't seem to think that anything like that really mattered.'

16

Eleanor lay on a mattress on the floor of Jason's kitchen. When she heard someone at the front door she closed her eyes. Whoever it was, waited: then went through to the sitting-room. She thought — It cannot be Jason: he will be with Lilia. Footsteps went to the bottom of the stairs. Eleanor thought — Perhaps he, if it is he, will think I have been trapped beneath rubble, and will bring me a cup of tea.

Whoever it was came into the kitchen. Eleanor lay with her eyes closed. She thought — But you can go on too long, like acrobats, trusting that hands will catch you —

After a time there was the sound of cupboards opening and shutting; of cups and plates being put on a table; of a kettle beginning to steam.

She thought — Love was often somewhat embarrassing.

The Professor said 'Would you like a cup of tea?'

'Yes please.'

'And so many lumps —'

'You remember?'

She thought — Lying here, with pleasure at my feet, like a dog, purring —

He said 'I always used to bring you cups of tea!'

She wondered if she might say — You never!

She lay on her back with her hands folded across her chest. She listened to the sounds of his moving about in the kitchen.

He said 'Ah those were the days!'

She thought — With the tanks in the streets —

— And little bells going —

There was the sound of a toaster making its springing noise: then the scraping of a knife against burnt bread.

He said 'You were so beautiful.'

She said 'And you were so powerful.'

He said 'I shouldn't have gone off, have let you go —'

She said 'Shouldn't you?'

He brought her a cup of tea. She sat up in her bed.

They were in the bombed house; the mattress was on floor-boards.

She said 'We were never really apart. We said that.'

He said 'In the sight of God —'

She said 'Who else do you want to be seen by?'

Taking an interest in Jason's kitchen — the table with the top at the level of her head; the dresser with cups and jugs on hooks; a dish-washer propped up at the front with a child's bricks; she thought — You know, of course, why we were such a good husband and wife; because in the sight of God we had a function.

She said 'We never really worked out what makes one set of chances different from others.'

He said 'Well it's what you see in them, isn't it?'

She said 'But they work on their own.'

He said 'I think happiness is dangerous because you get no warning; it's all there for you; the seagulls get you; you're not looking.'

She said 'I think real happiness is almost unbearable.'

She drank her tea.

She got off the bed. She and the Professor sat on either side of a table on which there were teapot, mugs, plates, toast, butter, honey.

She said 'And what are you doing now.'

He said 'Language. Patterns. Means of communication.'

She had the physical sensation, suddenly, of her brain in two halves like those of an apple: then coming together, slowly, to make one.

He said 'And what are you doing?'

She said 'Teaching.'

She thought — You mean if you went right round the world and then back again, to the Garden of Eden, there would still be that Tree of Life, which before, for some reason, they did not recognise?

After a time she said 'Where are those children —'

He said 'It wasn't that you didn't want children —'

She said 'What was it then?'

He said 'You didn't want a child. You wanted children. You wanted to look after the world.'

There was the sound of someone coming into the hall. He seemed to listen.

She said 'I would have liked a child.'

He said 'We've got that too.'

She thought — That head from which an eye is born, behind the forehead —

Then — It was because of your experiments, years ago, looking after the world, that we couldn't have children?

Anderson's voice called from the hall — 'I say, does anyone know who found my film?'

Anderson came into the kitchen. He was carrying his cardboard box. He looked round the room. Then he said 'What's that burning?'

The Professor said 'Toast.'

Anderson said 'And I thought it was the Old Science Buildings!'

He went to a bread bin on the dresser. He took a piece of bread and put it in the toaster.

Then he said 'How are you two doing, all right?'

The Professor said 'Well, who did find your film?'

Judith said 'I did.' She had put her head round the doorway. She looked round the room cautiously, like a child on the edge of a pantomime.

Anderson said 'Thank you.' Then — 'Why, what were you doing?'

Judith said 'Nothing.' Then — 'And who put the milk and things for Lilia?'

Eleanor said 'Jason did.'

The Professor said 'And who's got my typescript?'

Anderson said 'I have.'

Eleanor thought — This is ridiculous.

Judith said 'Well there we are then.'

Anderson said 'With both momentum and location.'

He came and sat at the table and poured out tea.

329

He said 'Bombs, guns, angels. Radioactivity —'

Judith said 'Peace; procreation —'

The Professor said 'I'm going!'

Eleanor thought she might say — Eat up your breakfast.

Judith said 'Where would you go to?'

The Professor said 'To a conference of Marxist determinist bacteriologists.'

Anderson said 'And I could make a film about my prophetic soul, my uncle.'

Judith said 'And I could act — The Liberation Army.'

Eleanor thought — We've always known that language is ridiculous: that something quite different is happening.

Then — We want not to be gods but those parts of us that are our children to be gods —

There was the sound of a car outside.

Eleanor said 'They were expecting us?'

After a time Jason's voice, in the hallway, said 'Look what's here!' Then — 'And I thought I'd lost it!'

Jason came into the kitchen. He was carrying a typescript. He said 'Hullo —'

Eleanor thought — Please God, no one say: I was afraid you might not remember me —

Lilia's voice, from the hallway, said 'It must be someone else's.'

Jason said 'Yes it must be someone else's.'

Eleanor held out her hand for the typescript. She said to Jason 'They're all your story anyway.'

Lilia came into the kitchen. She was carrying her baby. There were Eleanor, Anderson, Judith and the Professor sitting round the table.

Anderson said 'This is like the last act of a panto.'

Judith said 'Didn't Lenin act in a panto?'

Jason said 'It is not like the last act of a panto!'

The Professor said 'Can we all write our own stories then?'

Lilia held up her baby and seemed to be showing it the room. She said 'Look how pleased he is to see you!'

Jason said 'Yes, you write your stories.'

Eleanor said 'They'd still be about the same thing.'

330

Jason said 'What.' Then — 'Throw away the scripts!'

The baby stretched out its hands to the people in the room.

Lilia said 'He can walk! He was so bored of the people outside!'

Anderson said 'Can he not fly?'

Eleanor got up and went over to Jason. She thought — But at the end of the last act, in that construction like a telephone box, there is enough room for more than just us to come alive?

She put her hand on Jason's arm. She said 'We are your seeds. We are each other's children.'

Jason said 'We will be able to go out into the world?'

There was a banging on the door outside.

Eleanor thought — I'll go.

Lilia said 'Do you think they followed us?'

Jason went past Eleanor into the hallway. She heard him opening the front door. Then he was saying 'Oh do come in!'

Eleanor saw two men in the garden. She did not know if they were policemen, or those on the other side.

The Professor called 'Tell them we've been told to stay here, and not to say any more just now!'

One of the men came in and looked into the sitting-room. One looked up the staircase.

Anderson called '— And we're keeping in touch with them by telephone!'

Lilia said 'Have you had breakfast?'

Judith said 'There's room —'

Lilia held her baby out so that it was taken by Jason. Then she went out with the two men who had gone back into the garden, where there were splinters of glass like light.

Eleanor called 'You know where we are —'

The baby seemed to crow.

Jason said 'What goes on in that huge head!'

DALKEY ARCHIVE PAPERBACKS

Visit our website: www.dalkeyarchive.com

DALKEY ARCHIVE PAPERBACKS

Visit our website: www.dalkeyarchive.com